Rare Orchids:
written by:
Khadeja Hester-Storms
aka
D.D. Sherman

D.D. Sherman   Rare Orchids

*"If I speak in the tongues of men or of angels, but do not have love,
I am only a resounding gong or a clanging cymbal."*
                    Corinthians 13:1

Chapter 1

I was watching Amber try on the eleventh pair of shoes, a pair of sparkly and strappy stilettos. Colorful shopping bags of all shapes and sizes bunched up to my armpits and small mountains of footwear covered the floor before us.

Amber sprung up from her chair, did a hip-swinging runway-walk, spun before a mirror, flicked her voluminous weave over one shoulder, and headed back to me with her hand on her thigh and her diamond engagement ring shimmering in the soft lighting of Neiman Marcus's shoe department.

"So whattayah think?" she asked, twirling her foot and batting her naturally long eyelashes. "Am I freaking these babies or what?"

"They're too damn high. Five inches?"

"But they're soooo sexy."

"Shoes used to be made for walking. Only clowns wear stilts."

"Well call me Bozo 'cause I'm taking these bad boyz!" she replied, dropping in the chair beside me. "So, what are we doing to celebrate your thirty-eighth birthday?" Amber asked, beaming. She pointed to a box of shoes piled on top of many others. I picked them up and handed it to her.

"I hadn't planned on anything."

"Girl, it's your thirty-eighth birthday! The big four-oh is right around the corner. We've got to go big or stay our butts at home," she said, taking one of the flats out the box, closely examining its ornate design.

"Which I'd rather do to tell you the truth. Give me a warm bubble bath, a slice of Junior's cheesecake, a Scandal binge and I'm as happy as Idris Elba's next-door neighbor."

Amber playfully bumped shoulders with me. "Oh, stop being an old fuddy, duddy. You're turning thirty-eight, not eighty-eight."

I rolled my eyes at her repeated mentioning of my age. "Since when is growing older alone something to celebrate?"

Amber scoffed. "Well I'm throwing you a party whether you like it or not. I'll invite Devin Smith. The cutie pie from the fifth floor who just moved into my apartment building. You remember him? The one we rode the elevator with the other day?"

I furrowed my brows and cocked my head, pretending to be dumbfounded.

"The one I saw you checking out from the corner of your eye."

I pinched my chin and threw my head back as if struggling to remember.

Amber put her hand on her hip. "The tall, brown skinned brother with the mustache and goatee."

"Oh him?" I asked, playing it cool, even though my heart thumped at the mere mentioning of his name. "Yes, I think I'm starting to remember now."

Amber's soft hand clenched my wrist. "Come on, girl. We'll have a blast. I promise, it'll be fun."

"You can if you want." I shrugged to hide my excitement about the prospect of that gorgeous hunk of a man, Devin, attending my birthday party. "And where are we having this birthday extravaganza?"

Amber perked up at my apparent change of heart.

"Club Sapphire."

"Sapphire's? Amber do you know how much it costs to rent that place?"

"Don't worry girl." Amber nudged my arm with her elbow. "I gotchu!" she reassured me, tossing the flat back into the box, cradling them in the bend of her arm, and reaching down to scoop up two more boxes. "Can you grab those?" she asked, struggling up from her chair.

I grabbed a fourth box and the hoard of shopping bags, mostly Amber's, and trailed her to the register struggling to suppress a smile. I was envisioning Devin and me at my birthday party locked in an embrace, swaying to an Anthony Hamilton song. Suddenly, my thirty-eighth birthday couldn't come soon enough.

***

"Hap*py* Birthday to ya! Hap*py* Birthday to ya! Happy Beeerthday!" My mother and sister Charmagne crooned the Stevie Wonder's version of the happy birthday song in unison on the other end of the phone.

"Thanks, guys. Much appreciated."

"Too bad we couldn't get up there to celebrate your birthday with you this year, my sweet darling," my mother said in her babying voice.

"That's okay, Momma. I know you would've if you could've."

"The doctor said no flying 'til I get my blood pressure under control."

"That's right. That's exactly what he said." Charmagne put in. "But, we won't be missing your next big event—whenever and whatever that may be," she added. "I took momma completely off salt and got her drinking nothing but alkaline water."

I chuckled weakly. "Well, that's good to hear. I do hope to see you guys soon. Even if it's for no reason at all." My attention returned to my guests. A rather hefty woman, whom I did not know, had just executed the perfect split. A gathering of onlookers tossed change at her as she sat with her legs parted at a 180-degree angle. "Welp, let me rejoin the party. Don't want to be rude."

"Okay, baby. Momma loves you."

"Love you, too." I replied, cringing as my mother talked to me as if I were a child.

"I love you, Symone."

"Love you more, Charmagne."

I disconnected the call, and surveyed the room.

Waxed over crab dip, half a platter of hot wings, swipes of leftover potato salad in a colorful ceramic bowl, sticky plastic cups sitting or lying seemingly everywhere—these, were the relics of my dwindling thirty-eight birthday party.

Amber claimed Club Sapphire wanted a five-thousand-dollar deposit at the last minute, so the party got moved to my house, as I somehow knew it would. If hell was filled with good intentions, Amber already had a penthouse suite reserved.

Hours later, there were about ten to fifteen guests who, at three in the morning, had over-stayed their welcome; but there was no one I was more eager to see leave than Ebony. Ebony was my best friend Amber's close friend and everything I wasn't—loud, flirtatious, and a downright fool once she had a few drinks in her. At the peak of the party, before a wall-to-wall room full of guests, she had the gall to hop onto my granite countertop and stretch herself out so several male attendees could line up to suck melting Jell-O shots from her belly button. Shortly after that brazen move, she staggered to the middle of my polished hardwood floors and performed pirouettes like an inebriated ballerina. Then, in an exaggerated stupor, she fell helplessly onto the lap of Devin Smith, spilling her half-drank cup of wine onto the cushion of my sage-colored sofa. I didn't know what made me angrier, that she came on to the guy I had in my crosshairs all evening, or the red Moscato that marred the couch I had just paid off. You'd think he'd push her off of him, especially witnessing how liquor morphed her into a clowning klutz, but no more suave than King Kong in heat, he grabbed her around her generous hips and started kissing her instead.

Once the guests thinned out, I noticed a strikingly attractive young man discussing the Giants versus Cowboys game with Phillip Berman, a co-worker and good friend of mine. He seemed quite comfortable, perched on my loveseat with his arms spread across the top cushions like he owned it. I chalked it up to him probably being a guest of a guest and mentally counted how many stragglers were keeping me from a hot bath and my crisp, freshly laundered sheets. My cousin Felicia and her best friend Sonya sat at the kitchen counter sipping from plastic red cups, showing no signs of calling it a night. Amber and her fiancé were among five people marathon dancing in my converted dining room. Just the night before, Amber and I had somehow managed to move a dining room table, four chairs, and a large china closet into the spare room.

I was fed up watching people—half of whom I did not know—treat my house like the local sleaze joint. I lifted myself from the bar stool, where I had been planted for most of the evening, and grabbed a few garbage bags from the pantry. I tidied up, removing those ubiquitous plastic cups from my counter tops, window sills, and end tables that triggered my OCD and sent me into a cleaning frenzy. I dumped picked-over platters of chips and finger sandwiches, poured out half-drank bottles of cheap wine and put away what was left of the spirits. I shimmied through the cluster of two-steppers to sweep up food crumbs, wipe up random spillages of cola and alcohol and to finally work on the wine stain ditzy ass Ebony left soaking into the fabric of my sofa. Instinctively, I looked up and there she and Devin were preparing to leave together.

I bet he'll knock it out of the park tonight. The rascal, I thought with a sting of jealousy. I stood clenching a damp cloth in one hand while watching the happy new couple hug and shake hands with the remaining guests.

Ebony gave Amber a peck on the cheek then sashayed over to me with outspread arms. "Smooches, birthday momma!" She embraced me, her full, red hued lips planting a moist kiss on my cheek while I kept my hands pressed to my sides. She leaned back to look at me, clenching my upper arms. "What's that matter, Symone?" she asked, apparently noticing my dismay. "Now don't go feeling bad about turning forty—"

"Thirty-eight."

"Same thing," she replied with a chuckle.

"Not really," I fired back with a forced smile.

"Well, I'm on your heels either way. I'll be thirty-eight in …" She trailed off, placing her hand on her hip and tapping her chin with her index finger. "Let's see, I'm thirty-five, right?"

I bit down on my lip to keep an insult from slipping out. "From what I've been told." I said, wiping my face and noticing a smudge of red lipstick on the back of my hand.

"Oh yeah," she chuckled. "In three years. I was never any good in math," Amber said with a full-tooth smile.

Just rub it in, why don't you? I shot a glance at Devin who was standing by the front door with his blazer jacket draped over his arm, hoping he was taking note of Amber's mental deficiencies.

I led her over to him and opened the front door. "Well, thanks for coming."

"I had a nice time—wait, what did you say your name was again?" Devin asked.

"I didn't. It's Symone."

"Good party, Symone. Thanks for inviting me," Devin said, walking through the door, trailing so close behind Ebony he looked like an appendage to her backside. I could've sworn I heard him panting.

That was the most he had said to me all evening and to think I already had our breakfast menu plotted out.

Welp! there goes another future husband I hadn't even been formally introduced to, I thought closing the door behind them. I glanced at my reflection in the black flat T.V. screen and performed a quick assessment of myself. I could make out that my corkscrew curls had gone limp and my lipstick looked like it could have used a fresh coat, other than that I was pretty impressed with myself. I wondered about what was it that Devin saw in Ebony and not in me? Granted, she had big hips, thick lips, and an effervescent personality—to a fault at times. I, however, was more witty than flirtatious and liked to scale back when it came to makeup or other beauty enhancements. I preferred simple ponytails, a great pair of jeans, and good walking shoes to heels and dresses, but I immensely enjoyed playing dress up whenever I was inspired to.

Someone cracked a joke causing an eruption of laughter which jolted me back to the reality of my bust of a party. I walked over to my music player and powered off the poor man's deejay that was my iPod, instantly freezing Amber and her dancing cronies in the midst of a two-step. Surprised faces turned in my direction.

"Hey, wassup with the music?" asked Antoine, Amber's fiancé.

"I guess somebody's trying to tell us something." My cousin Felicia folded her arms across her chest while her friend Sonya sucked her teeth and cocked her neck to one side.

"Look people, it's past three in the morning and I really need to get some beauty rest," I said walking over to Amber and placing a hand on her shoulder. "E for effort girlie, but I'm truly tired."

Amber leaned in to hug me. "I feel you momma. I hope you had a good time."

"I really did. Thank you," I lied and wondered what part Amber played in pulling off this wannabe shindig. Outside of assembling a few sandwiches on a tray and buying a bag of chips and French onion dip, I was the one who did all the work. I made the potato salad and hot wings and it was my liquor, my house, and my streaming service that kept folks entertained all evening.

One by one, I walked guests to the front door and bid them farewell with cheek-to-cheek kisses. Amber and Antoine were the last to leave. About mid-way down the steps, Amber halted abruptly, telling Antoine to wait as she sprinted back up the steps into my house.

"I didn't forget about your gift," Amber informed me closing the door behind her.

I waved her off and forced a smile. "Chile, don't you worry about that. You know I'm not big on gifts."

"I know I screwed up with the whole Club Sapphire thing."

"Amber, it's okay. I'm fine. Don't worry about it."

"And I saw Devin leave with Ebony," she said, turning the corners of her mouth down.

A wave of heat washed over me as I dry-swallowed a lump in my throat. "Oh, did he? I hadn't noticed."

D.D. Sherman   Rare Orchids

"Come give me some love." Amber reached her arms toward me. We hugged. Even though the top notes of her perfume had waned, I could still smell the subtly sweet fragrance on her smooth brown skin.

Amber stood back to admire me. "You look amazing in that saffron, hip-hugging dress," she said, spinning me around, "that's got you all bootylicious and your girls sitting so perky and upright."

"Yeah, all the good it did." I tittered, struggling to push the thought of Devin and Amber leaving together to the recesses of my mind.

"I'll call you later, lovey," she said, opening the front door.

"Okay. I'm sure I'll be up for the next few hours cleaning up this mess and then I'm taking a bath and crawling right into bed."

"Well, enjoy your night—I mean—day, honey cakes." Amber winked at me, then sprinted down the steps to an awaiting Antoine.

It was no wonder Amber was two months away from being Mrs. Antoine James. Like me, she was thirty-eight, a bubbling brown sugar complexion with perky boobs and a caboose that made even women do double takes. Amber owed her superior figure to her frequent gym visits, something I could never really sink my teeth into despite her constant prodding. I figured I was just fine so long as I didn't exceed my 160-pound threshold, which wasn't criminal considering my five-foot-six height.

With everyone gone, I was able to survey the extent of the damage. Scuff marks dulled my once shiny hardwood floors. Remnants of spilt liquid from an overturned cup on my kitchen counter slowly dripped onto the cushion of a bar stool. My decorative pillows were strewn about the sofa and surrounding floor. Sadly, I saw that I had missed a few abandoned plates of chicken carcasses and hardening finger sandwiches during the initial cleanup.

"Well, this mess ain't gonna clean itself, Symone." I said.

D.D. Sherman   Rare Orchids

    I grabbed my Swiffer from the pantry and started the arduous task of restoring my usually tidy home to some semblance of normalcy. After about two hours of dusting, sanitizing the guest bathroom, wiping down the kitchen cabinets, and scrubbing the baseboards on my hands and knees, I dragged myself into the bathroom and ran a hot tub of water. While the tub filled, I returned to the kitchen and noticed the message indicator flashing on my phone and saw a missed call from Amber.

    "Guess I'll catch her later on today," I said to myself, placing my phone back on the counter.

    The water was so hot that wisps of steam rose from the tub. I undressed and cautiously tested the temperature with wiggling toes; one foot, the other foot, and finally, full immersion. I moved my legs up and down, agitating the water and creating tiny waves of soap suds.

    I scrubbed off the residue of a failed birthday party, washed away the image of an excited Devin leaving with Ebony, and the idea of having no one to grow old with. After the suds had evaporated and the water cooled, I reluctantly exited the tub, stepping onto the rubber mat. Water trickled down the length of my body. I shivered and reached for the towel rack, regretfully undoing a neatly folded towel display. I dried off then secured the towel around me by tucking it into a knot beneath my armpit. I walked out of the bathroom, a few feet up the hallway and into my bedroom. I stood before my dressing room mirror and brushed my hair.

    A passing blur in the mirror startled me. I glanced over my shoulder. "Stop being paranoid," I admonished myself and continued brushing my hair.

    Even still, I got the feeling someone was watching me and quickly spun around. A figure stood before me. I could feel my eyelids stretch and I choked on the urge to scream. It felt as if my heart was trying to beat a hole through my chest and I heard the brush fall from my stiffened fingers and crack against my wood floor.

D.D. Sherman   Rare Orchids

"Don't be afraid. I'm not here to hurt you. I swear." Despite the terror he'd evoked in me, the man's voice sounded gentle.

I re-secured the loosening towel around me and coached my feet backward, out of the room, and into the hall. My goal was the kitchen where I was planning to retrieve a knife from the butcher's block.

"You're that man from the party. The one I saw talking to my friend Phil."

"So you *did* notice me. That's a good thing," the tall, stranger said, slowly advancing upon me with his palms raised in the air. His shirt was undone, revealing sculpted abs the tone of hard caramel; abs, that, if things went according to plan, I'd soon be plunging my knife into.

"Yeah, I remember you and so does everyone else so you better not try nothing!"

I was just steps away from the kitchen, planning to leap over the counter, grab the sharpest knife from the butcher's block, and give that Henry Simmons doppelganger no more than five seconds to high-tail it out of there.

"Look, I'm not here to hurt you." He continued to pursue me with an easy, self-assured strut, lowering the palms of his hands so that his elbows were level with his shoulders.

I continued backward down the hall, occasionally glimpsing over my shoulder.

"So what are you here for? I don't have any money and I don't get paid for another two weeks. I blew everything on that dumb party."

I was in the kitchen now, prepping for an imminent bloodbath.

He giggled. "No. No. It's not like that."

"You think this is funny? Hiding in my apartment? This is trespassing. I hope you know you're breaking the law, my friend."

He chuckled, apparently unfazed by my assertion that he was committing a crime which frightened me and churned the contents of my stomach.

"How am I breaking the law when I was invited? In fact, it was you who let me in," he smirked cockily.

"Well, that doesn't mean you could just move in."

"You were so busy checking out the other dude that ended up leaving with that other chick that you barely noticed me."

His statement was like a jab to my heart. *Okay, it's time*, I thought. I had to get this right as I sensed there would be no margin for error. I leaped into the air and threw myself against the counter, striking the granite countertop with a painful thump. He grabbed me, struggling to subdue me.

"Wait a minute sweetheart! What in the world are you fit'n to do?"

"I'm *fit'n* to slice and dice me up some dark meat!"

I managed to wriggle from his grasp and slide to the opposite side of the counter. I lunged for the butcher's block, extracted a knife, noting that the blade was short and serrated and probably insufficient for the kind of butchery I had in mind. I pointed it in his direction regardless.

"You better keep it moving if you know like I know!" I warned, holding the knife while struggling to keep the towel secured.

He threw up his hands in surrender. "Look, I'm only doing my job, miss."

"Come again?" I asked, whipping my head to one side.

"Your friend Amber? She didn't tell you?"

I reaffirmed my grip on the knife. "What about Amber and what is it that she's supposed to tell me?"

"She hired me to spend the evening with you. I'm your gift. Here, look!" he went to reach in his back pocket.

"Wait!" I warned, still wielding the knife in his direction. "What are you doing?"

"Um. . . getting the receipt."

"The receipt?" I shook my head and furrowed my brows, acutely aware of his every movement.

"Yes. I want to show you the receipt. I'm paid off."

"You've got to be kidding me?"

"Look here!" he said, slowly reaching for his back pocket with one hand and protectively holding out the other. This time, I didn't stop him. He tossed what looked like a crinkly invoice onto the counter.

I snatched it up, still with knife in hand, and did a quick scan. "Jumping Jehoshaphat! Is that where the deposit for Sapphire's went?"

"I'm good." He smirked at me. "Reeeeaaaal good. Now can you put that knife down before a stick of butter gets hurt?"

"No!" I said, pushing the invoice back across the counter to him. "I don't want it—I-uh, I mean—not it. I don't want you or any part of this crazy arrangement you have with Amber."

"From what I hear, I may not be what you want but I'm damn sure what you need."

"Well, I don't give a hell what you've heard. I'm not interested."

"Look, I'm paid up for the night and it's after five in the morning."

"So?"

"So, don't you want to get your friend's money's worth? I mean, I am a little spent, but after a can of Red Bull, it'll be a first-round-knock-out." He leaned into the counter that separated us. "By the way I come with a one hundred percent satisfaction guarantee."

"Alright. I will admit I do find you slightly entertaining, perhaps a little on the attractive side, but frankly, I'm tired and have had about enough of this game." I came from around the counter still holding the knife while managing to keep the towel tucked under my arms. I placed my hand on the small of his back and led him into the hall and toward the front door.

In the foyer, he turned to face me, buttoning his shirt. "Seriously? You're throwing me out without even giving it—" he broke off, indicating his crotch with a nod. "A try?"

"I believe I am."

"Can I just stay for a couple of hours? Maybe crash on your sofa? It's almost morning and I'm exhausted, especially after that cougar I had to tame earlier. She was an animal *for real*."

"You were going to do two women back to back?"

"Look baby, a man's gotta eat."

"First of all, I'm not your *baby* and second, that's just nasty," I said fumbling with the door locks.

"Look miss, it's a job—"

I flung open the door. "Get out!"

His shoulders slumped as his eyes pleaded with me.

"Get...out!" I shouted, then prayed none of the neighbors heard me.

He smiled. "Don't you want to know my name?"

"No!" I answered opening the door wider.

He turned to leave then abruptly turned back to face me. "Tell me one thing before I go. How is it that a pretty ass lady like you is so alone in this big, ole house?"

"That's none of your business." I shot back with a squint and grind of my teeth.

He stood at the top of my stoop as if contemplating a response. "Right," he simply said before sprinting down the steps, halting midway to face me again. "By the way my name is Dontae. You enjoy the rest of your day." He turned away and continued down the steps.

I watched as he reached the landing, walked through the gate, up the street, and out of sight before I remembered I was standing in my doorway clad in nothing but a towel. Suddenly, my left hand felt numb. I looked down and saw that I was still clenching the hell out of that knife.

Chapter 2

"What, you didn't think he was cute?" Amber asked, hitting her third mile on the treadmill, her athletic form strong and upright, her spandex capris fitting her like a second skin, her pink and black work-out bra accentuating her tight abs.

"Well, yeah—I mean—no!" I said, running beside her, feeling as if I were gasping for my last breaths.

"You don't have to lie to me," Amber said effortlessly even though she seemed to be running twice as fast as I was.

"What he looks like has nothing to do with it." I reduced the speed on my treadmill and slowed to a walk.

"What are you doing?" Amber asked, glancing over at my machine with a raised brow.

"Um . . . slowing down my heart rate."

Amber stretched her neck to look at the electronic display on my treadmill. "You've only been running a half hour."

"And that's ten minutes longer than I intended to," I said, bringing the treadmill to a complete stop while trying to recover my breath.

"Another half hour wouldn't have killed you."

I stepped off, stood beside my treadmill, and stretched, pressing my calf to the back of my thigh. "Yes. It would have."

Amber shook her head. "I still don't get why you didn't just give him some," she said, maintaining her speed and showing no signs of tiring. "I would have if I were not engaged. He's just that gorgeous."

"You must really think I'm desperate." I stretched out my other leg.

"Well, it *has* been a good while. Hasn't it?"

"That's because I made up my mind to stop throwing it around to every Dick I meet. No pun intended."

"No pun taken."

I straightened my back and bent over. I had an epiphany as I touched my toes. "Wait a minute," I said looking up at Amber sideways. "If you knew I had the hots for Devin, how come you paid Dontae to sleep with me?"

"Devin was going to be hit or miss."

I straightened up to get a better look at Amber. "Why? You didn't think I could snag a tall, fine ass drink of water like Devin?"

"No, sugarplum. That had nothing to do with it."

I was astounded by Amber's stamina. She was barely sweating as she trotted along.

"Dontae was simply a back-up plan."

I shook my head and chuckled. "Boy, you were really on a mission to get me laid." I walked over to a dispenser and retrieved some sanitary wipes then returned to my treadmill.

"You know I have to look out for my girl."

Despite my disdain for pity of any kind, I did consider that at least Amber's intentions were good. "Thanks. But next time, save your money." I began wiping down the display, and then the cup holder, the television monitor, the arms, and the thingamajig that attaches to you and stops the treadmill if you trip or fall.

"Oh, you don't mean that," Amber said, still galloping along.

"Yeah, I do," I insisted, noticing where dust had accumulated on the floor around the treadmill and fighting an overwhelming urge to wipe it away. I lost that battle and quickly bent over to wipe the tiled floor.

"Girl, what are you doing?" Amber asked, still running. I could almost feel her rolling her eyes at me.

"This place can use a good cleaning." I went to get more wipes so I could clean the other side of the floor where the treadmill was positioned.

"You're not at home, Symone."

I stood up to dump the dirty wipes in a nearby trash can. I glanced at my watch. It was going on eight o'clock. "Look, I have to hit the shower. I got little more than an hour to get to work." I said, holding onto the ends of the towel I had draped around my neck.

Amber was still in her stride. "Look, Symone, you're one of my best friends...and you know I got nothing...but love you for you. I want you to have some fun...once in a while," she had said in between breaths. "It's *okay* to want to be caressed...and held by a man every now and then. Every woman wants that. Heck, every woman deserves that. You don't have to feel guilty...or ashamed because you get lonely sometimes. We've all been there."

"So Dontae is the answer to my prayers?" I shook my head at the mere thought of it. "A man that earns his money sleeping around with desperate women? A gigolo? Wait a minute. Do they even still call it that?"

"Dontae may be a momentary thing, but from what I hear…it'll be a moment you'll never forget." Amber said, smirking as if running forty minutes straight had no effect on her.

"Well, I'll never know."

"He'll always be there if you change your mind or if that fire burning between your thighs gets too hot and starts singing the hairs off your twat." Amber laughed, nearly tripping over her feet.

"That was so funny, I'm dying of laughter here."

Amber quickly regained her composure. "That's exactly your problem, Symone. You've forgotten how to have fun."

"Maybe I have," I responded hanging onto the ends of the towel still draped around my neck. "Tell me something, Amber?"

"What's that, sweet peach?"

"How did you come to know this Dontae?"

"He's Ebony's younger brother—"

"Ebony's younger brother? I shouted.

"Best friend."

"Huh?"

Amber sucked her teeth then repeated, "He's Ebony's younger brother's best friend."

My ears started to burn instantly, and every muscle in my body tensed up. I had to fight back a sudden impulse to snatch Amber off that treadmill and pound her head into it. She knew how much I despised that money-grubbing, man-stealing twit—especially after the other night.

"You paid ditzy, bitchy, Ebony's little brother's friend to have sex with me?" I only realized I was screaming when half the people in the gym turned to look at us.

Amber finally reached for the button on the display to slow her treadmill and fell into a swift walk, her elbows swinging at her sides. "Well, yeah, but what does that have to do with anything? It was Ebony who recommended him as a gift in the first place."

"That boy's a friggin baby compared to me!" I retorted, trying to be mindful of how loud I was talking.

"Dontae is twenty-seven. He's not *that* young."

"If I were thirty-thirty-five, maybe, but you're talking about an eleven-year age difference."

"So?" Amber said with a shrug. "What's wrong with being a sexy, hot cougar? Ro-oow!" she roared and clawed at me with one hand.

I shook my head. "Figures dingbat Ebony would think a roll in the hay with a perfect stranger is par for the course."

"Girl, you need to loosen up a bit before you pop a blood vessel."

"Look, I've got to get out of here or else I'll be late for work." I stormed off, damn near marching into the locker room, singed by the thought of Amber letting Ebony believe I was so hard up for it that she had to pay someone to sleep with me. Damn! I was really looking forward to a cold shower.

***

I'd just sat down and picked up a pre-sentencing report to review when the aroma of hazelnut coffee wafted to my nostrils and overwhelmed the usual stale air of my dusty office. I looked up to find Phil standing in the doorway with his requisite latte in tow.

"Oh good. You're *are* here. I was about to send out a search party," he said.

I shrugged. "I was five minutes late. Big deal." I lowered my head to continue reading the report, my lips moving to silent words.

"For *you* it is. You've never been late in the six years—"

"Seven," I corrected.

"I'm sorry, the *seven* years you've been here."

"Uh-huh," I simply stated, keeping my eyes glued to the report, hoping he'd get the message that I wasn't in the mood for early-morning chit-chat.

Instead, he walked into my office, sat in the wooden chair pressed up against the wall across from my desk, and crossed his legs.

"Why are you so bitchy this morning?" He probed, taking a sip of his do-it-yourself latte from a Styrofoam cup. Every morning, for seven years, Phil made the same flavor of instant coffee from liquid packets and milk that he heated in the microwave.

I finally looked up at Phil, taking note of how yuppyish he looked in a plaid shirt, tan suit, and hot pink bowtie. His sandy-blonde hair was shaved close on the sides and teased in the middle. Sunlight beamed through my office window, illuminating his green eyes so that they twinkled. I had always suspected Phil was gay, but never had the gall to ask and he didn't volunteer any information himself. He had shared custody of his eight-year-old daughter, but he never talked about his child's mother or any woman for that matter. He loved talking sports with the men around the office and equally enjoyed chatting it up with us ladies about the "real housewives" of this or that or the latest reality show centered around getting married.

"I'm *not* bitchy!" I snapped.

Phil smirked and leaned back in his chair. "Case closed."

"Okay, I'm sorry. I just had a weird weekend." I wrinkled my forehead trying vainly to focus on the report I held close to my face.

"What's the matter? You didn't enjoy your little soirée?"

"Not really. Especially since it set me back three hundred bucks."

"You're kiddin'? Three hundred dollars for a few bags of chips, dip and buffalo wings?"

"And wine and liquor—anyway, its water under the bridge."

"So whatever happened with…" Phil trailed off. "What was his name again? The nice-looking fellow who had his eyes planted on you for most of the evening? He had a really cool name. Oh, I remember. Dontae."

Phil's words electrified me. Suddenly, he had my undivided attention. "Wait, you know about Dontae?" I asked, laying the report on my desk while looking Phil square in the eyes.

"Of course." Phil laughed, crossing his arms and arching his wrist. "We talked half the night. I have to say, he was dead-set on snagging you. Did he make a move?"

I laughed, recalling the absurdity of Amber's so-called gift. "Oh yeah. He made a move alright."

Phil sat up, his arms as straight as arrows as his hands clenched the sides of his chair. "Do tell…puhleez." He leaned into my desk with perked ears, his sparkly eyes widening in anticipation of hot gossip.

"There's nothing *to* tell."

Phil's shoulders slumped. "You mean you didn't oblige him? Why? He was *adorable*." Phil crossed his legs and sat back in his chair reaching for the cup of latte he had placed on my desk, spilling some of it on my calendar blotter. I grabbed a few napkins from the drawer and went to work, feverishly rubbing the brown splat from April 23rd.

Phil pressed his palm to his chest. "Oh! Clumsy me. So sorry, Symone."

I tossed the napkins into a nearby waste basket. "You're forgiven."

"Good." Phil said, snuggling back in his chair. "Now back to Mr. All That and Then Some. Why didn't you guys hit it off?"

"Long story. Look Phil, can we take this up another time? I've got a shitload of work in front of me and somehow I have to find time to check in on one of my cases today."

D.D. Sherman   Rare Orchids

"Okay, okay. Not going to make you have to tell me twice." Phil stood. "But you've got to tell me all of the dirty details the very first minute you get," he insisted, pointing a finger at me.

"I promise."

Phil smiled and gulped down the last of his latte, tossing the empty cup into my trash can on his way out.

***

The neighborhood of East New York seemed to be the dumping ground for all those who were either gentrified out of the more coveted areas of Brooklyn, or who were the lottery winners of the sudden implosion of low-income housing. A few property owners doggedly held onto what they had, while the carcasses of boarded up, foreclosed homes awaited new ownership. My juvenile client lived up the block from a methadone clinic and if I visited him early enough I'd catch what looked like the backup cast of *The Walking Dead* staggering about in real time.

Godson Curry was one of forty-two cases I was tasked with supervising. My clients were mostly adolescent boys making their way through the foster care system, or otherwise the products of highly dysfunctional families. They all shared similar stories of growing up in fatherless homes or being churned through a capricious foster care, mental health or criminal justice system. At nine, Godson had already been labeled a juvenile delinquent and a reluctant truant afflicted with ADHD, which to me were all euphemisms for a misguided, unloved, and very confused child struggling to discern his place in a society that didn't quite know what to do with him. By the time his three-inch thick, tattered folder came across my desk, he had been in and out twelve foster homes. Typically, some petty misunderstanding—like taking extra food without asking or changing the television channel without permission—got him kicked to the curb. His biological mother was only sixteen when she had him and went on to pursue a career tricking for dope, leaving Godson home alone for days on end. A neighbor had reported her— and the thirty-year-old loafer she'd let shack up with her—to ACS. One day during an unannounced wellness visit, an agent found a hungry Godson frightened and home alone. He told the agent he hadn't seen his mother in days and couldn't remember the last time he had eaten. He was four years old and had been a ward of the state ever since while his mother and made-believe daddy did a brief stint in prison for child neglect.

I approached the old dilapidated brick-front building where Godson had lived for eight months. I found him sitting at the bottom of a concrete stoop that had no banisters. His head was buried between his thighs while a few small children tagged and chased each other on the sidewalk before him. His foster mother and her granddaughter sat at the top of the steps in lawn chairs and the mother vigorously waved to me as she saw me approaching.

Godson slowly lifted his head in my direction, a smile emerging on his face.

I sat beside him, opening my bag to retrieve a hand-held video game. It was against the rules, but Godson had confided to me long ago that he'd never been gifted with so much as a birthday card. So, with every visit I made it my business to pick him up a little something.

"Oh wow!" he exclaimed, his previously lethargic mood perking up as he snatched the game from my hand.

"What do you say, Godson?"

"Oh, I'm sorry." He looked up at me sheepishly. "Thanks, Miss Alexander." He held the game in his lap closely examining his new gadget.

"Put it away!" I urged, not wanting to call attention to the other playing children or his foster family who were sitting in earshot.

He hastily stuck the game in his pants pocket.

"How you doin' today, Miss Alexander?" Ms. Grace, Godson's foster mom asked sitting back in her lawn chair and fanning herself with a crumpled magazine.

I twisted my neck to look up at her, shielding my eyes from the piercing sun. "Trying to stay cool, like you."

She was a robust woman with a wide grin. "Godson tell you he passed all his classes 'cept fo' math?"

"Yes, he did." I turned in the direction of Godson. "Guess that means summer school for you, little man."

"Uh-huh," he replied ruefully. Suddenly, he sprang to his feet as if remembering something. "I gotta get somethin' outta the house! Wait right here, Miss A!" He turned, leaping two and three steps at a time then disappeared behind two rickety adjoining doors.

I stood and walked up a few steps to where Ms. Grace and her pregnant granddaughter, Jeanette, were sitting.

"How's he *really* doing?" I asked, trying to whisper.

"I mean, fo' the most part, he's a good chile. It's jus' that he gits restless and that's when he starts get'n into thangs. I mean, it seems like I gotta keep my eye on him ev'ry second of the day."

"Well, you're doing a phenomenal job. He's been from pillar to post the bulk of his life. I think eight months is the longest he's been with anyone."

"That's right. That's what his social worker told me."

"I'm going to look into some programs for him. Between that and school, he shouldn't be finding much time for trouble."

"Maybe we can wear him down," Ms. Grace said with a light sigh.

"That's the plan." I turned my attention to Jeanette, who had been thumbing through the screens on her phone. "So when's your due date?" I asked, figuring it polite to make small talk.

"August third," she mumbled, barely looking up at me.

"Wow! Two months. Are you excited?"

She shrugged. "A little."

I noted her bare ring finger and the fact that there was never a man in sight whenever I came to visit.

"Well, good luck with everything if I don't see you before then."

She smiled weakly, dropped her head and went back to playing with her phone.

D.D. Sherman   Rare Orchids

Godson swung open one of the doors, holding a piece of blue construction paper. "I made you a card for your birthday, Miss Alexander," he said, jumping the steps to where I stood and handing me the decorated piece of construction paper.

HAPPY BERTDAY TO THE BAST PRO B EVER! It read in large, awkward letters, finished with a few random sprinkles of glitter.

"He's been wanting to give you that thang since last month." Ms. Grace chuckled lethargically. "I told him that he had to be patient 'cause I knew you'd be stopping by here sometime soon."

"I love it!" I exclaimed, grabbing Godson into a generous hug. "I'm going to hang it on my fridge as soon as I get home." I kissed his cheek then released him.

Godson stood with his arms folded and a proud smile fixed on his face probably mirroring the wide smile I wore on mine.

"Well, I have to be getting back to the office." I turned to face Ms. Grace. "I'm so glad to see that he's doing well. I'll be contacting you about those programs, just as soon as I can find a suitable one." I said, folding the soft cardboard to stick it inside my handbag.

Ms. Grace nodded.

Godson grabbed on to my hand, leading me down the flight of steps.

"How come you ain't got no husband, Miss A?" he blurted as soon as we reached the landing. "Pretty ladies always have husbands."

"Well, how do you know that, young man?"

"Cause I don't see no ring on your finger 'cept for the one they give you when you graduate from school."

I took in a deep breath, searching my mind for an appropriate answer. "I had a husband once."

"What happened? Did he get kilt or somethin'? They tell me I had a uncle that got kilt."

25

I squatted to get eye level with Godson and placed a hand on his shoulder. "No, no, nothing like that. We decided that we would be happier just being friends."

Godson stood with his forehead crinkled, considering my answer.

I squeezed his small shoulder. "It's one of those things that you'll understand when you're older so try not to think too hard about it."

"Oh," he replied, relaxing his face.

"Keep up the good work. I'm proud of you."

"I will."

"And pay attention in summer school so you can pass math."

"An' den maybe I can graduate and make it to junior high school, right Miss A?"

"If you work hard."

I patted his cheek then walked to my car, praying that Godson's run of good behavior would not be short-lived and wondering what in the hell could I do to make things better for him.

Chapter 3

"You have *got* to be kidding me?" I said approaching my house, shocked to see Dontae sitting on the porch steps, leaning back on his elbows.

"Do you work all day long, lady? I've been waiting here for two hours." He glanced at his smart watch with a bright neon-orange band attached. "I mean, it's almost nine o'clock at night."

"Seriously, dude? You didn't get the message the last time I threw your behind out of here?"

He sluggishly rose to his feet with a grunt, dusting his rear off. "Boy, sis, you are sooo uptight. You really need to relax," he suggested, now looking down at me.

I titled my head back to look up at him. "Look *young* man, you had your fun the other day. I'm really not up for any games tonight. And you can tell your little friend's sister that I may be single, but I'll never be that hard up for—"

"Wait!" He interjected, tilting his head to one side and frowning. "Is that a gun in your waist?" He straightened his neck. "You a cop?"

"Listen, I don't owe you—"

"You mean to tell me you're packing that type of heat—" he broke off, squinting at my waist. "A Glock? And the best you could come up with the other night was a *butter knife*?"

"I didn't have the chance to get to it. I keep it in a safe. I mean, I *used* to keep it in a safe. Now I sleep with it under my pillow. You just never know what fool you may find hiding under your bed these days." I crossed my arms and pursed my lips.

"True, true," he affirmed nodding his head, choosing not to acknowledge the reference I was making to the other night.

A gentle breeze blew past and carried his scent to my nostrils. It was an odd but pleasant fragrance of fresh coconut and almonds. It was becoming darker and I took note of how his gleaming white teeth sparkled against his golden-brown skin which held the hue of a hot mocha latte.

D.D. Sherman				Rare Orchids

A tingle crept up my spine and a warmth between my thighs urged me closer to him.

". . . that's all."

Apparently, he had been speaking to me as I momentarily drifted on scented clouds of almonds and coconut. "That's all what?"

"I left my Nets baseball cap here and I just came by to pick it up. That's all."

"Yes, I found it lying on the floor at the foot of my bed and put it away. Wait here." I commanded as I brushed past him on my way up the steps.

"I guess this means that you *wanted* me to come back," he said, turning his head in my direction as I ascended the steps.

"No, it means that with all of the people in my house that evening, I didn't know who the hell it belonged to," I returned, unlocking my front door and stepping inside.

"You sure you want me to wait out here?" he shouted after me. "You can still claim your gift!"

I closed the front door behind me choosing not to entertain his offer. I tossed my handbag onto the sofa and started to unholster my gun but thought better of it. I walked up the hall, past the kitchen and guest bathroom, stopping at a hallway closet. I opened the door and pulled his
baseball cap that I had neatly stored in a Ziploc bag down from the shelf.

I hurried back to the front door and swung it open. "Here you go," I said, handing him the bag. He stood, smirking, at the top of the steps.

"I don't bite," he said taking the bag from me. He recovered his hat and discarded the Ziploc bag over his shoulder which was immediately taken up by a gentle wind.

"All dogs bite," I retorted, brushing past him and recapturing the wafting bag mid-air. "Ouch. That hurt."

"Good!" I remarked, feeling a sense of accomplishment for doing my part to spare the environment of more senseless waste.

"Wait! You for real?" he asked with a perplexed look.

"What? Somebody's gotta be environmentally conscientious," I said, walking back up the steps with bag in hand.

"Look at you, all worried about our planet. That's just the cutest thing." It had gotten darker so Dontae's bright whites were really gleaming.

I maneuvered past him and stepped inside the foyer. He placed his foot at the threshold as I attempted to close the door.

"No need to be rude, hon. I'm just trying to get to know you," he said, still with his foot stuck between the door and frame. In a fleeting moment, I thought about slamming that door on his fancy sneaker.

"Why? Because someone paid you to?"

He chuckled sexily. "No, because I think you're a cool person. You're just putting up a front."

I glanced down at his foot planted in my doorway. "Um. . . can you move your foot, please?"

There was that irresistible smirk again. "Yeah, I can move my foot, but it's going to cost you something."

"Boy, you really are persistent."

"A closed mouth can't get fed."

"What do you want from me, *young* man?" I said, hoping he'd understand that my emphasis on young meant I wasn't into games.

"To get to know you better. That's not asking for a lot, right?"

"I ain't fixin' to be nobody's sugah momma."

He chuckled. Hey, I make my own money."

"So, I've heard. . . Look, bro, we have *nothing* in common."

"Sure we do," he said with a smile, revealing those radiant teeth.

"Like what?"

His smile broadened. "Like this moment."

I was quickly becoming bewitched and weak in the knees as if Dontae were putting some kind of spell on me. I wanted to say something sarcastic, but words evaded me.

Apparently taking advantage of my moment of vulnerability, his soft, luscious lips pressed against mine. I was savoring the sweetness of his gentle kiss when I found the gumption to push him off me.

He chuckled and then smiled softly, his lips still moist with my saliva. He put his baseball cap on. "You *sure* you don't want me to come in?"

I cleared my throat, trying to ignore the heat between my thighs and the erratic thumping of my heart. "Look, I don't know what came over me. I'm usually not like this. It's just—"

"Look, baby. You don't have to explain yourself to me. It's okay—"

"No, it's *not* okay. I don't know what in the hell I was thinking." I looked down at his foot still blocking the doorway. "For the last time, can you please move your foot from my doorway?"

He smiled, as if debating whether he should honor my request. After a moment or two he slid his foot back.

"Goodnight, Symone."

A thrill came over me and I shivered when he said my name, but for some reason I felt too weak to reply.

He pulled his baseball cap down on his head. I watched as he turned away and raced down the flight of steps. He reached the landing, spun in my direction, and kissed the air.

I quickly closed the door, praying he wouldn't use my few moments of vulnerability against me at some future date. I collapsed against the door and inhaled deeply. The smell of fresh coconut and almonds lingered on my skin.

***

Even though it was nearly twelve in the morning, after a long hot shower and dinner—chicken breast, cucumber, and tomato salad, I decided to pull all the food items out of my pantry and sort them by expiration date.

D.D. Sherman   Rare Orchids

    At the stroke of midnight, I was sitting on a chair in the middle of the kitchen floor surrounded by an ocean of boxed cereals, pastas, rice, cans of sauces, jars of peanut butter, bottles of dressings and other food paraphernalia. I was dismayed that a few items had somehow remained past their expiration dates and inwardly admonished myself while tossing them into a nearby trashcan. I worked tirelessly, placing the good items back into the pantry with the oldest dates to the right and the more recent dates to the left. I entertained the thought of perfecting the system by developing a spreadsheet and logging groceries into the computer as I bought them, but quickly dismissed the idea, figuring the task would be too daunting and time-consuming. *You're just going to have to learn to stay on top of things!* I scolded myself.

    I thought my preoccupation with organizing my pantry would keep thoughts of Dontae at bay, but that kiss we shared kept flashing in my mind and whenever it did a wave of euphoria surged through me.

    It was nearly two in the morning when I finally completed the pantry task and crawled into bed. I was too exhausted to think of anything that had happened the previous day and grateful to have fallen asleep the moment my head hit the pillow.

***

    "It makes me look fat!" I protested, looking at my side profile in a full-length mirror.

    "Well, *I* like it." Ebony spun around before the full-length mirror at the Forever & Ever Bridal Boutique.

    Amber had chosen a metallic-gray, chiffon dress with a black sash for us to wear as bridesmaids in her upcoming August wedding.

    The dress fit Ebony like it was made for her, but I found that it added excessive girth to my already size twelve figure.

Amber, who had been sitting on the edge of a sofa—anxiously blurting out orders for us to sashay, twirl, pause and strike a pose—looked up at me wearily. "I'm sorry Symone. I love the dress and the other girls who tried it on all agree."

"Why couldn't you just go for a simple black dress?" I asked, placing my hands on my hips and slumping my shoulders.

"Black?" Ebony retorted, shifting her weight to one side and placing a hand on her voluptuous hip. "Black is boring."

"Black is chic!" I insisted.

"Well, you've got until August to try and knock off twenty pounds," Ebony suggested, turning back to face the mirror where she primped and admired herself from all angles.

I shot Amber a warning look.

"Okay, let's not go there, Ebony," Amber warned. Ebony shrugged in response.

Another of Amber's bridesmaids, Lacey, a happy-go-lucky, grey-eyed girl, with sandy-brown tresses, was also trying on her bridesmaid gown.

"I lost twenty pounds in one month on the Fast Drop Diet," she said, turning from her mirror to face me, her dress clinging nicely to her petite frame. "If you want, I can give you their website. It wasn't hard to follow. You just eat a lot of protein and very little carbs. It's something like the Paleo diet."

"No, but thanks anyway. Skeletons belong in graveyards." I mumbled under my breath, turning away from her and stepping off the platform to sit next to Amber.

Lacey shrugged and turned toward the mirror again, tugging on the sweetheart neckline of her gown so that it made her boobs look fuller.

"I'm sorry about Eb," Amber leaned over to whisper.

"It's okay. This is supposed to be about you. I'll wear this dress, even though it makes me look like a beached whale," I cajoled her with a chuckle.

"You can never look like a whale. You're just being hard on yourself, sweet peach."

D.D. Sherman   Rare Orchids

I placed my arm around Amber's neck and pulled her to me in a friendly embrace, noting how fresh and clean her hair always smelled. The massive diamond twinkling on her soft, neatly French manicured finger reminded me of something.

"You wouldn't believe who stopped by my house last night I said to Amber, releasing her and kicking off the pair of glittering four-inch stilettos she'd picked out for us.

Amber's eyes lit up. "Did you give him some?"

"Girl, I told you I ain't messing with that kid. He left his baseball cap there the other night and was just stopping by to pick it up."

"Are you sure that's *all* that happened?" Amber asked with a raised brow.

I averted my gaze. "Of course I'm sure," I said bending over to scoop up my shoes.

Amber shook her head. "Well, I might as well tell you now."

"Tell me what?" I asked lifting myself up from the sofa.

A giggling Ebony and Lacey stepped down from the platform and headed toward the dressing room. I thought maybe their inside joke was about me. Amber watched until they were out of sight.

"Devin's accompanying Ebony to the wedding."

"So," I shrugged, standing before her, barefoot, holding those high heels by their ankle straps.

Amber stood and placed a hand on my shoulder. "I know how much you liked him, and I didn't want you to be surprised, especially since you don't have a companion for the wedding."

"Come on, Amb. You threw me a pity party last week. Girl, I'll be fine. Besides, I still got about two months. Anything can happen."

Amber shrugged. "Yeah, you never know, right?"

"And there's always Phil if I get desperate."

Amber turned her head to give me side eye. "Ain't he gay?"

"The hell if I know. I'm not trying to sleep with him. I just don't want to be there alone and looking stupid."

Amber nodded. "I feel ya, pumpkin."

"Anyway, it's not about me. It's your day."

Amber smiled and we hugged again. After that, I made a beeline for the dressing room. I couldn't wait to peel that vice grip of a dress off me.

***

I had been sitting in my Rover with the driver's side window cracked for more than an hour trying to muster up enough courage to ring Nathan's bell. It would have been all good under normal circumstances. In fact, he used to love when I surprised him. Like the one time I was feeling all Robin Givens*nish* in *Boomerang* and showed up on his doorstep with a black trench and less lingerie than she wore in the movie. But just last week I told him to lose my phone number, deleted his from my list of contacts and damned myself to hell should I ever pick up the phone to call him again, much less go see him.

I sat, trying to remember what sparked my angry outburst. We always fought over frivolous stuff like how it irked me that he always kept his phone on silent, or how he typically gave one-word answers to my questions. He hated that I popped gum, referring to it as my 'suppressed inner ghetto child struggling to come out.' He detested whenever I reminded him about upcoming holidays. 'You suppose to let the man surprise you. A man doesn't like to feel like he's being pressured into something,' was his reply. Then he'd go out of his way to prove his point by not making much of the holidays which just peed me off even more.

Nathan was an Aries and I a Taurus. Have you ever seen a raging bull and a mighty ram frolicking through the pastures of life without incident? According to Linda Goodman, our relationship was doomed by the cosmos before we even met.

It was a Tuesday evening and I was taking a chance on him being home. He was usually in the gym a few nights a week. Other days he stayed home searching the computer for cheap houses that he could rehab and flip.

An anxious tapping on the car window jolted me, calling my attention to a grungy man in a black hoodie who was sweating profusely. He made circular motions with his fist, urging me to roll down my window. I complied, gripping the butt of the gun I had concealed in my opened shoulder bag sitting on the passenger seat next to me.

"I'm sorry miss. I haven't ate nufin' all day. I was wondering if you could spare a dollah so I can get some'n to eat?"

I reached into a compartment I used for spare change and scrambled for a few coins. I dropped about a dollar's worth of change in his filthy, calloused palm.

He glanced down, then back up at me. "Anotha fifteen cents would make a dollah."

"Well, you're almost there." I rolled up my window.

"Thanks, sis. God bless you anyway," he replied with censure.

I nodded as he turned to walk away. I watched him in the side view mirror. He scuttled up the block with a gait that favored his right leg as if the other one was too short.

I reached for my hand sanitizer and squeezed half the bottle into my palm, rubbing them vigorously.

I had a change of heart and started the engine. Just as I did, Nathan's black Suburban pulled into an empty space in front of his brownstone.

My heart pounded and I could hear blood rushing through my ears. My slippery palms slid along the steering wheel. *Maybe I should offer to treat him to dinner and a movie?* I thought. After all, it was me who cussed him out and told him that if he ever called me again, or so much as walked down my block, I was heading right to court and taking out a restraining order. 'Just try me,' I warned him. 'I know lots of people in the system.'

'There you go again, acting like a cop,' he'd said with a shake of his head. 'Get this straight, woman, I'm not one of your clients!' That was the last thing he said before leaving me looking

like a fool—all alone at an upscale French restaurant—on the lower east side.

I took in a deep breath, opened the car door and felt my opened-toe heels make contact with the pavement. I coached my feet over to his vehicle, remembering to keep a sweet smile on my face. It always worked for me in the past, but then again, that was before I threatened him with a restraining order.

He darted out of his vehicle, wearing a gray jogging suit and jiggling his keys in his hand. He crossed in front of his car and mounted the curb not noticing that I trailed him by just a few feet away. I was about to call out to him when he walked over to the passenger side and swung open the door, through which emerged a pink pair of stilettos at the end of long, shapely legs which propelled a green-eyed, platinum blonde in a white jumpsuit into view.

I halted as my jaw dropped. It was as if someone had glued my soles to the ground. I just stood there watching the two of them giggle playfully as they walked hand in hand through the gate and up to his front door. He stuck his key in a lock, paused to give her a peck on the lips, and then turned the cylinder. They both stepped inside. Nathan glanced over his shoulder before closing the door behind them never noticing me.

Now he's into White girls? I could feel a wave of heat rise up from within me. My ears burned. I ground my teeth, struggling to suppress the urge to run over to his house, leap the gate, kick the door in, grab Blondie by her platinum locks, slam her to the ground and give her an ass kicking she wouldn't soon for—

The blaring of a car horn and the errrrrrrr of screeching tires jolted me aware that I was standing in the middle of the street. I leapt out of the way of a charging silver and black mustang. My upper body arched over and clutched the hood of Nathan's truck.

"You stupid motherfucker!" The driver shouted as he sped off.

I remained in that position for a few moments, frightened and gasping for breaths, with the words *stupid motherfucker* ringing in my ears. Perhaps he was right.

Chapter 4

"Well, you can't blame him." Phil sat at his desk adding his coffee packet to his Styrofoam cup of steaming milk. He wore a new hairstyle, parted on the side and combed flat. He looked nice, as always, in a mauve short-sleeved linen shirt and crisp, white slacks.

I sat across from him, leaning my head against my palm with my elbow propped on his desk. I was dressed in a soft yellow linen suit and flowery turquoise tank—peppy bright colors that nicely contrasted the mood I was in. I often confided in Phil because he was great at keeping secrets. Amber had been under the impression that I had left Nathan alone months ago and would have been quick to shake her finger in my face.

"I guess you're right." I finally said.

"I mean, threatening the guy with an order of protection?" Phil stirred his coffee with a plastic spoon. "Sounds a little extreme, hon," he added, tossing the spoon in a nearby wastebasket then cautiously sipped his coffee.

"I know. I know. He just gets me so riled up sometimes." I folded my arms over my chest and swung my crossed leg. "And then to take up with a *white* girl."

"What does the fact that she's white have to do with anything?"

"Because that is what these black men do the minute they get a little bit of money. Like sisters aren't good enough. Hmph!" I swung my leg faster.

"Maybe he finds the white lady a bit more docile."

"Bullcrap! Black women can be docile…sometimes…on very rare occasions."

"Exactly what I mean. Personally, I like the fact that black women are strong and don't take crap."

"What do you know anyway? What interactions have you had with black women other than here in the office? And you can't go by us. We're just always amped up from having to deal with the worst society has to offer day in and day out."

"My mom's best friend, Barbara, is black," Phil said confidently as if that made him some kind of authority on being black.

"Do you find Barbara aggressive?"

"Actually, she's the sweetest, little old lady you'll ever meet. But that's just comparing apples to oranges."

"Men often think of black women as aggressive. I like to call us resilient."

"Well, you've had to be."

"Amen to that."

"Ugh. White women are always stealing the best of our men!" I retorted.

Phil shrugged. "Well, steal some of theirs." There was a pause and then the both of us looked at each other and laughed.

"Are *you* available?" I asked, jokingly.

"Nah, you don't want me. I'm much too anal," Phil sipped his coffee.

"So am I?" I replied, wondering if he meant that literally. "We'd be perfect together."

"Gee, I hadn't noticed the way you sanitize your office three times a day."

We laughed again. "No seriously, Phil. I'm gonna need a date for Amber's upcoming wedding. I'm a bridesmaid and everyone's coupled up."

Phil sighed and took a few long sips from his cup. "What about the groomsmen?"

"Of course I have a partner to walk down the aisle with but it's not like I know the guy. Somebody named Melvin."

"Hey, I know." Phil wriggled around in his seat and straightened in his chair, his green eyes twinkling. "What about that young guy I met at your party the other—"

"Don't even go there, Phil!" I pointed my finger at him.

"You said you would give me all the dirty details."

"Amber hired him to sleep with me."

Phil dropped his shoulders and arched his back. "Noooo," he said placing his cup on the desk before him.

"Yeeaah. He was supposed to be my birthday gift."

Phil cackled uncontrollably. After about a minute, he finally composed himself. "Come on, you're not serious, are you?" he asked, teary eyed.

"As the IRS."

"That's great!"

"What's great?" I asked with brow raised.

"I wish someone would pay a hot bod to have sex with me. I think that was very thoughtful of Amber."

"It's not funny, Phil."

Phil studied me for a moment, then grinned. "Alright, alright. I'll be your beau for the evening, but the cake had better be good."

"Eight-tiered, red wine cake with chocolate ganache and buttercream frosting," I said, almost tasting the piece I'd sampled at Amber's cake testing.

"Would you stop!" he started in with his May West impression. "You're getting me all hot and bothered," Phil said, fanning himself with his hand.

A ringing phone line cut in on us giggling. Phil answered. "Officer Phillip Berman, speaking," he said in a deep, masculine voice which hit the ear oddly coming immediately after the sultry, feminine voice he'd just spoken in. "Yes, she is. Please hold on."

"Who is it?" I asked accepting the phone.

"The 79th precinct." Phil answered, turning the corners of his mouth down and shrugging.

"Yes, this is Officer Symone Alexander."

***

Lieutenant Lance McMillian's eyes seem to light up when I burst through the doors of the precinct, but his body remained ultra-relaxed, leaned back in a swiveling armchair. He smirked cockily, which I took to mean that either he was recalling our last tryst—

which ended in drunken sex even after I had bet him dinner and a Broadway show that it wouldn't—or was assuming that my flustered appearance meant I needed a favor—a big one. Lance seemed to enjoy seeing me vulnerable. I think it gave him a fleeting sense of superiority since we were both in law enforcement and butted heads because of that.

Lance had been divorced for three years and had since run through throngs of women like a drunk at a bar during happy hour.

'After almost ten years of marriage, I realized that it ain't for me! I'm just out here having fun for now.' He revealed over the lost bet dinner date before plunging a chunk of lobster between his impeccably straight teeth. He made sure I spared no expense on him.

A twinge of disappointment had sank to the pit of my stomach and churned my insides. After all, Lance was exceptionally good looking. He was forty-one with sprouts of grey in his moustache and goatee, tall and slender with a Hershey's Kiss complexion. In my mind's eye, he was at the top of the list of potentials to father my future children; though it seemed we could never get past the on again off again FWB status. Our unstable relationship all depended on my current dating situation and his finicky mood. I'd put him on pause whenever a new actor showed up, assuming role of boyfriend in my life and when he was done playing the part, I'd hit play and resume my pseudo relationship with Lance. We had been going on like that for a couple of years. It was pure bliss and absolute torture, but damn was he everything a girl could dream of—now whether that dream was a nightmare is whole another story.

I rushed over to the central desk behind which he was seated.

"Your client's in pen five," Lance said, sounding smug.

"What did he do now?" I asked, exasperated.

Lance swiveled in the direction of an officer standing on a lower platform. "Carmine, hand me the arrest paperwork on Godson Curry."

"Yes, sir," The dark-haired, blue-eyed officer responded.

Lance's eyes scanned over the report. "Petty larceny. The complainant, Annabelle Grace, claimed he stole a hundred sixty dollars from her."

I sighed. "That's his foster mother."

Lance tossed the report on the desk in front of me. I perused it quickly, not because I doubted anything Lance told me, but because I needed to see it in writing so the reality of the situation could sink in.

"Ugh." I groaned before sliding the paper back over to Lance. "He wouldn't do this. He's looking forward to junior high. He knows I'm counting on him to do the right thing. There has to be a reasonable explanation."

"The arresting officer found the money on him." The over-zealous officer handed Lance a padded envelope. Lance shook it in my face. "Here's the evidence."

"Can I talk with him?" I asked.

Lance looked at the officer again. "Put cell five in an interview room." The officer nodded, then scurried to the back of the precinct with a chunky set of keys jingling at his hip.

I noticed Lance glaring at me with a one-sided smirk. His eyes ran the length of my body, rolling up to focus on my face as if remembering I had one. "So whachu doin' tonight?"

"Laundry. Lots of laundry."

"Oh, thought maybe you wanted to catch a Netflix movie or somethin'."

I thought for a moment, trying to discern if Lance's question was an invitation or merely a statement. He was tricky like that, always holding back just enough to abort the mission if—for any frivolous reason under God's great sun—he had a change of heart. He was an emotionally tenuous guy, always with one foot in your door and the other in the fastest track shoe on the market.

"My client's waiting," I said dismissively. I knew better than to fall for Lance's shenanigans. It had been almost two years since our last drunken encounter and in that time I had come to understand that Lance was never going to be more than a quick romp in my silk sheets.

42

Godson sheepishly looked up at me when I walked into the room. His heavy-lidded eyes drooped, and he appeared older than his eleven years. I observed that he needed a haircut—not that his hair was too long, but rather that it was coiled into tight kinky knots that looked almost matted. There were random sprinkles of lint in his hair that resembled remnants of cheap bed linen, and a ring of ash encircled his dry lips.

"I didn't take Ms. Grace's money, Miss A," he informed me before I could sit opposite him at a wooden desk marred with coffee rings.

"I know you didn't, Godson," I said, dropping into an armless wooden chair.

He perked up, seeming surprised that I believed him. A weak grin appeared on his face and the crusty ring around his mouth cracked as if that were the first time he'd smiled that day.

"Are you thirsty?"

He nodded rigorously.

I looked through the open door and summoned an officer standing by. I reached into my wallet and extracted two dollars and handed it out to him as he trudged over to me. "Can I get a can of—"

I broke off to look at Godson. "What flavor soda do you like?"

"Cherry!" he exclaimed, sitting erect in his chair.

"Can I get a Cherry Coke?" I asked. The lackluster and frumpy appearing officer nodded, snatching the two dollars from my hand.

"How you know I didn't stole the money, Miss A?" Godson asked as I turned in my chair to face him.

"Because I know you want to do better in life. And I know you want to be very successful."

"Yeah, like a airplane driver—"

"You mean pilot. Pilots are the people who fly airplanes, they don't drive them. You drive cars and trucks. You ride bikes and motorcycles. You sail boats. But you *fly* airplanes. Understand?"

Godson ruminated over my explanation then nodded once it apparently clicked in his mind. "I got it," he affirmed with a yellow and plague-caked smile.

"So, tell me what happened? How did you end up with Ms. Grace's one-hundred-sixty dollars?"

"Cuz her grandson Marvin put it in my jeans pocket while I was sleep."

"Why would he do a thing like that?"

"Cuz he don't like me and wanna get me outta his house."

"Well, why wouldn't he like you? You're smart. Friendly. Nice."

Godson propped his elbow on the desk, leaned his head in his ashy hand, and shrugged his shoulders. "Guess some time people just don't like you," he mumbled.

"True," I reluctantly agreed.

"And maybe cuz I wouldn't let him see my video game. He wanted to know where I got it from, but I ain't tell 'im nothan cuz I didn't wanna get you in trouble, Miss A."

"Thank you, Godson." I felt a bit guilty, knowing that the whole misunderstanding was due to the gift I'd bought him.

The sluggish officer returned with a can of regular Coke in hand. "They didn't have cherry," he said, sitting the can before Godson then turning to exit the room, but remaining in close proximity to the opened door.

"Sorry about that," I said, but Godson smiled gratefully.

"I like this flavor too," he said, popping off the tab and releasing a *whish* of air before taking a few slurps.

"Well, let me go and make a phone call to Ms. Grace and see if I can straighten this whole thing out. She seems like an understanding lady."

"Yeah, Ms. Grace is cool, but sometimes she yells too loud and it hurts my eardrums," Godson informed me then resumed slurping his soda and smacking his lips in a way that would test the nerves of any adult not used to the myriad quirks of children.

"Look," I started, walking over to Lance who was reclined in his chair with his bent leg propped across the other. "I need a favor." I hated admitting to myself that I was still hopelessly attracted to him. It was his easy self-assuredness. He had it, knew it, and didn't give a damn if anybody begged to differ.

"Here it goes." he stated, unfolding his leg to sit upright.

"Yup! You knew it was coming." I said, hoping he'd take that as an admission that he was right and not sarcasm.

"Go 'head," he sighed as if bracing himself for something arduous.

"It's not that bad."

"Go 'head," he insisted.

"I need you to release Godson and sweep this whole incident under the table."

Lance straightened his shoulders from their previously slumped position. "Nah! Not going to happen."

"Why not? His arrest is unwarranted."

Lance jerked up the envelope and shook it in my face again. "Unwarranted? Here's the evidence!"

"He was set up!"

"This is the third time he's been in trouble since I've been assigned to this precinct. So don't go pretending he's just a poor victim of circumstance."

"Well, he is."

Lance tittered. "Gimme a break. That kid's a crook. Look, he's even got you conned."

I felt my shoulders droop. I needed to think of something...and fast. Lance was not the type to change his mind once it had been set.

I inhaled through my nose and forced a smile. "You know, I *did* want to catch up on Insecure. I'm a season behind."

"Really?" Lance asked, but more in a *woman-how-dare-you-insult-my-intelligence* tone.

"Reaaaly," I affirmed with a twang of sexy.

"I don't watch Insecure," he said leaning back in his chair clearly enjoying the sudden shift in power.

"You don't have to watch it," I baited.

"Hmm...not sure. Gotta be up at five in the morning. Firearms training."

"Don't worry. I'll make sure you don't oversleep."

Lance ruminated a minute or two then glanced over at the previous austere officer who seemed unaware of the wide grin stretched across his own face.

"Carmine!"

"Yes, sir."

"Process Curry for release," Lance ordered.

The officer's smile dropped, and his face resumed its serious expression. He pivoted in the opposite direction, stepped out from behind the desk and promptly scuttled toward the holding pen area.

"See you tonight?" Lance asked, eyeing me hungrily.

I nodded, inwardly cursing myself for being weak.

***

I rang the doorbell of apartment 2A and put a finger to my lip to shush Godson who stood next to me with his tattered backpack slung over one shoulder. His eyes looked upward, then wandered to the side, and back around as he chewed his lower lip in angst.

Phil flung open the door clad in a satin robe that hung open to reveal a pair of tight, silk briefs.

Godson gaped at him.

Surprised to see us there, he snatched his robe closed and fumbled with his belt, securing it tightly around his waist.

"Were you expecting someone?" I teased.

"Yes, the pizza delivery boy. What are you doing here, Symone?" he questioned, not bothering to hide his annoyance. "Ever heard of a courtesy call?"

Godson dropped his head, looking down at his worn sneakers and frayed laces.

"And who is this?" Phil asked.

"Godson Curry. You know, the nice kid I'm always talking about?"

"Nice kid?" he questioned, totally baffled. "I know about a kid that you're always complaining stays in trouble—"

I placed a hand on Phil's shoulder to stifle him. "Um...can we come in?"

"For what?"

I clenched my teeth. "Because we need to talk."

"I was just running a bath."

I shot Phil a wicked side-eye. He was deathly afraid of my side-eye—or any other black girl's side-eye for that matter.

"Come on in." He sighed, stepping back to open the door wider.

I walked in, half-expecting to see an assortment of male blow-up dolls, a rack of neatly assembled S&M blue rays, and a torture room fully equipped with metal contraptions, leather whips, and a video recorder.

I hadn't envisioned this simply because I thought Phil was gay, but rather that he seemed too perfectly put together. He fit the paradigm of the quintessential nice neighbor who had decade's worth of corpses buried deep within the cement floors of the building's laundry room. My imagination had run amuck, thanks to a marathon of crime shows I had OD'd on the prior weekend.

Instead, Phil's home was rather quaint; clean lines and sparsely, but tastefully, decorated. There were pictures of him and his eight-year-old daughter sitting on the mantle of a faux fireplace. Another one of a younger him with—who I surmised—to be his older sister and their parents. There was a Buddha flanked by two decorative candles, your typical flat screen television mounted to the wall, and a white leather sofa and love seat with soft, furry ornamented pillows strewn about them. From the living room I could partially see his bathroom. It was silver and black with a small, burgundy chandelier hanging from a textured ceiling. I noted that there was no water running; but who could blame him for lying about running himself a bath? I was impeding on his privacy, with a complete stranger, no less. I appreciated his graciousness in even allowing us in.

"Well, you might as well get comfortable." Phil suggested, moving some pillows off to the side so we could sit on the sofa. "While I go change into something apropos."

"I'm sorry for intruding, Phil. Really I am."

"I know you've got something up your sleeve. I'm just hesitant to find out what it is."

The doorbell rang, to my surprise.

"Can you get that?" Phil asked me, disappearing into a room at the end of a short hallway.

I opened the door and gave the tattooed, dark-haired, tall, and lanky pizza boy—who I guesstimated was no more than twenty-two—twenty-three max—the once-over. I thought Phil was just teasing about expecting him. He was a little too cute for that line of work. My deviant mind surmised he was probably slinging more than just pizza boxes.

He looked surprised to see me.

"Um...um..." he started, double-checking the receipt in his hand and looking at the mounted apartment number above the doorbell. "Um…I *think* I got the wrong apartment."

"No, you're in the right place," I assured him.

"Oh. Um..." he started, lowering his head between his shoulders. "Doesn't an older gentleman live here?" he whispered, for whatever reason.

"He does," I confirmed.

He smiled, relieved. "Oh. Thought I was going crazy."

"How much?"

He held the receipt before his eyes. "Eight cheesy knots, an order of eggplant parmigiana, and a liter of Diet Coke comes to $18.75."

I gave the man a twenty, took the order, and went to close the door when he raised his hand to stop me.

"'Scuse me, miss?"

"Yes?"

D.D. Sherman   Rare Orchids

He leaned in and shielded his mouth as if about to tell me a secret. "The older guy usually tips me a twenty." Then said in a normal tone, "'Cause I gotta ride my bike like thirty blocks just to get here."

"Oh, I'm sorry. Was I being presumptuous by tipping you?"

He sulked, looked as if he wanted to say something, but shook his head as he scuttled away.

I chuckled to myself. I'm usually a generous tipper, but the twenty dollars was all the cash I had on me that day and the fact that he kind of called me out on it just made matters worse for him.

I walked into Phil's small kitchen and placed the food on the counter, then glanced over at Godson. He was leaned forward on the sofa with his head propped in his hands and his elbows resting on his skinny thighs.

Phil was tuned in to an old black and white movie with the sound barely audible. He appeared in the entryway of the kitchen, his palms pressed against the door frame. He'd changed into a pair of distressed jeans, flip flops, and a v-neck t-shirt.

"Did you tip him?"

My forehead creased. "Of course I tipped him. Why?" I questioned, feeling a little insulted that he would even ask me that.

"Great! How much do I owe you?"

"It's on me."

"Bet I'll end up paying for it one way or the other," Phil said under his breath but loud enough for me to hear him. "Anywho, what's this surprise visit all about?"

"Well—"

"And give it to me in doses. I've got a migraine."

Oh Lord! He's being a diva, I thought.

I hesitated, trying to organize a succinct, yet compassion-provoking explanation in my head. "Well, let me see. What's the best way to put this? Okay. Godson Curry's foster mother's grandson planted a hundred-sixty-dollars on him and told her Godson stole it. She called the police, they searched him, and sure enough, found it on him. So he ends up getting arrested—by the way—that was the phone call I took in your office earlier. Anyway, I had to swing by the 79th to get him released. And then I called Ms. Grace and begged, and pleaded—"

"Doses please. *Small...doses.*"

"Ms. Grace refuses to take him back in and he needs a place to stay for a night...or two...or three, until I can find him a suitable home." I gabbled, then tucked my head between my shoulders and raked my teeth over my lower lip.

"So what does this have to do with Phillip Berman?"

Oh no! I thought. *He's referring to himself in third person.* Whenever Phil referred to himself in third person, he meant business. It seemed he had the uncanny ability to instantly stuff the ole light-hearted and playfully animated Phil into the crevices of non-existence and conjure up his staunchly serious and dour evil twin, Phillip, in an instant.

"You're like the only one I can count on."

"No. I'm not." Phil dropped his hands, walked into the kitchen, and scrambled through the cabinets and drawers for plates and silverware.

"Look, Phil, I wouldn't have asked if I didn't really—"

"First off," He started, but leaned his head back to glance at a restive Godson who had interlocked his fingers and placed his hands—palms up—on his head. He continued in a lowered voice. "First off, I'm not too keen on putting my job in jeopardy. This is textbook conflict of interest!" he snapped in a strained whisper.

"How are you putting your job in jeopardy? He's not your case. He's mine."

"For Pete's sake, woman. Don't go blonde on me now," he stated, pulling the container of food from the plastic bag. "Did you tip him?"

"You asked me that."

His eyes wandered upward. "Right. I did." he said, ladling out a heap of food onto a plate that I suspected would be mine. Phil knew how much I loved to eat.

"Look, Phil. Who's going to know? I have his case. All information concerning Godson is filtered through me."

"Cheesy knots?" he asked.

"Yes. Thank you." He handed me a plate then nodded at one of two chairs positioned at a metal bistro table that looked more like patio furniture. I went to set it down while he started on the second plate. "Can I use your bathroom? I need to wash up."

"Wash up?" Phil asked, perplexed.

I held my palms up and wiggled my fingers. "Just my hands."

"Oh." He nodded, his brow raised in skepticism. "Sure, go right ahead. Bathroom's straight down the hall."

Phil had a decorative dispenser for his hand soap, like I somehow knew he would. I pumped out a generous amount and massaged the fruity smelling liquid into my hands before rubbing them together under the tap to work up a good lather. I rinsed and repeated, three times for good measure.

"You think Godson likes eggplant?" Phil asked as I walked back into the kitchen drying my hands on a paper towel.

I shrugged, slumped down in my chair, and bit into a cheesy knot.

"I mean it tastes almost exactly like chicken...soft, moist chicken. I guess if we don't mention eggplant."

"Just give him a little bit. I'm sure it won't go to waste."

Phil left the kitchen to set up a folding table before Godson and bring him his dinner.

"Thank you, mister sir," I heard Godson say from the living room.

"No problema!" Phil replied before re-entering the kitchen and making his own plate.

"You're being evasive, Phil." I stated.

"Why can't he go into a foster center for the next few days?" he asked, walking over to the table to set his plate down, then back to a wine cooler positioned under the counter. "Red or white?" he asked flinging the door open.

"White. Moscato if you have it."

"Nope." He extracted a bottle from the cooler and held it up. "Chardonnay?"

"That's fine. Whatever. Look, Godson's gullible personality makes him an easy target for bullies. The last time he was in one of those homes, someone took a bottle to his head which is why he has that nasty scar behind his left ear. And set his sneakers afire."

Phil left the kitchen to bring Godson a can of some kind of organic soda. I snickered.

"What's so funny?" He asked stepping back into the kitchen, pouring out two glasses of the recently uncorked wine, and taking his seat at the minuscule table.

"Nothing."

"I did see the scar," he said with a hint of pity, then snarled. "Yeah, it's a nasty one alright." Phil stuffed a forkful of eggplant in his mouth and chewed slowly. "This is exactly what I needed," he said with a full mouth, then took a sip of wine.

"Can he stay?"

Phil inhaled and held onto that breath.

"Tomorrow's Friday and then there's the weekend," I noted.

Phil released a protracted breath and took another bite of food.

"Come on, Phil. I promise to have him placed first thing next week."

Phil swallowed. "I don't get you. Why do you care so much?"

"Because I'm an underdog fighter. I was picked on and bullied for most of my childhood and even into my early adult life. I know how it is to feel as if the entire world's conspiring against you."

The despondent look on Phil's face told me that he also related to what I was saying. "But what will he do here most of the day by himself?" he asked, taking another bite of food.

"Tomorrow's Friday. He'll be alone for just the one day." I shrugged. "Just give 'im a Cherry Coke, a few snacks and sit him in front of the TV."

"So I have to cancel my weekend plans?"

"I'll make it up to you," I pleaded.

Phil sat back in his chair and folded his arms across his chest while chewing. After some deliberation, he swallowed. "Okay." He shook his head and threw his hands up. "He can stay until Monday. Max!" He jabbed his fork at me. "And you're lucky it's not my weekend to watch Amy."

I leapt from my seat and ran over to hug Phil.

"And you're replacing whatever he steals."

"Godson's not a thief. He's only got two petty larcenies on his record. One time he ordered a sandwich from a deli and ran out without paying because he had gone the entire day without eating. The other time is when he hopped a turn style in search of his drug-addicted mother."

"I'm absolutely positive this is going to end up costing me big time."

I continued to hug Phil tightly. He smelled so nice, like freshly bathed skin and a Fifth Avenue fragrance boutique.

I straightened up and walked into the living room. Godson had eaten all his cheesy knots, but it looked as if he'd picked over the eggplant and his glass of soda was nearly full. I sat down beside him.

"Didn't like the eggplant, huh?"

"Da what?"

I pointed to his leftovers. "That's eggplant."

"It don't look like no egg. How can eggs be a plant?"

I patted his bony thigh. "Never mind. Look, Mr. Berman is kind enough to let you stay here a few days until I can find you a suitable home."

Godson's shoulders slumped. "He's weird," he mumbled and picked up his glass of soda holding it out before him. "And this soda tastes funny."

"Yes, he is a little strange, but he's very, very nice and you can trust him."

Godson shrugged.

I leaned over to whisper in his ear. "I'll tell him to let you watch all the anime you can stomach."

Godson looked revived, his droopy eyelids widening. "He got cable?"

"Yup! But I want you on your best behavior," I said, shaking a finger at him.

Godson nodded.

Phil appeared in the living room with glass of wine in hand. "Is this a party and no one invited me?" he asked, slapping a palm over his chest in exaggeration then dropping to sit on the shag rug before Godson and me. "Who's got the remote? I hear someone likes anime."

Chapter 5

Lance's erection greeted me at the front door. He was naked. He was Adam in the Garden of Eden naked. Before the fig leaves naked. His body was sculpted, defined and statuesque, like the Thinking Man, but standing up. His brown eyes seem to peer straight through me and I couldn't cool the heat between my thighs, nor calm the butterflies fluttering in my stomach.

He was chewing on the wrong end of a dental flosser and I don't know why that turned me on even more. Maybe it was because he was meticulous about his health and hygiene or maybe because he was cockily self-assured.

"Come in," he had to say in order to jar me from my stupor.

I pulled my eyes from his erect penis, brushing up against its firmness as I stepped inside the apartment and into his living room. The spectacular view of a shimmering Brooklyn Bridge juxtaposing the Manhattan skyline was as wonderfully jolting as his stiff organ.

I stood before the sliding-glass-window, marveling from twenty-one stories above at myriad streets that looked like veins snaking through a bustling metropolis, illuminated skyscrapers challenging the heavens, and throngs of harried people too hurried to take it all in.

Lance came up behind me and pressed himself into my backside. He rubbed his hardness against my firm buttocks and everything in me pulsated.

I spun around to face him and placed a hand on his chest pushing him an arm's distance away. "What are you doing?"

He dropped his hands from my hips in resignation. "Oh boy, here we go." His eyes rolled upward.

"What do you mean, 'oh boy here we go?'"

"Nothing," he replied, sounding annoyed.

"And why are you naked?"

"I just got out of the shower when you buzzed the doorbell."

I could sense a rising agitation in his voice that singed me a little, but I was hopelessly aroused, and I didn't want to do or say anything to spoil the evening.

"You hungry?" he asked, snatching the flosser from his mouth and tossing it into a nearby waste basket.

"Not really."

"Oh, 'cause I ordered Chinese food. Chicken lo' mein and shrimp dumplings."

"Maybe later," I said, plopping down onto his plush leather sofa.

He tossed the remote to me. "Here, watch whatever you want. I'm going to put some clothes on." He sounded disappointed, as if I had foiled his strategic plan to hit it the minute I walked through the door.

I turned on Netflix and scanned the menu for a movie, a romantic comedy perhaps. I felt my spirits tanking and had a yen for something funny.

I heard Lance rummaging through his chest of drawers. I started to debate if going there had been a good idea after all. Something about him answering the door with his private member fully extended rubbed me the wrong way. Like maybe that was the sole reason he invited me over but damn, did he have to make it so blatantly obvious?

He stepped back into the living room clad in boxers and a wife-beater carrying two paper plates in one hand and three Chinese food containers in the other, with the ends of two plastic forks clenched between his teeth. He set the food down before me on an art-deco coffee table that looked like a giant wooden spool with thick, silver rope wound around it to resemble thread. It was a cool piece of furniture. Previously, I asked him where he had found such a unique piece. He told me his artist friend Gustavo had designed it. Since that time Gustavo had designed a couple originals for me. One was a cocktail table which was a naked woman made of wax wood lying on her belly with her arms and feet curved upward to support a glass top. The other was a small totem pole made of teak wood that concealed salt and pepper shakers.

Lance made himself a plate, disappeared into the kitchen again, and then reappeared clutching two ice-cold Coronas.

I thought you might like a beer," he said, using a bottle opener to lift the cap off one of the beers, the action flexing his arm muscles.

I nodded. "Thanks. Appreciate it."

The cap popped off, releasing a wisp of vapor into the air. He handed it to me as condensation bubbled to the top and started to roll over the side.

He popped opened his own beer then dropped down beside me, grabbing his plate, and propping the balls of his feet up on the edge of the coffee table.

His toes were nice—cute even—with tiny coils of hair sprouting from the big ones. The nails were clean, evenly filed, which meant that he was probably keeping up with his routine pedicures. *He's so vain*, I thought. *So sickening, yet so impressively vain.*

I reveled in his muscular arm pressing against mine. It made me feel…well… protected.

"So what are we watching?" he mumbled with food in his mouth.

"I don't know." I shrugged, skipping through the choices.

"Not that girly stuff. You know I'm a shoot 'em up, bang, bang, kinda guy," he stated, plowing through his food like he hadn't eaten in days.

"Thought you said I can watch whatever I wanted?"

"Knock yourself out!" he said, plunging a fork full of food in his mouth.

"So Insecure is out?"

"Unless you want to watch TV alone." He chewed his food ravenously.

"What about the Dave Chappelle or Chris Rock comedy special?"

"Saw them both. But I'm down to watch them again."

"Oh, wait a minute!" he exclaimed, looking down at this watch. "I'm missing Luke Cage."

"Sorry, but I'm really not into superhero shows."

"I can catch it in the other room." He got up and placed his half-eaten plate of food on the spool top."

"You're just going to leave me here?" I asked, sitting my quarter drank Corona on the table. "That's rude, you know."

"Naaaaah," he tittered. "You're welcome to come watch it with me."

My eyes vacillated between the Netflix menu screen and the tall, lean bod standing over me.

"Whachu gon' do?" He sounded exasperated.

Well I didn't come here to watch TV by myself. I reasoned. *But I know where this is going to lead.*

"So whachu gon' do?" he asked again impatiently, placing his hands on his hips.

God give me strength! I thought, aiming the remote at the TV to turn it off and popping up from the sofa, following Lance up the hall into his bedroom.

He grabbed the remote, flicked on the TV, and fell back onto the middle of his bed with outstretched arms. His gold chain fell aside and hugged his neck. I stood at the edge of the bed looking down at him, trying to figure out if there was enough space for me. He fluttered his fingers, beckoning me to him.

"Move over!" I demanded.

"Ugh!" he grunted, scooting over on his behind. "You're so damn difficult."

I slid my heel straps from my ankles and kicked off my shoes before plopping in bed beside him and laying my head in the crevice of his underarm, which smelled like freshly washed skin and a manly deodorant. "Am I?" I asked rhetorically.

Lance propped up on his elbows to watch a scene wherein Luke Cage fought a crew of Jamaicans in a warehouse. He'd been swung at with a baseball bat, attacked with a machete, shot multiple times at point blank range, and tossed a grenade in which he crushed in his hand, then walked calmly away without so much as a papercut to the mortification of his opponents.

"Damn! My man!" Lance blurted, relaxing his neck and wriggling against the quilted blanket to get comfortable.

His warm palm crept up under my dress, ultimately resting against my thigh. His heart pulsated through his T-shirt and a sudden rush of blood bolted through my veins making me flush. I raised my head from his arm and shook out my thick mane, raking my fingers through it.

Lance turned on his side to face me as his delicate hand sneakily slid up my thigh and halted at the prize he was seeking. I drug up my heels, bending my knees, hoping to deter him, but he pulled my leg toward him and lifted himself from the bed to mount me.

Nothing's gonna happen. I coached myself. *But ain't nothin' wrong with a little bit of dry humping.*

"Can I pull your panties down?" he whispered in my ear, his moist breath sending trembles through my tense body.

"No," I protested weakly. He started to grind against me.

"Why not?" His deep, sultry voice was hard to resist.

"Because I don't think this is a good idea," I said near breathless, finding myself grinding back in perfect synchronization.

He sucked air between his teeth and pressed himself against me harder. "Come on!" he urged in a strained whisper.

"Nah. No can do," I protested though still in rhythm.

"Come on, baby. Let me get that."

Fight! I urged myself. *If you give in, you'll hate yourself in the morning—better yet, you'll hate yourself the minute it's over!*

He paused, sprung up on his knees, and pulled his wife beater over his head flinging it behind him. He reached both hands under my dress, and just like that, was tossing my red lace thong aside. He pushed my dress up and collapsed between my thighs with penis in hand. The head poked around in an almost frantic search for my opening. He aligned himself then commenced to—

"Stop!" I demanded, pushing against my elbows to sit up in bed.

Lance shut his eyes, dropped his head, and released a hard puff of air through flared nostrils. He lifted his head to look at me. "What's the matter, Symone?"

"You were going in raw dog?" I craned my neck to one side and folded my arms over my erect nipples. "You should *know* I don't do raw dog."

Lance exhaled and turned on his side to scramble through a drawer in a nightstand. "Wait. I got Magnums."

By that time the inferno blazing within me had started to cool. "Look," I began, swinging my legs across the edge of the bed. "I had a long day so I'm just gonna cut out." I reached for my shoes and panties, then slipped them on. "You can go ahead and watch your program undisturbed."

A look of disappointment darkened Lance's countenance as he tossed the unopened condom packet back in the drawer. "Hmph!" he groaned. "If I hada known this I would've ordered takeout for one."

"You can have the leftovers for lunch tomorrow."

He shook his head. "You're too damn melodramatic." He grudgingly lifted himself up from the bed. His erection had started to wither and in my mind's eye I patted myself on the back.

Ha! Ha! Good job! The sassy female voice that I often attributed to either my deceased grandmother—or some elementary school teacher I thought of as a mentor—celebrated in my head. "Sorry, I'm just not in the mood to be your fuck buddy today."

"Whatever!" Lance said exhaustingly while following me up the hall to the front door.

"Take care!" I said walking through it.

"Hey!" he called after me.

I turned to face him.

"I'm not mad at you. I'm here for whenever you're ready."

"I don't think I'll ever be ready for what you have to offer, Lance."

He shrugged and flashed a cocky smirk. That cavalier gesture sliced through me, momentarily siphoning me of something—dignity, pride, self-worth—hell, I couldn't tell. My emotions were clouding my mind. I just needed to get away from Lance and all the failed relationships he reminded me of.

***

The bubbly waitress sat two frozen margaritas down before Stephanie and me, then rubbed her palms against her apron.

"I'll be back with your nachos grandé and waffle fries, okay ladies?" The flickering light from the candle on our table twinkled in her crystal blue eyes. I tapped her arm as she went to turn away. She spun back around to face me.

"Can I get an order of fried calamari with that?"

"Sure!" she said with a quick flash of her braces.

"And can we look at some dessert menus?" I asked sheepishly.

"Yep!" she replied, and then scuttled off towards the back of the bar/eatery, her long, blonde, ponytail swinging to her peppy gait.

"Calmari too?" Stephanie questioned, pulling her phone from her handbag to check the message indicator. The illuminated screen made her overly made-up face look ghost-like in the dimly-lit bar. She was a bit of a contradiction in that she sported a short, natural afro, but wore long, fake eyelashes and globs of foundation.

"Yup! Guess I'm blowing my diet." I braced myself, waiting for her admonishment, but she instead texted something then slipped her phone into the side pocket of her handbag.

"So what's been up with you?" she asked without judging my decision to gorge myself on useless carbs and sugar. I suddenly remembered why I liked her so much.

Stephanie was a clerk in one of the courts I frequented. We weren't close like Amber and me, just casual acquaintances who did lunch every now and again. I never filled her in on my mostly non-existent love life like I did with Phil. I would only tell her that I went on a date here and there with this one or that one when we passed each other in the lobby or corridor. Never any spicy specifics. Just brief overviews.

"Oh, nothing much." I shrugged. *There is something going on. A lot going on, but I don't know if I'm comfortable sharing my deepest, border-line disturbing thoughts with a mere acquaintance.* "What about you?"

"I'm good. Thinking about getting dreads."

"That's going to take a while," I put in, more out of courtesy than interest.

She sipped her frozen margarita, then puckered and swallowed. "The fake ones."

"Oh!" I chuckled. "I've seen those." I grasped my frost-covered jar, sipped, and then smacked my lips. "Nice."

"I love your hair. So thick and long."

"Awww, thank you." I managed a smile though my heart was heavy. I couldn't erase that cocky image of Lance smirking one-sidedly from my memory. It was stuck on repeat. It seemed it would take a few more margaritas, a line of blow, and perhaps a lobotomy to help me forget.

I was so upset after leaving his apartment, I blew up Amber's phone; but of course, she was out somewhere being all lovey-dovey with her fiancé, so I settled for Stephanie because I knew—like me—she'd almost never say no to an opportunity to eat, though she managed to maintain a cute, but nicely robust figure.

"You heard about Judge Fuller?" Stephanie asked, leaning into the table as if she was about to reveal some big secret.

"Antonio R. Fuller?"

Stephanie nodded.

"I work with him all the time. Why? Something happened?"

She shook her head because she was sucking her frozen drink through a straw. "Mmmph." She set the glass jar down on the wooden table. I watched her smack her lips a few times, waiting for her to continue. "He's retiring."

"Oh no! Don't tell me that! He's always looked out for Godson. Helped me get him into a lot of great programs."

"Who?"

"Just one of my clients." I picked up my straw and whipped it around in my icy cocktail, feeling even worse hearing about Judge Fuller. "He's very fair and wants the best for a lot of people."

"Even the ones who don't want the best for themselves," Stephanie added.

"Tell me about it. You know how many used-to-be-thugs told me they've turned their lives around because of Judge Fuller?"

"I know. I know." Stephanie nodded, still sipping her half-full drink through her straw. She smacked her lips again. "I know quite a few of them."

Our waitress returned balancing three large platters. "Here ya goooo!" she sang out, sitting the mound of nachos drenched in oozing cheese, golden-fried calamari, and piping hot waffle fries on the table.

I wanted to dive in—headfirst, but I calmly reached for my silverware, unrolling my fork from a napkin which I submerged in the glass of scalding hot water I had asked for when we first sat down.

"Can I get you ladies another round?" Bright eyes asked with one hand on hip.

"Yes, I'll have another," I readily answered.

"Me too," Stephanie added.

"Alrighty then. Be back with those dessert menus!"

Good girl. I thought. *She remembered.* I flipped through my mind's rolodex of desserts. I had been to O'Keefe's multiple times and usually ordered the caramel-drizzled, chocolate chip brownie with a side of vanilla bean ice cream. But my taste buds were longing for something tart like maybe something along the lines of a warm apple pie alamode.

My phone buzzed in my purse, jolting me from the borderline pornographic thoughts I was having about food. I grabbed for it. Amber's modelesque profile dominated my screen. I accepted the call and pressed the phone to my ear.

"Hey!" I said, realizing how lackluster I sounded.

"What's the matter boo boo?" Amber could always detect when something was off with me. "How did the date with Lance go?"

"Date? What date?" I glanced up at Stephanie who I believed was pretending to be engrossed in her phone.

"Didn't you go by his house?"

"I did but listen. Let me talk to you about that another time."

"Oh, somebody must be in your midst."

"Uh-huh."

"Okay, honey dew. Hit me later."

"Will do." I disconnected the call, picked up my fork, and went to stab a wingette when I realized I had not washed my hands. *I'm slipping.* I thought. "Be right back," I told Stephanie, then excused myself from the table.

I burst through the door of the unisex bathroom and headed over to the single sink. I pushed up at the soap dispenser. Nothing. I pushed again. Nothing again. I pushed even harder. A little bit of something, but certainly not enough to adequately wash my hands. I was angry—no livid—no enraged. "How could they?" I mistakenly cried aloud.

"Don't tell me there's no soap." I noted that the voice belonged to someone wearing a pair of flowery, cloth wedge heels in one of the two stalls.

"Nope!" I confirmed.

"And this is supposed to be a restaurant? They should have people constantly checking these things," the voice grumbled as I listened to the snap of panties being pulled up.

"Yep."

"Well, I'm going to complain to management." A brown-eyed, brunette emerged from within the stall adjusting the straps of her sundress.

D.D. Sherman   Rare Orchids

"I don't blame you," I said, doing the best that I could with the miniscule trickle of soap I did manage to coax from the dispenser. I filled my palms with the warm water repetitively, grabbed for a few paper towels, and returned to my table.

I dug into my handbag and extracted a small bottle of hand sanitizer. I squeezed half its contents into my palm and rubbed my hands—one over the other—vigorously. I decided to eat my finger food with my fork for safe measure.

The waitress returned with our second round of drinks and the dessert menus tucked between her arm and side.

"Okay, you ladies just let me know as soon as you decide what you want for dessert, which I imagine will probably be a while."

Stephanie handed her menu back to the waitress. "No dessert for me."

Dammit! I thought. *This chick's blowing my high. Doesn't she realize gluttony loves company?*

The waitress turned her head toward me. "Whenever your fat, greedy, gelatinous ass decide what you'd like to inhale, just please let me know," I imagined her saying.

"I'll have the warm apple pie."

"Ice cream?" Her eyes sparkled.

"Yes, please," I heard myself say from a vortex of shame.

"I'll give it a few minutes before putting the order in. Is that okay?"

"Sure." I replied, already feeling regretful.

After eating half a mound of nachos smothered in cheese and jalapenos, a half platter of waffle fries, nearly all of the calamari, a serving of apple pie topped with two scoops of ice cream, three frozen margaritas which produced two bouts of brain freeze, I was on a food and alcohol induced high.

"So the MF comes to the door with his johnson out like here baby—" I broke off, spread my legs, and glanced down at my crotch while my hands grasped the invisible body that mounted me. "Jump *on* it! Jump *on* it! Jump *on* it!" I sang in my Sugarhill Apache voice while making up and down motions with my hands.

D.D. Sherman   Rare Orchids

    Stephanie was leaned back in her bar stool cracking up while her fist banged the table. "Gurl, you are *too* funny!"

    "I mean, what the fuck was that all about?"

    Stephanie shook her head, still chuckling.

    "At least spend a few duckets if you want some ass. Chinese takeout? Really, dude? And you didn't even have the common decency to ask me what I wanted? Chicken lo mein and shrimp dumplings? I mean like where they do that at?" I stated ebonically, the tequila high jacking my moral compass and robbing me of the ounce of dignity I had left.

    The remaining two percent of my sober brain told me I was revealing too much to this virtual stranger, but I was on a roll and her belly-bursting laughter did little to discourage me.

    "But he was hung like a horse, I tell ya. That's the only thing that I'm going to miss."

    "Really?" Stephanie asked with a wide grin.

    "Uh-huh. Wanna see?" I asked, reaching in my handbag for my phone.

    "Hell yeah, I wanna see!" she exclaimed craning her neck forward and cocking her head to one side to look at a picture of Lance sprawled out on his bed with a stiff one in hand. "Well, damn!" she exclaimed with widened eyes.

    "Now you see why I'm so upset." I pulled my phone away from Stephanie's mesmerized gaze and dropped it inside my handbag. "My last boyfriend had it going on too. I've been lucking out with that lately."

    "I need one of those in my life."

    "Men these damn days. That's about all they're good for." I stated, suddenly aware of a sadness clenching at my heart.

    Stephanie pressed her lips together and shook her head empathetically.

    I sighed. I didn't like any form of pity. "Well," I started glancing at my watch and already feeling a bit foolish for the way I had just acted. "One more work day, then home free."

"Thank God." Stephanie glanced at her phone to see the time. "Oh wow! It's almost twelve o'clock! You need a ride?" she asked, tossing her phone back in her bag, prepping to leave.

"Nah, my car's parked outside. I'm just gonna call an Uber."

"Good," she stated scooting out from under the high-legged table.

"Well,thanks for hanging out," I said throwing my arm across her shoulders.

She pressed her cheek against mine and kissed the air. "No problem, sweetie."

"Yeah, gotta do it again."

"Yep. I had fun."

I bet you did. And I bet you can't wait to tell everyone at work about the show little Miss Pretty and Proper Symone Alexander put on tonight.

'Damn sure can't.' I imagined her thinking

Chapter 6

Dottie James shuffled through a folder of papers. Her glasses sat to the edge of her nose and the beaded chain they were attached to draped along the sides of her sagging cheeks. Her eyes swept over my disciplinary report—moving from left to right as she silently mouthed the words on the paper.

She was a hefty African-American woman with a large, pointy bosom who wore an over-used pageboy wig that sat on her head like a helmet and flipped around her gold-studded earlobes. Her lips were painted a red hue which did little to enhance her looks. She was the only one I knew on planet Earth who still wore rouge—the liquid kind, and like the lipstick, it was a cosmetic bust.

I fidgeted in my chair and glanced at a wall clock above her head. It was just after nine in the morning and I had been sitting there for a good ten to fifteen minutes in virtual silence watching her peruse my write-up. I had taken note of her wedding band which was a plain gold sphere and thought she must've been a looker in her day. My eyes roamed over elegantly framed family pictures of who I surmised were her adult children and grands, but there were no apparent pictures of her husband who I was most curious about.

I noted how she was dressed—how she was always dressed—in a too tight pants suit as if she refused to accept the fact that she had ballooned three sizes bigger a very long time ago. Her dress shirts always gaped at the center of her bosom and I often wondered if it was an industrial-strength thread that kept her buttons from popping off and putting someone's eye out from sheer velocity.

"Okay," she started, sliding her glasses off and closing the folder with a protracted exhale. "I've read the report and have come to a decision."

I cringed, flashing back to when I was younger and my mother forewarned me of an impending whooping which was simply, 'go get a switch 'cause I'm about to beat yo ass.'

"I'm giving you a verbal reprimand and taking you off Godson Curry's case. In fact," she paused to breathe in deeply. "I'm going to reassign you. You'll be working with adults henceforth."

Something inside me broke apart and shattered. I had affinity for all my forty-two clients, but Godson was special and kind of like the son I always wanted. Unlike the men in my life, he stayed around, trusted me and I believed had genuine love for me. I needed him as much as he needed me. He gave me purpose, a reason to keep fighting and to get out of bed in the mornings.

"Please don't do this, Ms. James," I pleaded. "That kid depends on me. If I'm reassigned, he'll feel like I let him down."

"You did," she stated, sitting back in her chair and clasping her hands over her protruding mid-section.

I cupped my face in my hands.

"You had neither right, nor the authority to bypass the way that things are rightfully done here. We don't get personal with our clients and we *certainly* don't take them into our homes."

"Wasn't my home—"

"Doesn't matter one bit. It was your decision to side-step policy and procedure and to get Officer Berman involved in this mess."

"Oh, please!" I clasped my hands together and pleaded. "Puhleeeeez, don't go after Officer Berman. It was all my idea. I forced him into it."

She leaned forward and glanced at another folder on her desk. "He's getting a verbal reprimand."

I pulled a deep breath in through my nose. "He's going to hate me for this," I said collapsing back in my chair.

Ms. James folded her hands atop her desk. "If anything had happened to Godson Curry under Officer Berman's watch, it would've been a lot more than a verbal reprimand. It could've cost him his job...and yours too."

I slapped a palm to my forehead and shook my head. "Can't believe he had an appointment with his social worker last Friday. I didn't think to ask Ms. Grace about his schedule."

"Uh-huh. And you're lucky Judge Fuller is overseeing his case. Anyone else would've brought the gavel down on your head, Berman's head, *my head*, and maybe even the director's head."

All I could do was sigh deeply at the thought of getting Phil into trouble and never seeing Godson again.

"Okay," Ms. James said, sliding the folder across the polished wood desk and propping her glasses onto the bridge of her nose. "Sign, attesting that you accept the charges."

"Shouldn't I be speaking to my delegate or something?"

"Listen, I'm being very lenient. If you want to go getting the union involved, I'll just go for a thirty-day suspension and call it a day. Believe me, you're getting off easy, young lady."

"Young lady?" I considered her statement. *"Compared to your sixty-five, sixty-six-year-old-self, I guess I am a young lady,"* I thought with censure. I scribbled my signature on the piece of paper, not even bothering to read it over. Like Ms. James said, I was getting off easy, all things considered.

"Good luck on your new assignment."

New assignment. Ugh! So it is real. I thought, rising from my chair as if in a trance. "Thank you," was all I could muster to say before slumping my shoulders and dragging, what felt like my cemented feet, from her office.

***

I followed Amber's red-dress-hugged physique, a petite, but shapely Asian woman with her phone pressed to her ear and the building's concierge on a tour of the nearly three-million-dollar loft that was up for sale in Tribeca. I strolled the pricey apartment with my brows furrowed. I wasn't impressed but confounded as to why someone would pay that much money to live in a slightly above average apartment other than the fact that it was situated in a zone of uppity snobs with hordes of money.

The finishes were a fusion of traditional, futuristic and Spartan. There was a normal—but aesthetically appealing stove with huge knobs and regular burners, knob-less, corrugated tinted-glass cabinets, counters with sharp lines, boxy hallways, and angles of open space. It whispered clinical with its furniture and accents being either bone, pale grey, or white, with a random appearance of muted bronze that framed the kitchen cabinets and was the color of a bowl set that rested on a stone countertop. There was more of the same lackluster color scheme in the two bedrooms. Some interior designer—probably with an over-inflated ego—did, at least, think to add fabric to a back wall and paint the rooms a blue-grey, but the modest attempt lost its momentum against dull, tawny-colored hardwood floors.

The Asian woman placed a hand over the mouthpiece of her phone. "My client want to know if price negotiable?" she asked in pretty well-spoken English, though her native tongue was still predominant.

Amber shook her head. "I'm sorry. The price on this loft is firm. We already have four offers."

Hmph! I thought. *And to think there are people starving in Africa.* But who the hell was I? Wait, did anyone even realize I was there?

The Asian woman spoke Mandarin into her phone. I knew because I was able to make out the Chinese version of *I am sorry*—*duì bù qǐ*—which actually sounds like *three boo chee* phonetically. I had taken a few courses in Mandarin back in college but dropped it in sophomore year. The rest of what she said was indiscernible, but I noticed abrupt pauses in her dialogue as if she were being interrupted.

Amber stood effortlessly in four-inch pumps bumping her firm thighs against the faux alligator-skin clutch she held before her. She was as cool as a refrigerated cucumber, flicking her costly weave over one shoulder. That was the thing about New York real estate; properties practically sold themselves. Realtors were just there to mediate between the spoiled and sense-of-entitlement bidders who just wanted to add a Manhattan property to their list of prodigal assets, and the bosses who paid their salaries.

But there was something invigorating about money being spent in droves, I had to admit. Although I was as far removed from these species of humans as the barrister brewing up a caramel macchiato at the Starbucks across the street, I didn't mind pretending—no imagining— that I was part of this big money fray.

"If everything goes right, this'll be my biggest deal yet!" Amber beamed when she had stopped by my new office earlier in the week with a good-luck plant in tow.

She was at the peak of her career and I was tanking in mine. It had been a month since my reassignment and chasing after adults—grown men included—to ensure they were doing the right thing was just not my cup of Joe.

The concierge stood at-the-ready with his hands clasped behind his back and a fixed smile planted on his middle-aged face. His sandy blonde hair against his reddish, tanned skin gave him a tropical complexion. His teeth were white—too white and straight—pretentiously straight. He looked past me, above me, to the side of me, but never at me and in my head, I told him to *go F himself in the middle of Macy's store window*, which was something my deceased grandmother would often say.

The Asian woman disconnected the call. "My client say he will let you know."

Amber smiled. "You have my email address, correct?"

"Yes, yes, I do. I will pro-ba-bly contact you at end of week."

"That'll be fine." Amber responded, as we all exited the apartment in a cluster.

"So whattayah think? Was that crib amazing or what?" Amber asked, sliding on her Miu Miu sunglasses once we were back on the street amid the rush of hurried New Yorkers.

"It was aiight. Not worth an hour's drive into the city." I reached for my Raybans and mentally compared her glasses to mine. Hers were flamboyant with animal print temples and ostentatiously shaped oval lenses. Mine were much more straightforward, sloping circles for lenses and sleek, narrow temples that were basically one solid color.

"You said you wanted to talk to me about something."

"I do, but I don't think you're going to like it."

Amber looked at me over the rim of her glasses. "Come on. Let's hear it."

"I want to sit the wedding out."

"You wanna do what? Wait!" Amber jerked off her shades. "Say that again."

I cringed, gritting my teeth. "I can't get into my dress." I tucked my head and raised my shoulders in shame.

"What do you mean, you can't get into your dress?"

"I mean I can, but it's tight. Like super tight. Like a sumo wrestler in a cat suit tight."

"And where am I supposed to find a replacement on such short notice?"

"Why do you need one?"

"Because Melvin already rented his tux."

I sighed. "Oh, forgot about that. I'm just not in the celebratory mood with all that's happening. The transfer, losing Godson's case, and getting Phil into trouble."

"Are you two still cool?"

"I mean yeah, but it's not the same."

"Not the same? How so?"

"I called to invite him out to lunch the other day and he made up some excuse about having to leave work early for some chiropractor appointment."

"You're just being paranoid. Phil doesn't seem like the type to hold grudges."

"Maybe not, but my being pissed at Lance isn't helping the situation either. It just feels like I've got way too much going on and I don't want that to bring the mood of your bridal party down."

"Listen," Amber started, shifting her weight to one side. "You betta get over yourself. The wedding's next month so you've got plenty of time to knock off those few extra pounds and try a few sessions of psychotherapy or something."

"Psychotherapy? You for real?"

Amber shrugged. "It worked for me at a point in my life."

It was shocking to hear that seemingly all-put-together *Amber* had been on someone's couch. I thought we knew everything about each other. I guessed I was wrong. I readjusted my sunglasses. "Okay. I'll try and pull it together. I'd really hate to disappoint you."

"Anyway, I've got to run to this closing, snookums!" Amber said, flinging her arm around my neck to hug me. We pressed cheeks and kissed the air. Air kisses. I liked them. They were germ free.

***

Nathan's name and number popped up onto the screen in my dashboard, near causing me to swerve into oncoming traffic. A surge of adrenaline sent my heart into overdrive and my head whirled with racing thoughts. I pressed a button on my steering wheel to connect the call and said hello in the most casual voice I could muster.

"Wassup, Symone?"

"Nothing. Just coming back from the city. How are you?" I replied coolly.

"I'm good. Am I violating some kind of order of protection by calling you? I ain't trying to go to jail or nothing like that," he tittered.

"You still thinking 'bout that? I was just angry that day."

"To say the least."

We're talking again. This is great. No, not great, it's wonderful.

"Look, let me be the first to apologize. I'm sorry if I said or did anything to offend you 'cause at the end of the day, you're really a good woman. And I mean that."

This can't be. Nathan apologizing? This is too damn good to be true.

"Well, I do put my best stiletto forward." I chuckled, just to keep in sync with the pleasant mood of our conversation.

"But you *do* have a temper."

"Guess it's the bull in me."

Nathan laughed. "Must be."

There was a mutual silence and I used that time to search my thoughts for what to say. I didn't want to sound overly desperate, yet I did want to make it clear how much I missed just being with him.

"You know, Symone, I couldn't even tell you what we last argued about."

Oh, but I can—word for word—line for line. "I think we got into something about me wanting to do a dinner cruise on Valentine's Day and you misconstruing that as me trying to dictate when and how things happen in our relationship."

Nathan chuckled weakly. "Sounds about right, I guess. You know I've never been into holidays. It's just another way to control the masses and I'm definitely not one to be controlled."

Ugggggh! There it was, the old Nathan creeping back into view.

"Tell me about it."

"But anyway, I just called to let you know how much I've always admired and respected you. I mean you're a smart and independent woman that's out here doing her own thing."

Okay, enough with all the ego stroking. Let's kiss, makeup, and get it on and poppin'. It's been a while, old boy. I suggested in my head.

"Awww…that's sweet of you. Thanks."

"So like I said, I'm just calling to say sorry if I've hurt you in any way. That was never my intentions."

Sounds like a deathbed confession. "Trust me, I'm over it. I've got much more important things going on than worrying about a stupid lovers' quarrel."

"I'm so relieved to hear you say that you've forgiven me."

Nathan seemed to be stalling so I just went for it. "I know you are, sugah. You know I'd be happy to discuss this more over a nice dinner? Thai, Jap, Italian, Vietnamese? Just say when and where?"

"Symone, I'm married."

*Errrrr...*I slammed on my breaks, narrowly missing rear-ending the car in front of me. *What did that fool just say?* I asked myself. I wasn't sure if I heard him correctly and I was deathly afraid to ask for clarification. I just sat there listening to him squirm on the other end, surely wracking his brains for what to say next.

"Hello?" he continued cautiously.

"Yes, I'm here." I tried to be nonchalant, but that was kind of difficult considering how my once whole and functioning heart felt like a two-ton weight had fallen on it, crushing it into disrepair.

"Look, I know you're in shock. I'm sure you probably thought I'd never take the big leap, but I met this girl—I mean like, *dude*, she changed my whole thought process, turned me inside out."

Really? You're actually going to wax poetic about this woman's virtues to me? "That's nice. Well, I got another call coming through," I lied.

"I just wanted to clear the air between us so that we can *hopefully* remain friends."

"Yeah, okay. No problem. Look, I really gotta grab this call."

"Alright, sweetie. You take—"

I disconnected him, pulled over to a curb, and let my forehead collapse against the steering wheel. An onslaught of thoughts assaulted my brain. *Why wasn't you good enough?* My grandmother's voice or the empathetic elementary school teacher I subconsciously latched on to, asked. *Did he even care about you the person or was he just interested in what you got going on between those thighs? An entire year and a half you've wasted on that loser.* The voice admonished. *And then he runs off and marries someone else in record time?* It felt as if I were looking at the world through foggy lenses then realized why when I caught a glimpse of my watery, bloodshot eyes in the rearview mirror. I looked pitiful. There I was, acting the fool over a guy—no a friggin' moron—who didn't even think I was wife worthy, but good enough to stay friends with just in case he had a hankering for a little throwback. Instead of crying, I should have been celebrating, and celebrate I did.

D.D. Sherman   Rare Orchids

Chapter 7

COME ON IN AND GET LAID the hand-written sign featured on the bulky, metal door of a tacky strip joint called TEAZE suggested. The building was located on a dark and sinister corner in very unlikely Astoria, Queens.

Phil, who I practically dragged from his apartment, Stephanie, who was down for almost anything, and myself stood before the door, cringing like children about to enter a haunted house.

"Look, we can't stand here all night," I finally spoke up.

"Well, you have to be patient with me. This is my first time," Phil stated turning red at the ears.

"Mine too," Stephanie revealed.

We probably looked more like a freak show than the sideshow that was going on inside. Phil was dressed in a flamingo pink suit with short pants that rose just above his knees and a single-button blazer. He wore a white button-down shirt and a blue, polka dot bow tie. Stephanie was packed into a form-fitting glimmering dress made from some kind of gold spandex material, and I wore an orangey-rust colored skirt suit that looked more appropriate for a courtroom than a strip club.

"See, we're virgins. You've got to break us in gently," Phil said.

"Well, I'm going in," I stated firmly, while opening the bulky door, whose hinges cried out in agony.

"Gently, I said," cried Phil, clasping his ears in exaggeration.

I shook my head as we climbed a tight flight of metal steps. The place smelled of incense and alcohol. Kelis's *Milkshake* thumped in my ears and chest.

"'La-la...la-la...la, warm it up! La-la...la-la...la, the boys are waiting."

D.D. Sherman					Rare Orchids

I glanced down at Phil and Stephanie who were behind me looking anxious as if depending on me to lead them safely through a dangerous expedition.

There was a vestibule area at the top of the steps and a little room for coat check and to buy tickets. A big, black guy with a shiny bald head grinding a toothpick between his teeth, checked our bags and conducted a cursory pat frisk of Phil. I watched Phil from the corner of my eye to see if he was enjoying it, but there were no telltale signs as far as I could see.

The bald bouncer stepped back so that a near-nude female in a fishnet dress, lace bra, and pink thongs could pat Stephanie and me down. Her wig was big, blonde and curly and seemed to overwhelm her petite frame.

Once we paid and received our paper wrist bands from the also scantily clad ticket seller behind the desk wearing a faux leather tube top and tight mini skirt halfway up her thighs, we got laid.

The leis around our necks made us a hodgepodge of weird. Phil's orange and pink flowers clashed with his pink short suit. My deep purple necklace against my rust-orange wardrobe would've been more appropriate had it been Halloween, and the closest leis they could find to match Stephanie's shimmering gold spandex dress were a bright yellow.

We trailed inside the club, with me still leading the way. Even though I had been acting brave, it was also my first venture into a strip joint. It had always been on my bucket list and not because I was all that interested in looking at bouncing tits and gyrating asses. I secretly wanted to learn pole dancing and felt who better to pick up some pointers from than those who did it for a living.

The dancers, most of whom looked more like whores out of retirement with sagging tits and cellulite-flecked thighs, danced on wooden platforms from which black paint chipped off. There were smudged mirrored walls at the rear of each platform and only the stages in the middle had stripper poles.

D.D. Sherman   Rare Orchids

    There were two younger strippers strategically placed at the center of the club. They had pretty faces and toned bodies and would've been nice looking had it not been for the jagged teeth one of them had and the keloid scar running from ear tip to jaw line marring the face of the other.

    "'My milkshake brings all the boys to the yard and there like it's better than yours. Damn right it's better than yours. I can teach you but I have to charge.'" Kelis sang.

    The three of us stood in a shameful knot, not quite sure what do. I rocked my hips attempting to look nonchalant, and Stephanie bobbed her head. Phil just thrust his hands into the pockets of his shorts and stood with his knees touching like he had to pee.

    We watched the dancing women. One slid on her behind, legs spread, six-inch clear heels in the air and tummy undulating like that of a serpent's. Another stripper was making her butt cheeks bounce in an alternating motion while a cluster of men hungrily reached for it, grabbing their crotches and making obscene gestures.

    Another near naked waitress approached us, toting a wooden serving tray. "Can I get you guys something to drink?" she asked with a friendly smile that made me feel a bit more relaxed and it seemed to loosen Phil and Stephanie up as well.

    The waitress wore makeup caked on so thick that it made even Stephanie's face paint appear conservative. It was a failed attempt at concealing the fine lines that sprouted from the edges of her probably once-attractive eyes.

    "I'll have a regular martini. Two olives. Dry," Phil ordered up over the thumping music.

    "I feel like an apple martini. Frothy," I said.

    "What kind of margaritas do you have?" Stephanie asked.

    "We have strawberry and coconut. We may have peach, but I'm not sure. I'd have to ask the bartender."

    "Don't bother. Just make it a strawberry," Stephanie said loudly, competing with the booming bass.

"This'll be on one tab," Phil advised the barmaid who nodded and smiled.

We thanked her and watched her prance away. Feeling bolder, we migrated farther into the club. There were a few old, washed-up sugar daddies drunkenly leaning over the platforms and extending their dollar bearing hands up toward the dancing strippers who sensually thrusted their hips and wrapped their legs around the poles. Young wannabe ballers casually tossed a few crumpled dollars onto the stages and copped themselves a squeeze of butt cheek or breast in compensation.

Once we had our fill of alcohol, three drinks each for Phil and Stephanie, and my one- drink max since I was the designated driver—something I had bartered away earlier to convince them to accompany me—we were all over the place.

Phil was sandwiched between the two younger strippers. Jagged teeth was bent at a ninety degree angle, grinding her atomic booty against his crotch. Phil wriggled and jiggled off-beat behind her as if seizing while scar face repetitively slapped his backside.

For some ungodly reason, Stephanie was dancing butt to butt with one of the older strippers whose sagging tits were basically deflated flaps of stretched out skin held in place with a metallic-silver bustier.

I walked the sleaze joint, covertly filming Phil, Stephanie, and the pole dancers. I recorded Stephanie because I needed some form of blackmail since that was the second time she'd seen me in a vulnerable state and I didn't know her well enough to trust that she wouldn't go blabbing my business to everyone she knew. I filmed Phil so we could laugh about it later and I recorded the pole dancers for instructional purposes only.

That one strong margarita and the hookah-infused atmosphere of the outré club had me in a tailspin. I laughed so hard watching Phil and Stephanie make complete arses out of themselves that I forgot all about psychopath Nathan and the surprise revelation that he'd recently married.

I walked and Phil and Stephanie staggered a couple of blocks up to a nearby diner. My ears were still burning and vibrating from the loud music. It was a great time and it only set me back thirty dollars; twenty dollars for the ticket and the ten dollars' worth of singles I stuck in the G-strings of the dancers.

Phil had bought all of our drinks at the club and Stephanie splurged on a platter of mozzarella and zucchini sticks at the diner. I treated Phil to a steak dinner hoping to make up for my costing him a write-up.

After dropping Stephanie and Phil off at their houses, I was alone with my thoughts. The memory of my earlier conversation with Nathan surged to the surface and took center stage in my mind like a buoy that refused to sink. *Why in heavens wouldn't he consider you wife-worthy?* The empathetic voice in my head questioned. *Oh, don't go feeling sorry for yourself. He was never worth the time you did give him. Luckily, you dodged that bullet.* And then the channel in my head flicked to Godson. *Is he safe? Is he angry with me? Has he found a new family or is he stuck in some foster care facility? Is this all my fault? Is everything all my fault?* I wondered relentlessly.

***

I thought it was a ridiculous idea to have a bridal party two-step down a church aisle which is why I was sick with embarrassment when it was Melvin's and my turn. He went right when I went left and when I went right, *he* went left. A sea of intense faces watched us from the pews as we bounced and swayed to Jodeci's, *Forever My Lady*, finally falling into step about midway down the aisle.

Amber flashed a nervous smile from the altar as Melvin and I took our places before the pulpit next to ditzy, bitchy Ebony and none other than—drumroll please—Devin Smith. I was seething. Amber told me that he had been invited to the wedding, not that he would be in the *actual* wedding party. I had a hunch that she was trying to spare my feelings, but I hated pity. Empathy was tolerable, but pity made me feel weak.

Lacey and her partner, Roderick—her hazel-eyed, dark-haired boyfriend and one of Antoine's myriad friends—

mechanically strode down the aisle doing the best version of the two-step they could pull off. They appeared hyper focused with their eyes darting, necks stiff, and noses pointed straight ahead as if turning their heads ever so slightly would knock them off rhythm. They took their places next to Melvin and me with obvious sighs of relief.

Marisol and her groomsman, Miguel, were next. They bobbed down the aisle smoothly, with a little Latin flair in the sway of their hips and placement of their pointed toes. Seated folk smiled and even clapped as they sauntered down the aisle, making it look easy. The stars had come to steal the show, until Marisol tripped over a slight raise in the carpeted runner that sent her whirling forward, striking the old hardwood floors with a very audible *thump*.

Amber gasped then covered her mouth as most of the bridal party fled their stations to assist Miguel in picking her up. Some of the observers shot up from the benches and ran over to the scene, uselessly exacerbating the expanding knot of confusion.

"I'm sorry Amber, but my dogs are barking!" I announced, limping toward a wooden bench and plopping down.

"Well, y'all need to get your two-step together!" Bridezilla demanded, craning her neck to one side and folding her arms over her chest.

"I don't see why we have to practice in heels anyway," I protested, taking off my shoe to rub my throbbing toes. The surviving bridesmaids nodded in agreement.

"Because I want y'all to get used to the feel of the shoe!" A seemingly flustered Amber retorted, shaking her head rapidly as if to say, *duh*. "I don't need no tripping, *falling*—" she stopped to shoot a glance at red-faced Marisol who was being helped to her feet. "Or stumbling on my wedding day!"

Antoine tried to cajole his fiancée by placing a hand on her shoulder, but Amber just sucked her teeth, marched up the aisle, and disappeared through the chapel doors. He looked around embarrassed, shrugged, then hurried up the aisle after her.

D.D. Sherman   Rare Orchids

    My head followed Antoine for a moment and then spun forward to notice Melvin eyeing me with a silly smirk. I understood why Amber had never suggested we meet prior. He just wasn't my type. I mean he could've been attractive had it not been for his awkwardly shaped head that started off as a square and expanded into a round shape just below his temples. It made him appear fat, even though he wasn't. It was also a little flat when he turned sideways. He had a very thin mustache—which I despised on a man—wide, meaty fingers, and clammy hands that kept reaching for mine when we "danced" down the aisle. I had heard that he had his own business brewing craft beer and that his brand was carried in a few local taverns including some Wholefood stores, but that just wasn't enough to shake the nuts off my tree.

    Marisol, assisted by Miguel and Devin, limped over to a bench. They sat her down gently while Lacey ran somewhere to get an icepack. I started to get up, but there were already enough people crowding poor Marisol who I surmised was suffering more from embarrassment than the pain in her knee.

    Melvin finally mustered enough courage to come sit next to me. I scooted over to the end of the bench even though there was already plenty space for him to sit down. He smelled really good; masculine sweet. A thrill went through me. A good smelling men's cologne always had an aphrodisiacal effect on me, even if the man resembled the Frankenstein monster.

    "She looks like she messed her knee up pretty bad," Melvin said, craning his neck to try and look over at Marisol and her cluster of caregivers.

    "Looks like it." I shrugged, disinterested in small talk.

    "Hope this doesn't keep her out of the wedding."

    "She's got a month to recover," I replied tersely, praying that Melvin got the hint.

    "True," he agreed, and rubbing his palms together, he actually started to whistle. I supposed he was struggling with what to say next and I wasn't about to help him out. Frankly, I was tired and wanted nothing more than a hot, sudsy bath in my claw foot tub, all by my lonesome.

I felt him leering at me and kept my eyes peeled on the goings on around Marisol.

Probably shuddering from the cold-shoulder I gave him, he finally thought of something to say; "I guess rehearsal's over."

From my peripheral I could see him glance at his watch. A Breitling. *Hmmm, somewhat impressive.* I said in my mind. "I guess so," I replied, keeping my head turned in the direction of the Marisol saga.

"Well," he started, getting up. "Let me go try and find Antoine and let him know I'm out."

I finally turned to look at him. "Okay, see you at the ceremony."

He leaned over to whisper in my ear and I cringed. "We better get our two-step together or your friend's gonna have us knocked off."

I chuckled. He straightened and walked away, leaving his good-smelling scent to linger in my nostrils.

Chapter 8

"You sure you had enough?"

"After a huge seafood platter, two pina coladas, a basket of bread and a slice of cheesecake, do you really think I have room in my stomach for anything else?" I asked Melvin, and then wondered if I did.

He chuckled in a way that irked me. It was slow and over-exaggerated and sounded something like uh-huh, uh-huh, uh-huh, as if he were trying to expel something from his throat.

"I'm just making sure," he responded, his meaty fingers opening the jacket and scanning the one-hundred-eighty-nine-dollar receipt without flinching. He scrambled through his pocket for his wallet, extracted a gold American Express Card, and slipped it in between the jacket covers.

He had quite a few drinks, so his dull eyes looked a little bloodshot and glassy.

Melvin wasn't my type, but boredom and borderline desperation made me agree to a date with him. Amber had called and asked if it was okay for her to give him my number because he had been—in her words—'aggravating the *shit* out of her for it all week.' I said no a few times, but finally acquiesced under the guise of me just getting him off Amber's back. Truthfully, I peeped that Breitling and knew that he had a few dollars, so I thought, *what the hell, at least I'd get a good meal out of him.*

The waiter came over to our table, covertly cracked open the leather jacket to glance at his tip, thanked us with a slight nod of his head, and then happily scurried away.

"Welp," I started. "Best be getting on my way. I've got reports to do."

"On a Saturday?" Melvin asked in a way that almost disputed my statement.

"Every day is a workday for Probation Officers."

"Oh yeah? he asked, sliding his legs from under the table."

"Yep," I responded, already standing up over him, full, satiated and anxious to hop in his car and high-tail it home.

When we left the restaurant, night had trumped day and God had flicked on the celestial lights of Heaven. The piercing white stars appeared to waft and glimmer against an atmospheric sea of midnight blue. The seafood restaurant was an actual boat docked at a pier. The slightly pungent smell of sea water and fish coupled with a crisp wind made that a night for lovers. Only, I wasn't with the person I loved, or even liked for that matter.

Melvin grabbed for my hand as we waited for valet. I didn't resist. I figured I owed him at least that much.

"Nice tonight," he said with a grateful sigh.

For you. I thought. "Yeah, it is," I stated, raking my splayed fingers through my tresses to push the windblown hair from my face.

His white Mercedes SUV pulled up, so he finally had to let go of my hand, which I wiped down my jean mini-skirt to rid my palm of his excess sweat.

Melvin started for the driver's side.

"Oh no!" I protested. "You've had one too many, my friend." I hoped he got the *friend* part. "I'm driving."

"Waaait," he slurred a little. "What 'bout when it comes time for me to drive myself home?"

"We're like an hour and change away from my house. Hopefully, you'll be a bit more sobered up by then." I stuck out my palm, he dropped the keys in it, then staggered to the passenger side.

I tried my best to keep a superficial conversation going, anything to distract Melvin from any romantic ideations.

We talked—well mostly I talked—about everything from the Game of Thrones, to the current political climate, from slavery to the civil rights movement, to how to cook a turducken to how to prepare Thanksgiving stuffing. We chatted about the time I clamped a combination lock on my big toe, forgot the combination, and ended up getting the lock sawed off at the local hospital, and of course, I chatted it up about Amber's upcoming wedding.

D.D. Sherman   Rare Orchids

He must've took my loquacious demeanor for familiarity and commenced to placing his moist hand on my thigh, then pushing my skirt up a bit.

I grasped his hand and flung it at him. "Don't do that!"

He sucked his teeth and wriggled angrily back against the plush passenger seat.

"You're getting mad because I moved your unsolicited hand from near my private region?" I was seething.

He darted forward in his chair. "Your private area? When was my hand near your private area?"

"So I'm imagining things?" I shot him a wicked side glance, then returned my focus to the road.

"Must be. Listen, I'm not a desperate man. I don't have to be."

"Well, don't go putting your hands where they don't belong!" I retorted.

"Please, just drive the car," Melvin ordered, pushing a button on the dashboard to loudly play Will Downing's CD.

I put pedal to metal, wishing I had a pair of ruby slippers so I could click my heels three times and be home and away from the likes of Melvin. He apparently thought that a seafood dinner had earned his hand a trip up my thighs. Wrong!

We said a combined ten words since our big blowout; thank you, you're welcome, take care and you take care too. I practically leapt from his vehicle thanking God I only had to see him one more time. I wondered how in tarnation I was going to make it through Amber's wedding day. I decided to not even mention the disastrous date to her. I didn't want anything dampening her nuptials.

***

Amber's wedding was held in a historic church in Manhattan, reminiscent of Gothic architecture with its flying buttresses, rising spires, pointed arched windows and artistically carved gables. Inside were ribbed-vaulted ceilings embellished with swirling shapes of gold. The floor was a dark color wood and Amber's must-have-red-carpeted-runner ran the length of the long aisle. There were pedestals at the end of every other pew supporting vases of tall, white hydrangeas and an arch of clinging vines and dangling jars of softly lit candles positioned before the altar.

Once the estimated two hundred some odd guests were seated, the bridal party assembled in the church's vestibule area. I thought I would gag and die when I saw Dontae, all dressed up in the groomsman tux, take his place beside me. I whipped my head around, trying to catch Amber's attention, but she was clearly nervous and distracted, with someone coming up to her seemingly every second to whisper something in her ear.

"Pssst, pssst, pssst." No matter how hard I tried, I just couldn't get Amber to lock eyes with me.

"Wassup, cutie?" Dontae leaned over to whisper in my ear.

"What do you think you're doing?"

"What does it look like I'm doing?"

"You're not my partner. Where's Melvin?" I questioned, not knowing which was worse, a walk down the aisle with clammy hands or a gigolo wannabe.

"Your boy broke his ankle. Lucky you."

"For real?" I asked, choosing not to feed into his antics.

"Dead up. I heard trying to play basketball. Old dudes should be in the bleachers, not on the court."

"But you don't know the steps," I protested in a strained whisper, the worry in my voice palpable.

Dontae reached in his pants pocket, extracted a blue and white cylinder, and then shot two bursts of minty liquid into his opened mouth. He smacked his lips, then turned to look at me, sticking the canister of mint back down in his pants pocket. "Honey, it's a two-step, not the moonwalk."

"Okay, everyone!" Amber's wedding planner, Arlene—a short lady—with thick hips, a small waistline and what I guessed to be C-cup breasts, called for our attention. She was dressed in a form-hugging gown that opened and flowed below the knees. "We're about to go in."

D.D. Sherman   Rare Orchids

    She darted around, anxiously fixing the boutonnières on the groomsmen's lapels and gave all of us bridesmaids the once-over. She straightened the beaded hair clip that Amber's sister, and maid-of-honor, wore to keep her chignon in place and then gave the thumbs up to proceed.

    The doors flung open.

    "I'm nervous," I confided to Dontae.

    "I have that effect on ladies."

    I elbowed him in the side.

    "Oh, *now* you wanna play rough?"

    "I'm not nervous because of you—I mean yes, because of you—not you-*you* per se. I mean, I'm nervous because you and I have never practiced."

    The music started.

    I privately thanked God that Dontae and I were third in line to go and even suggested that we do a quick sixty second rehearsal.

    "Just follow my lead," Dontae suggested.

    "Yeah, right off a cliff."

    "And I promise, it'll be one helluva fall." He turned his head to give me a quick scan and something in his hazel eyes captivated me.

    He was undeniably as fine as homemade wine with his piercing eyes, smooth, decadent skin, and a killer physique that made that tux look like it was tailored to every movement of his body. He caught me staring at him and flashed a straight-toothed smile.

    I snapped myself out of it, realizing that the couple before us was already half up the aisle. The wedding planner nodded in our direction. Dontae grabbed me by the hand, coaxing me from a state of bewilderment and led me down the aisle. We flowed on beat, never missing a
step, and about a quarter way down, I was brimming with assuredness. One, two...One, two. I rocked my hips. One, two...One, two. My head bobbed smoothly to the rhythm. One, two...One, two. I was even able to smile confidently and make eye contact with the gathering of onlookers.

D.D. Sherman   Rare Orchids

Dontae's two-step was sexy as he strutted beside me. Occasionally, he flashed me a quick smile to let me know that I was doing okay. We made it to the end and took our places next to Devin and Ebony. The remainder of the bridal party glided in without a hitch, including a fully-recovered Marisol—albeit less salsa in her meringue.

The music changed to Jodeci's, *Forever My Lady*. When Amber and her dad made their appearance in the doorway of the chapel everyone stood and turned their heads to the rear to receive them. There was a look of wanderlust in Amber's eyes and a gentle smile illuminating her father's face.

Amber looked ravishing in her Lazaro beaded and laced gown with wide see-through slits running down the sides of it. She opted for a pearl and silver, intricately designed headband rather than the trite veil. She was radiant. Her white teeth and the whites of her eyes beamed with soft candlelight. Her father proudly led her by the hand, his white hair emphasizing his toffee complexion.

I ethereally drifted into Amber's body and saw myself wafting toward the altar, hand in hand with my bridegroom; only I did not know who he was, so I floated back into my physical self and sorely remembered who I actually stood next to.

We were almost an hour into the ceremony and Pastor Timothy Grayson had still not gotten to the vows. Instead, he used Amber's wedding as an opportunity to proselytize to a gathering of about two-hundred-fifty people, half of whom I surmised suffered in pain from hours of wearing stilettos, needle-point pumps, platforms, and very high wedged heels.

"This is not simply a joining of two people, folks," the suave pastor started, clad in a white and gold satin robe. "This is the joining of two lifetimes, two ideologies, and two generations. This is not a wedding, my friends. *This…* is a merger."

He was an attractive man, sugar-daddy-lollipop brown with neat sideburns and goatee. He was relatively young for his station in life; I guessed about thirty-eight, forty, max. I'd heard that he had his own church, and a rather sizeable one, in Harlem with a congregation of five thousand plus members which included Amber and her soon-to-be husband.

"Mergers happen when two individual parties realize that they are *stronger* together. They are *happier* together. They are more *profitable* together and they are more *powerful* together than they are apart."

The pastor extracted a handkerchief from a hidden pocket in his fancy robe and swiped his sweat-beaded forehead, keeping it clenched in his hand. "I know some of you are saying, 'now, Pastor Timothy I hear you, but where are you going with this?' Listen up! 'Cause I'm about to school you on some thangs. If the person you're with doesn't make you—" he broke off, turned his huge palm up, and pressed his pointer finger to the tips of his splayed fingers for every word. "Stronger, better, happier, more profitable, and more importantly, more spiritual, then you're not in a marriage, you're in a relationship and a relationship can mean all sorts of thangs these days."

A chorus of amens broke throughout the chapel.

"Come on y'all. Let's call it what it is!" The Pastor roared. "Let's not go sugarcoating facts."

I glanced up at Dontae who was nodding, but then quickly turned my head away when he'd noticed me looking at him.

"There's the sex relationship."

My feet were throbbing.

"Then we have these relationships of convenience." Pastor Timothy leaned back, clenched his side then shook his head. "Mmmp, Mmmp, Mmmph. Somebody help us."

My toes felt as if they were going to explode in those sparkly straps.

"There's the, *we're doing everything as if in a relationship but let's not call it a relationship*, relationship."

Some of the wedding-guests-slash-church-congregation shouted praises of affirmations and clapped their hands, which only served to egg the long-winded pastor on more.

D.D. Sherman　　　　　　　　　　　Rare Orchids

"And what's this friends with benefits thing all about?" Pastor Timothy whipped his head from side to side as if looking for someone to answer his question.

Some attendees giggled at his ostentatious delivery while my poor feet went up in flames.

After another half hour of a Sunday morning sermon, Amber and Antoine finally got to read their heart-tugging vows and Pastor Timothy pronounced them man and wife.

A shower of white balloons and streamers floated down from the ceiling and I was pleasantly surprised. It was just like Amber to go over the top in almost everything she did.

I hobbled over to her and tried to get a hug in, but Antoine and she were accosted by a mob of camera wielding photographers and well-wishers while I kind of faded into a non-essential extra in the film of Amber's Monumental Moment.

Chapter 9

After three hours of picture taking, the stretched Lincoln limousine whisked us over to the Brooklyn Botanic Garden. I had finally emancipated my feet from those evil heels and slipped into some sparkly, black flats that went virtually unnoticed under my long, fitted gown. A few glasses of champagne helped salve the sting of jealousy I felt at seeing Devin and Ebony all smooched up in the gray, plush leather seat across from me. In fact, almost everyone was coupled up except for me, Arlene the wedding planner, and a girl name Rasheeda who had an extremely big butt and a tattoo on her arm that was the words LOVE and HATE with a jagged line drawn between them. Sure, it was a little gaudy and lacked creativity, but at least you got its meaning at a glance.

    Dontae opted out of the limo ride, simply stating that he'll, 'see everyone a little later.' I was a bit disappointed. Obviously, we weren't a couple, but having someone—anyone at that point—fawning over me would have done wonders for my ego.

    Arlene was the first to pop her petite, curvy self out of the limo. "Is everyone here? Who are we missing?" she started, barking like a Chihuahua.

    We exited the vehicle, one by one.

    "You took your heels off?" Arlene blurted, looking down at my flats peeking out from the hem of my dress.

    "I couldn't take it anymore. They were killing me. I think I got blisters on the soles of my feet." I slipped a foot out of my flat and went to hold up my leg to show her my sole, but my clinging gown impeded me.

    "I'm sorry about your feet and all, but we're still taking pictures. And right now, we're going on a break then heading to the Rose Garden in the next half hour. So pull it together, Miss Thang," the little Chihuahua snapped before sashaying off in her heels to go bark at other bridal party members.

I crossed my arms over my chest, pouted like a six-year-old, and stood there debating if I was going to comply with Arlene's demands. "Who died and left her boss?" I asked under my breath. "I don't have to take orders from that runt?" I stated a little bit louder, catching the attention of Lacey who bounced over to me like her heels were as soft as ballerina slippers. *Am I'm the only one suffering here?* I couldn't help but think.

She put a delicate hand on my shoulder. "That little powerhouse packs a punch," she playfully alliterated.

"That little powerhouse is about to *get* punched!" I retorted.

"*Awww*...I know how you're feeling, girl. Trust me," she said, pressing her palm to her chest for emphasis. "But it's half way over. She's just doing her job. I guess we have to just try and hang in there." Lacey's pretty gray eyes flickered in the setting sun.

Her attempt at cajoling me just made me angrier. Apparently, her feet felt fine. "Yeah, whatever." I shrugged, undecided if I would put the heels back on only to take pictures or toss them in the first trash receptacle I saw.

The chihuahua scuttled back over to me. "Where is what's his name?" she asked with both hands on her hips.

"Who's what's his name?"

"The guy with the pretty eyes. Your partner?"

"Oh him? I don't know." I shrugged. "Maybe somewhere banging an older chick."

"EX...*cuuuse* me?" Arlene shifted her weight to one side.

"I don't know where he is. It wasn't my turn to babysit."

Lacey snickered, then rejoined Roderick as everyone took off in the direction of the Palm House.

"Why don't you ask Amber? Better yet, Ebony should know."

Arlene glanced at her watch. "We have *got* to keep it moving," she said, mostly to herself before marching off, her voluptuous hips swaying from side to side.

D.D. Sherman   Rare Orchids

    The *vroom, vroom* of a motorcycle snagged my attention. In fact, the entire bridal party was alerted. Who comes riding up on a red and black Ducati? None other than Dontae, in his tux, no less.

    He *zoomed* in my direction and swerved mere feet in front of me, nearly turning the bike on its side.

    He pulled off his helmet, looked up at me and flashed a bright, white smile. "Did you miss me?"

    "You could've run me over. Not cute!" I retorted, feeling my heart drumming against my chest, all the while suspecting the black-rimmed Ducati with its illuminated red fairings was probably gifted to him by some desperate older woman.

    "You're holding us up!" Arlene shouted, nearly stomping back in our direction.

    Dontae, still sitting on his motorcycle, twisted his torso to look at her. "Holding you up? From what?"

    Arlene shook her head. "We're all meeting in the Rose Garden in a half hour," she huffed. "That means you've got a—" she broke off to glance at her watch, then yanked her head up to look up at him. "*Now* just a twenty-minute break. So you should start making your way there in a few," she ordered, before strutting away.

    "Well, damn!" he exclaimed, watching her hips rise and fall. "Sounds like something's freaky going down in the Rose Garden?" He turned his head to look at me, then twisted around to look at a fleeing Arlene. "Are other men going to be there?" he yelled out after her. "Looks like I'ma need back up!"

    "Your mind is always in the gutter," I put in.

    "It takes a dirty mind to know one."

    "You're hopeless," I retorted, before sprinting away to catch up with everyone else.

***

The Palm House was an enclosure of glass panes that afforded guests a spectacular view of the violet-blue sky stroked with hues of orange, courtesy of the setting sun. Next to the venue was a serene pool of pink and purple water lilies, green water clovers and leafy fairy moss. Beside the pool was a lush green garden illuminated with hanging globe-shaped paper lanterns that lit a pathway to a large white tent with a string of softly glowing lights dangling from its canopy. The tables and chairs inside the venue were draped in white silk, and floating candles flickered from clear vases of long-stemmed white orchids. The backs of the chairs were tied in faintly iridescent, pink sashes formed into elegantly crafted love knots. Each guest received an embellished, silver-framed picture of the married couple which featured Amber and Antoine superimposed over an image of the friend or relative, which I thought was supercool.

    Amber chose the picture we took from our trip to the Bahamas three years earlier. It was sort of embarrassing; a grimacing dwarf had picked me up and hoisted me over his head in a perfect horizontal when Amber, hysterical with laughter, managed to get a shot of it. I looked around the reception room and noticed that nearly all the guests were slapping their palms to their mouths and doubled over laughing at the pictures, which made me feel a bit better. People were passing around the frames, pointing, guffawing or shaking their heads in embarrassment at what they saw.

    "Let's see yours." I heard a voice, too close to my ear, say. I jerked around to find Dontae standing almost groin to butt cheeks behind me.

    "Nope!" I retorted before attempting to stick the 5x7 frame in my beaded clutch. It still stuck halfway out.

    Before I realized it, he'd reached over my shoulder, snatched it from my purse, and held it before his face before doubling over with laughter. He straightened, started to say something, scrunched his face and collapsed, palms against table, with laughter again.

    I crossed my arms over my chest and watched until he finally pulled himself together. "Welp, your immature side sure as hell didn't take any time to show up!" I scowled, snatching the frame from his hand.

"It's not you I'm laughing at. It's the midget—"

"Dwarf!" I corrected.

"Okay, okay." He wound down off his laughing high. "The vertically challenged dude in the pic."

Vertically challenged. Better. "So, what about him?"

"Dude's got a crazy grin on his face. He's really straining, but he's trying to cover it up with that crazy, crooked tooth smile."

"Well, you may think it's funny—"

"No, I actually think it's hilarious."

"Whatever! That's how he makes his money. People place bets on whether he can pick a thick girl up or not. The thicker the girl, the bigger the pot."

"Hey, I understand. A man's got to eat," Dontae said, sliding back one of the chairs at the table.

Where have I heard that before? I wondered.

He sat down and clasped his hands atop the table, his brownish-green eyes taking in the ambiance of the room.

"Please don't tell me you're sitting here all night? You *do* know this is my assigned table."

"That's okay, I don't mind you sitting here. This is the bridal's party table, and I'm part of the bridal party. Just don't be cock-blocking me if my radar picks up on some cutie I may wanna take back to the crib and smash tonight." He slipped off his tuxedo jacket and turned around to hang it on the back of the chair. The elegant white shirt he wore clung to every contour of his muscular arms. "I wouldn't want you to go getting that walk down the aisle twisted."

"Trust me, you're the furthest thing from my mind," I lied.

"Then and again, you still got a twenty-five-hundred-dollar credit, but that's only good for one night. Anything over that, and I'ma need a credit card on file."

"You know what," I started, sitting down to relax my feet. "I'm going to ignore you. You're just ignorant."

"If ignorant is bliss, then keep me unenlightened."

All I could muster was a shake of my head.

"Heeey there!"

I heard someone behind me sing. I turned around to see a half-lit Phil with cocktail in hand. I sprung from my chair and gave him a generous hug.

"What's up, honey?" he asked, hugging me back.

"Sit down!" I urged.

He walked over to a chair and held on to the back of it. "After I get a refresher." He swirled his drink in his hand.

"Where've you been? Did you make the nuptials?"

"I did not. Traffic was horrendous."

I turned to look at Dontae who was oddly stroking the petal of an orchid. "You do remember my co-worker and friend, Phil, right?"

Dontae looked at Phil with furrowed brows, then a wide smile emerged on his face. "Yes! Yes! I remember you!" He shot up from his chair, came around the table and attempted to fist bump Phil who just stood there with a perplexed look on his face. "You're a Cowboys fan, right?" Dontae asked, dropping his hand when he realized Phil wasn't getting the fist-bump thing.

"Not so loud. I'd like to leave here in one piece, you know," Phil said, placing a palm behind his neck and turning his head aside.

"Don't worry. Even though I'm a Giant's fan, I still got your back."

"I *guess* that's good to know."

"We're cool." Dontae slapped Phil on the back so hard he heaved.

Phil downed the rest of his formerly olive-littered drink, then shook his glass. "Uh-oh, look who's on empty. Gotta go fill her up." He stabbed the last olive with a toothpick then popped it in his mouth.

As Dontae worked his way back around the table, Phil leaned over to quickly whisper in my ear. "Do him!" was all he said before prancing toward the bar.

A giggly Ebony and Devin finally joined us at the table, soon followed by Lacey and Roderick, Marisol and Manuel and then Rasheeda and her partner, Amir.

D.D. Sherman   Rare Orchids

    The table was a huge round circle large enough to accommodate twelve people. The other two chairs belonged to Phil, of course, and to my dismay, salty, bossy, Arlene who showed up about fifteen minutes later trying to rearrange our seats. It apparently annoyed her that Phil sat between Dontae and me.

    "It's not going to look right in pictures!" she said angrily.

    "Actually, Phil is my date tonight," I interjected, looping my arm around his.

    Phil cleared his throat. "Don't mind me. I'm just here for the cocktails." I elbowed Phil in the side. "And to accompany my lovely date, of course," he said, taking a sip of his drink.

    "Well, I don't want y'all getting too comfortable. We're all getting up in like ten minutes."

    "Just ten minutes already?" Ebony asked wearily.

    "It'll be dark soon. We don't have time to waste, *miss thing*!" Arlene snapped.

    "Oh yeah." Ebony glanced at her watch. "It is almost six o'clock." She sighed. Devin rubbed her shoulder to comfort her and I wanted to throw up in my mouth.

    "Ten minutes!" Arlene reiterated, flashing her ten fingers before storming away.

    "Well, I don't know about everyone else, but I'm using five of these ten minutes for a bathroom break. I've been holding it in for *hours*," Rasheeda announced, getting up from her chair.

    "Wait a minute. I'll go with you." A seemingly upbeat Marisol said, following Rasheeda.

    "So how you liking my little brother's best friend?" Ditzy Ebony blurted out of nowhere, placing her elbow on the table and leaning her chin in her hand.

    I looked over at a smiling Dontae, embarrassed. "Oh, you mean him?"

    Ebony dizzily nodded her head. "Uh huh."

    "He's alright." I sat, cringing, hoping the broad had sense enough not to bring up that whole bit about Amber hiring Dontae to sleep with me in front of a table full of men and Lacey.

Ebony looked at me from the side of her eye. "Just alright?" she asked, smirking.

Gosh, she is dumb enough to bring it up in front of a table full of men and Lacey. I thought nervously.

"Yes. He's *just* alright." I reached for my cocktail with a shaky hand and took a sip, hoping she'd just drop the subject; all the while Dontae sat there cockily, apparently taking pleasure in watching me squirm.

Ebony turned her line of questioning to Dontae. "Does someone owe Amber a refund?" She squinted at him.

Dontae turned to face me. "How you gon' ask for a refund when you never sampled the merchandise?"

Phil nearly spat his drink out, laughing. I poked him in the side, instantly stifling him.

"Hey, if there's some kind of inside joke going on here, let the rest of us in on it," Devin suggested, leaning into the table as if prepping to hear a secret.

"Yeah, I wanna know too," Miguel agreed. "Sounds like some interesting shit's going on."

Amir shook his head, then looked over at Phil. "Hey my man, where'd you get your drink? Looks like it's going to be a long night."

Phil turned and pointed to the rear of the room. "The bar is right behind that curtain partition."

"Thanks," Amir said getting up and excusing himself from the table.

"You know, there are over twenty-five thousand species of orchids?" Dontae said to no one in particular while caressing a petal between his thumb and forefinger.

We all turned in his direction with inquisitive expressions on our faces.

"There are over seven hundred types of orchids and more than a hundred thousand hybrids," he continued, lifting his head to look up at us with the candlelight flickering against his dark pupils.

"You have your Phalaenopsis or what some refer to as the moth orchid. And then there's the Cymbidium, or your boat orchid.

The Paphiopedilum better known as…" he broke off to look at me. "The *lady slipper*."

He returned his attention to the table. "You see, the thing about the lady slipper is that she has to be rooted ever-so precisely or this very delicate and deciduous flower will shed her petals prematurely."

"Wow!" Phil exclaimed.

I just sat with a glazed-over expression on my face. I know because it's the look I typically assume when I am shockingly amazed by something.

"Yo, this shit is deep," Miguel exclaimed with surprising interest.

Ebony sat with her mouth open while Devin leaned back in his chair with his forehead gathered as if trying to figure something out.

Dontae looked at Lacey. "You might like the Oncidium or what some may refer to as the dancing lady orchid."

Roderick placed his arm protectively around Lacey's shoulders.

"The Dancing Lady emits a *sensuous* fragrance of sweet cocoa, filling your nostrils with a unique aroma you won't soon forget."

Roderick pulled Lacey closer to him.

"But not every orchid is innocent," he continued, this time looking at Ebony. "Thus the Lycaste Orchid. Such a pretty white, pink, red, or lavender flower." His gaze moved to Devin. "But watch out! If you proceed carelessly it will prick your fingers with its spikey petals and then drink your blood for nutrients.

Ebony shifted in her chair and Devin loosened his tie.

Dontae smirked.

Marisol and Rasheeda returned to the table looking puzzled at how we were all captivated by whatever Dontae was saying.

"Who cares about Orchids?" Roderick asked.

Amir returned to the table with drink in hand.

"Yeah, man," began Devin. "I couldn't care less about an orchid." He waved his hand dismissively.

"And then there's my favorite orchid of all times," Dontae continued, apparently unfazed by Roderick's and Devin's comments. "The Vanilla Orchid."

"That's a cool name. *Vanilla Orchid*," Marisol repeated.

Donte plucked a cookie from the tiered serving tray, set on the table as a centerpiece, and held it before his eyes. "This is an orchid. He turned his head and pointed to the eight-tiered tuft and beaded wedding cake sitting on a table of draped silk at the far end of the room. "*That's* an orchid."

"What's he talking about?" Rasheeda asked, looking around the table for an answer.

"All different types of orchids, I guess," Lacey answered. "It's really interesting."

Roderick sucked his teeth, threw his head back and got up from the table. "I'm going to get a drink."

"Hurry up! Arlene, the drill sergeant should be back any minute!" Lacey called after him.

"The vanilla flavoring that most of us consume—unwittingly or otherwise—almost on a daily basis, comes from the pods of the Vanilla Orchid Plant."

"Okay." Amir shrugged.

"The Vanilla Orchid was indigenous to Mexico and used by the Aztecs mainly for medicinal purposes until the early 1500s when a Spanish Conqueror by the name of Hernando Cortés defeated the Aztecs and introduced the vanilla bean to Spain."

I could not believe I was listening to the same man who almost ran me over with his tricked-out Ducati barely fifteen minutes ago.

"Queen Elizabeth The First and most of the rich and royal of Europe developed an extreme liking for vanilla. The French tried to grow the Vanilla Orchid but failed because the bee that pollenated the plant only existed in *meheeko*," Dontae said, pronouncing Mexico with a Spanish accent. "Charles Morrens, a professor of botany, attempted hand-pollenating the plant and failed because his method was way too time-consuming and costly."

D.D. Sherman   Rare Orchids

"You can flunk me out of this history lesson," Miguel said, dropping back against his chair.

"The year is 1841," Dontae continued unbothered. "In walks a twelve-year-old *slave* by the name of Edmond Albius who's from a place called Réunion Island. He discovers a way to pollinate the Vanilla Orchid by the use of a thin blade of grass and his little...black...thumb." Dontae wiggled his thumb for emphasis. "Because of his methods, the Vanilla Orchid thrives all over the world in abundance. And you people—" Dontae stopped short to look around the table. "Get to eat cake."

Roderick returned to the table with a beer in hand. "Are we still talking about flowers?" he asked taking his seat.

Dontae looked at him. "You're back in time for the most important part of this horticulture lesson, my brother."

"Geez, I feel so lucky," Roderick responded.

"And then you have the Bucket Orchid. But this story's not about the orchid per se. It's about the orchid bee. You see, this particular bee is trying his hardest to get laid— "

An implosion of laughter from the table cuts Dontae off mid-sentence, mostly from the women while the men appeared intimidated.

"…but he needs a little help. That's where the bucket orchid comes in. So this bee flies under the hood of the bucket orchid flower and scales her slippery walls to reach these fragrant oils. In doing so, the dumb shmuck slips into a bucket of accumulated oils coating himself with a scent female bees find *absolutely* irresistible." More chuckles from the women.

"Now to keep himself from drowning this poor son of a bee has to figure out the one and only escape route, a narrow tunnel-like opening. As he squeezes through this tunnel—now so fresh and so clean with this sweet-smelling perfume—the bucket orchid deposits two pollen sacks onto the bee's back. He escapes to get laid another day, but not without the burden of another woman riding his back. Moral of the story, if you're going to be rolling around in another woman's juices, be sure to check your sacks before leaving."

Phil howled leading a chorus of laughter from everyone at the table, including me who was chuckling under my breath."

Dontae smirked. His gaze travelled to the vase of White Orchids. "And there's the white egret orchid, the rarest orchid of them all." he said, the back of his fingers stroking the soft petals of the flower.

His eyes focused on me again. "Can anyone tell me how does one *rare* orchid stand out in a field of hundreds of thousands?"

Our gaze locked. I felt damn foolish. I could not pull my eyes from his glare, even though I sensed that everyone at the table was staring at us.

"Chop! Chop!" I heard Arlene's bark in the distance even though she stood over our table. "Let's make this happen, folks!"

Chapter 10

Arlene was piping mad that I chucked my shoes and had to improvise by standing on my tiptoes in the Rose Garden pictures. I refused to let her know where they were by telling her I had forgotten which receptacle I'd tossed them in for fear she'd go fish them out.

As the bridal party dissipated, I stealthily lagged behind because I noticed Dontae squatted before a trail of rose bushes, leaning forward to sniff their fragrance.

I wanted to approach him and say something bitingly sarcastic, but things seemed different between us. There was a respect I was reluctantly developing for him; a nascent attraction that now included his intellect as well as his Greek god-like biceps.

He turned his head as if he sensed me standing behind him, glanced up at the dwindling sun, then back at me. "The sun," he started. "And the rain are the sine qua non of growing plants. Too much of—*or* not enough of either will always result in a plant's demise; therefore, it is essential that the caregiver knows when to be generous and when to hold back."

"How do you know so much about these things?"

"About plants, you mean?"

I nodded.

He motioned me over to him with a quick tilt of his head. I complied, squatting beside him.

He stared into my eyes relentlessly, so much so that I could see the brownish flesh behind his brown-green irises. "I have a predilection for beautiful things that often go unnoticed," he continued. "And then I'm prompted to study them, analyze them, dissect them to get to the very core of what or *who* they are."

I looked away embarrassed and caressed a rose. "I don't know if that's an answer."

"Look, can I be straight-up with you?" Dontae asked abruptly. "I mean about who I really am?"

"You mean that whole bad-boy persona is just an act?"

Dontae tittered. "Kind of." He sidled up to a display of bright yellow flowers, their delicate petals in gentle bloom. "These are Sunsprites," he informed me, gently pulling on the stem.

"They're gorgeous." I crouched beside him and leaned in to sniff.

"I dated a wealthy woman once—a much older woman. I guessed that she was somewhere in her mid to late fifties. Anyway, she had this expansive garden with almost every plant in there that you can imagine. I mean it was one of the most beautiful gardens I'd ever seen in someone's home. One of my duties—besides pleasing her—" his smirk was devilish. "Was to care for her garden." He took a minute to chuckle. "I was just a thug from the hood. What did I know about caring for plants?"

He looked at me as if expecting a reply, but I just nodded for him to continue.

"She told me I could make a lot of money as a landscaper and that it would behoove me to learn some kind of a skill. She offered to pay me a thousand dollars a week to care for her flowers and offered to send me to school to learn botany."

I laughed. I couldn't help it. His story sounded far-fetched.

"So I did," he continued unfazed. "And when I started learning about all the different kinds of plants and plant hybrids in the world, I became increasingly fascinated. I eventually earned a degree in botany."

"Wow," was all my brain could offer up.

"You see here." He pointed to a section of golden-yellow roses with dark green leaves. "These are Floribunda roses. They're a cross between a hybrid tea and a polyantha. This particular Floribunda is called *Amber Queen*." He delicately pulled the rose toward me so that I could sniff it.

"Mmm, that's nice. It has a spicy-sweet fragrance."

"And so it does." He smiled. His white, near perfect teeth reminding me of why he was almost irresistibly attractive. He pointed to another cluster of flowers. "And these are Grandifloras. Your cross between a Floribunda and a hybrid tea. Smell this."

D.D. Sherman   Rare Orchids

    He gently pulled on the stem. I got up to walk to the other side of him and squatted before the flower, pushing my hair behind my ear and leaning in my head to catch a whiff.

    "Oh my! Now that's amazingly strong and sweet," I cooed, imagining that there must've been some really strong pheromones in the area because my attraction toward Dontae was racing to the surface and on the verge of boiling over.

    We both stood to walk along a cobble path with bushels and vines of roses flanking us on both sides. Along the walkway were embellished iron archways covered in greenery with colorful arrays of roses dangling from them.

    "Ah, there she is," he started as we sauntered dreamily, pointing to a grouping of burnt orange roses blossoming from long thorny stems. "The Tuscan Sun. Unquestionably one of my favorites."

    "I can certainly see why," I said, marveling at the flower then copping a covert glance at him.

    He pinched the petals of a rose belonging to a cluster of leaning pink flowers. "And here we have the Rosa Smarty."

    "Looks more like some kind of sophisticated hibiscus to me." I chuckled.

    "You see, the Rosa Smarty grows prostrate as if submitting to the will of God."

    "Interesting," I said as we continued our walk, stopping under one of the floral covered arches.

    Dontae looked up and reached his hand to stroke a pinkish white leafy flower. "And what do you think these beauties are called?"

    "You got me," I said, suddenly feeling a bit dumb.

    "Come on, baby. It's obvious."

    I liked that he called me baby. A trill bolted through me. "Um…hanging vines? I don't know." I laughed, hoping to conceal my ignorance.

    "Close. These are called climbing roses. Do you notice how they scale this arch, intertwining its vines ever so lovely?"

"Yes, I do." I nodded excitedly. "God's handiwork is nothing short of amazing."

"I won't disagree with you there," he affirmed as our eyes locked under that flowery archway. "I want to kiss you. No, I don't!" he rescinded abruptly. "I want to *taste* you."

He closed in on me. I wanted—I mean I should've withdrawn, but something about his scent of almonds and coconut, his gleaming white smile, his seductive eyes and sultry brown lips, neutralized my defenses.

"I want to savor you." He neared me so close I could feel his heart pound against mine.

"I want to inhale you."

Before I could muster any objections, our lips were pressed together, and our tongues met in even exchange. They encircled slowly. He took mine in and I took in his, rhythmically to a silent cadence. His large, warm hands cupped my backside and his groin grew exponentially against my thighs.

I could hear passerby in the distance, conversing about the flowers, probably trying not to notice our heated display of passion.

We finally pulled apart. Dontae's eyes examined the length of my body in my hip-hugging dress, his sumptuous lips moist with my saliva.

"After that kiss, I can just imagine." He tucked his lips and shook his head. "Mmph, mmph, mmph."

"What?" I asked, trying to play oblivious even though I knew very well what he meant.

"Nothing," he whispered, moving his face toward mine. We kissed again, the same as we had before, but now with more fervor and intention as if there were some unspoken consensus.

I pulled away abruptly, grasped his wrists and removed his hands from my rump. I glanced down at my watch. "They're going to be sending out a search party for us any second now."

"It's okay. I have to be cutting out in a minute anyway."

My heart sank at this revelation and I instantly felt embarrassed for my prior moments of vulnerability.

"Thought you at least wanted to stay for dinner?"

"Nah, I'm good." The whites of his eyes shimmered in the onset of darkness.

I guess this was all a ploy to see how far you could get me to go, huh youngan? I angrily thought.

"I'm sure Amber and Antoine will be looking for you. There's still the walk-in, the first dance where the bridal party is supposed to be joining them. And oh, the garter belt thing."

Dontae tittered sexily. "Do I look like I want to catch a garter belt?" he asked, apparently amused by my naiveté.

"I guess not." I shrugged, hoping I didn't sound too pitiful.

"I'm sorry, but I have somewhere I have to be, sweetheart."

Sweetheart? I'm not your effin sweetheart, sweetheart! I spat that thought in my head.

"Oh, your line of work. How can I forget? Silly me."

"Nah, that has nothing to do with it. Look, let me walk you back over there," he suggested, placing his strong hand on the small of my back and coaxing me in the direction of the venue.

The walk back was sobering. There was no more talk of flowers, not even of the kiss we shared. There was only small, cordial-like chatter. He joked a bit about how he couldn't wait to get out of his tux and how riding a motorcycle with it on drew a lot of inquisitive stares and he snickered a little when I talked about tossing my shoes in the trash mainly to piss Arlene off.

The double-domed shaped, glass-paneled Palm House looked like an illuminated oasis. It was nestled in a thicket of lush green trees, sprawling lawns, and circular-shaped flower beds. The serene pool of water lilies dazzled in the night.

We walked the path of lit paper lanterns and stopped before an illuminated staircase that spiraled up the side of the building.

"Will you bid everyone a goodnight for me?"

"Yes, though I think you're more than capable of doing that yourself," I replied, with something heavy tugging at my heart.

I ascended the first three steps and wearily leaned against the glass wall. Dontae's dreamy eyes looked up at me.

"You know what?"

I crossed my arms to steel myself. "What?" I asked with as much nonchalance as I could muster.

"I think you like me."

"Boy, bye!" I retorted, waving my hand dismissively as I ascended the remaining steps to go inside. I turned to look at him. "Because I kissed you?"

"No. Because you tried to swallow me whole." He stuck his hands in his front pockets and giggled.

My cheeks burned. "You're ridiculous." I turned back around and continued toward the reception area.

"Hey!" he called after me.

I turned again to face him. "What is it?" I asked, tired. His shenanigans were starting to gnaw at me.

"What happens when you cross a thirty-eight-year-old, single cougar with a twenty-nine—"

"Twenty-eight." I corrected him.

"Twenty-*nine*." he insisted. "Today's my birthday."

"Oh," I uttered, feeling a little foolish. "Happy Birthday!" I mustered a tinge of excitement.

"That's why I have to leave. My grandmother planned a little birthday party. A few friends and family are at her house waiting for me. You see, I have to go to eat cake, otherwise I'll be disappointing my grammy."

And there it is. The immaturity. I mean like, what grown man calls his grandmother grammy? Symone, why in the blazing hell fires are you even giving this juvenile the time of day? I scolded myself.

"That's nice," I said, continuing up the steps.

"You never gave me the chance to ask my question."

I stopped and faced him again. Don't quite know why, but I did.

"Go ahead. Ask your silly question."

"Okay. What happens when you cross a thirty-eight-year-old-cougar with a twenty-nine-year-old tiger?"

"We claw each other's eyes out."

D.D. Sherman   Rare Orchids

"Close, but no cigar.

I rolled my eyes, took in deep aromatic breath, and sighed. "Go ahead and tell me then. I give up."

"We simply learn to play nice." He smiled broadly, which made his eyes seem to twinkle. His near-perfect choppers gleamed at me.

I melted as he turned to leave. I stood there watching him walk away until his black suit became an indiscernible figure moving in the darkness. I ran my fingers through my hair and felt something that startled me. I cautiously groped at it. It snagged at my strands a little as I pulled its prickly stem from the thick of my tresses. I don't know how or when, but Dontae had inserted a perfectly shaped golden-yellow Amber Queen in my hair. I pressed it to my nose and inhaled deeply, kissed it and placed it back in my hair before going inside.

CHAPTER 11

I pounded on the elevator button. An elderly woman and I had been waiting in the dingy lobby of a project building for more than fifteen minutes. She'd watched me wipe down the button panel with a sanitizing wipe from my trusty travel pack. From my peripheral I noticed that the old woman had one brow lifted as she disapprovingly looked on.

Hey lady, did you not see the drips of dried spit or snot—take your best guess—and what looked like blood spatter, on the button panel? I silently asked her. But I got it. Bodily fluids marring the walls, doors, elevators, and floors of project developments in Brooklyn was just part of the daily decor.

After thirty minutes, the small crowd that had gathered around the elevators finally conceded that neither one was working by way of mutual sighs and a few choice cuss words.

"What floor are you on?" I asked the old woman, the broken elevators now making us allies against a mutual nemesis.

"Seven!" she huffed. "How am I s'posed to get up these stairs..." she nodded at the dismally gray painted stairwell door, "with this here walker?"

I sighed with empathy and evaluated her stout and bent-over frame. "I don't think you can." Two half-filled plastic bags of groceries dangled from her meaty wrists.

"This is a damn shame! Especially for disabled people like myself. But they don't care about us," she grumbled, then sucked her teeth.

I nodded in agreement then shook my head for lack of a viable solution to her problem. My client lived on the twelfth floor. For me it was just a minor inconvenience. For that poor woman, it was crucial.

"Do you know a neighbor on the first floor whose house you can stay in until the elevators are repaired?" It was a flimsy alternative, but I didn't know what else to suggest.

D.D. Sherman   Rare Orchids

"Hmph!" she grunted. "I got two pints of rum raisin ice cream in here." She lifted her arm to show me, letting one of the bags dangle. "They be done melted by the time I get upstairs."

"Maybe you can ask your neighbor to at least store your ice cream in their freezer for you?"

"Look, I don't talk to none of these people in this building!" she replied sharply. "You got ole nosey Mary Jenkins in 1H. She don't do nothin' but hang out her winda all day tryna see what she can see so she can go run and tell the whole neighborhood. And that's where Mr. Pitkins live." She nodded toward an apartment door at the end of a short hallway. "But you see, he done went blind 'cause he wasn't taking his insulin like he s'pose tah. He got sugah. And I ain't fixin' to go knockin' on no blind man's door asking him to put my ice cream in his freezer!" she retorted, with a jerk of her head.

"How about if I carry your bags, your walker, and let you lean on me? We'll take a break mid-way each flight of steps."

"Well, it don't seem like I got much of a choice now do it?" she replied bitterly as if blaming me for the broken elevators.

Escorting Mrs. Della Johnson was a harrowing experience. Every time we'd take a step or two, she'd stop me so she could catch her breath, weighing me down with all of her girth; and whenever I addressed her as Miss Johnson, she readily corrected me with a fiery attitude.

"I done had three husbands! I ain't nobody's miss. Tho' they all dead now."

Yeah, and I bet it was you that killed them. I had to exercise extreme precaution when addressing Mrs. Johnson for fear of being chastised. Luckily, a young man entered the stairwell at the second floor and offered to give us a hand, grabbing the bags from me and then getting on the other side of Mrs. Johnson.

Three husbands, huh? I thought with a bit of intrigue. "How you managed to get three husbands and I'm struggling with just finding one?" I asked, surprising my ears with my very candid question.

"'Cause I ain't never looked at *what* they was. I looked at *who* they was."

With that tidbit, Mrs. Johnson and her walker struggled through the bulky metal door to her apartment before slamming it in our faces without so much as a thank you.

The young man looked at me and shrugged. "You think maybe I can get a couple of dollars? I was on my way to take care of some business when I saw y'all struggling."

I scrambled around in the side pocket of my handbag, found a few folded singles and handed them to him.

"Thanks, miss." He scuttled off and burst through a stairwell door. I heard the thumps of his feet racing down the steps.

I repeated Mrs. Johnson's answer in my head, making it grammatically correct. "*'Because I looked at who they were and disregarded what they were.'*"

Eureka! I thought I found the answer to Dontae's question. 'How does one rare orchid stand out in a field of many?'

***

By the time I got to the twelfth floor I was hot, sweaty, and gasping the marijuana infused air. I staggered to apartment 12G and knocked on the door. A muffled television played on the other side that sounded like midday talk show buffoonery. I pounded my fist harder against the door. I heard the TV lower and someone grumbling.

"Who's knockin' on my door like that?" an irritated voice questioned.

A young, petite woman sporting a kinky afro answered with an infant on her hip and a runny-nose toddler grasping her leg.

"Yeah?" she looked annoyed.

"I'm looking for Maurice Griffith. Does he live here?"

"Yeah, but he ain't here right now."

"Who are you to him? If you don't mind my asking?"

"I'm his fiancée," she replied proudly, taking in a deep breath to puff her small chest, though I saw no ring on her finger.

I noted that she looked rather young to be in a relationship with a forty-year-old. "Oh, sorry. My name is Symone Alexander. I'm his probation officer." I went to extend my hand but thought better of it. God only knew when I'd be passing the next restroom and I certainly wasn't going to ask to use hers.

"Do you know where I may find him?"

"He's at work right now."

"Work?" I frowned and turned my head to the side.

"Yeah, he's working."

"Well, he never reported that to me."

The young lady shrugged.

"Where does Mr. Griffith work?"

"At Home Depot."

"Oh, Home Depot is a legitimate business."

"No, he don't work at Home Depot. *I* work at Home Depot as an evening cashier."

"Huh? I'm sorry. I seem to be confused."

"He does deliveries at Home Depot."

"Does deliveries for them, but he doesn't work there?"

"Just go to the Home Depot at Gateway Mall and you'll find him there." She sounded exasperated.

"Well, thank you for the information."

"You're welcome," she mumbled before closing the door in my face.

A fifteen-minute drive brought me to the congested Gateway Mall. I parked my car in the crowded lot and sat scanning the Home Depot pickup area for Mr. Griffith. After a good while I decided to get out of the car and look for him. Just as I approached the bustling exit, I spotted him toting panels of sheet rock into the back of an old, rusty van.

"Mr. Griffith!" I called out as I approached him.

He snatched his head in my direction. "Damn!" he retorted.

"What do we have going on here?" I asked, now standing face to face with him.

"Hey, Officer Alexander. How you doin'?"

"I'm doing okay. What's this all about?"

"Look," he started with a lop-sided grin. "You told me to get a job."

"A legal, recognizable, tax-paying job. Soliciting Home Depot customers for home deliveries is not it."

"Look, this my hustle, ma'am."

"I'm going to have to report this, you know?"

"Come on, Officer Alexander. This is how I'm feeding my kids," he expostulated with clasped hands.

"I get that, but I also have to protect my job," I retorted, ruefully remembering what landed me working with adults in the first place. "I know you don't expect me to just look the other way when you're doing something unlawful?"

"Ok, listen." he stated, pressing the back of his rough hand against my forearm. "It's Monday, right? Let me finish out the week, and I promise to start looking for legit work come next Tuesday."

I took in a deep breath and let it out with a slump of my shoulders. "Okay. You've got until next week. You have to find something on the books. Something I can present to the courts to show that you're making progress in the right direction."

"You got it, Officer."

"And keep me updated with how you're doing. I know the job market is tight and all, but unless you make this a legal business, the judge is not going for it."

"I understand. You're right."

"And Fuller's retired so you can forget about leniency."

"Oh man!" he exclaimed, running his hand over his closely-shaved head. "That judge was a cool dude."

"One of the last compassionate ones."

"I promise, Officer Alexander. I'm gonna do the right thing."

"Okay, then. Have a nice day and I'll be looking to hear from you soon with some positive updates."

D.D. Sherman   Rare Orchids

"You got it." He forced a smile and tossed the last square of sheet rock into the old van. He waved bye, sprinted off to the driver's side of the vehicle, and started the engine with a *vroom vroom*. Exhaust fumes billowed from the car's rusty tailpipe as he sped off.

Well, at least he's trying, I thought to myself. I empathized with guys like Maurice. It was difficult to find work with a felony offense haunting you like relentless ghosts. That is the Achilles Heel of the criminal justice system. The courts advocated rehabilitation but did not provide viable resources for facilitating such; ergo more crime; ergo recidivism; and ergo probation officers like me who waded in the cloudy waters of ambiguity.

***

That evening I luxuriated in a tub of honey cream and lavender-scented suds. I owed it to myself after having washed all nine windows on the first floor of my brownstone. I gave myself an extra pat on the back because I had done it on a weekday, capturing the attention of some of my neighbors who looked on with what I perceived to be astonishment. *Wonder where she gets the energy after having worked all day*? I imagined them thinking. *That woman is really something.* Though, *look at that fool washing windows in the dark,* was probably more accurate. Whatever the case, it felt gratifying. I thought of how it would be getting dark earlier due to the impending fall season which always made me a bit sullen. There was nothing like a sudsy warm bath, fresh-smelling skin, and squeaky-clean hair to buoy my mood.

After getting out of the tub and oiling myself from head to toe, I slipped into my Giants Jersey, which was really a nightgown made to look like the real thing, plopped on the sofa with remote in hand, and scanned the menu.

My phone pinged a few times on the naked woman coffee table. I leaned over to grab it and saw that Amber had sent me several pics of her and Antoine. One was of them lounging on the beach in Aruba with gargantuan frozen drinks in hand. Another was a snapshot of them snorkeling amid huge sea turtles and other underwater creatures. The last ones were various flicks of their posh honeymoon suite; a heart made from rose petals decorated the center of a canopy bed, a table with ice-filled buckets of champagne and decorative saucers of fancy hors d' oeuvres sat on a balcony overlooking a crystal-blue ocean; and Mr. and Mrs. Robes hanging from brass hooks in a Victorian-inspired parlor room.

  I texted her back. *"Stop! You're making me jeaaaaaalous! Have a nice time, girlie!"*

  After a few seconds my phone pinged. *"Don't be jealous. Your turn is coming! 🙆"*

  I texted back. *"Well, let me know when you meet him. ☹ lol,"* then tossed my phone aside.

  After a few minutes, I heard another ping. I reached for my phone between the sofa cushions and read Amber's text.

  "I'm calling maid of honor!" ☺

  "You know it!" I texted back perfunctorily.

  "Lol. Antoine and I are getting ready to go get our massage on. TTYL, snookums!" 💋

  "Sounds amazing! Have fun! TTYL." I texted back, replacing my phone on the coffee table.

  I found a good documentary on NETFLIX and started watching it when I drifted off into a deep sleep, only to be interrupted by the persistent ringing of my doorbell. I sat up on the sofa and tripped over an arca rug as I stumbled to the front door. I flung it open with no shortage of annoyance.

  "Yes!" I demanded before I noticed the perplexed, frumpy looking guy standing there cradling a bouquet of white orchids in the bend of his arm.

  Something jolted through me and I stood frozen in place with my jaw hung open. *Flowers? For me? Not possible.* "Who are you looking for?"

D.D. Sherman   Rare Orchids

"These are for somebody by the name of Sa-sa—," he broke off and pressed his fingers to his temple. "I think he said, Symone Alexander."

"That would be me," I said with my heart pounding so hard I was sure he could see my night shirt vibrating.

I snatched the crystal vase as he handed it to me. Sure it was rude, but I couldn't help myself. I was overjoyed. "You know who they're from?" I asked, though I had my suspicions.

The man shrugged. "I was just told to deliver these to you. Should be a card in there."

"Yes, of course." I was sure he could tell I wasn't used to having flowers sent to me.

"Have a goodnight," the man stated, turning to leave.

"Thank you," I replied before closing the door.

I carried the arrangement to my cocktail table and gently sat them down. My trembling hand reached for the small envelope and it seemed I raised the tiny flap and extracted the card in slow motion. Nothing. The blank note had a floral border, but there were no words of endearment like I thought it would be.

"Son-of-a..." I said aloud. "That's just like his ole, cocky behind. I mean who does that? Send someone flowers without out a note!" I griped to myself. "If I ever see his black behind again, I'm going to let—"

My doorbell rang again, interrupting my internal tirade. *Oops...forgot to tip him.* I thought, as I reached for my handbag and retrieved a ten-dollar-bill. I flung opened the door. "I'm so sorry. Here's—"

My heart stopped. Literally. At least for a few seconds.

"Why you lookin' mad?" Dontae asked, standing there dressed in an all-black suit, black dress shirt, red silk tie and showing off his million-dollar smile.

My body felt ignited in a flash of heat. "I'm not mad. Why are you here and where are you coming from all dressed up?"

"Do you like your flowers?" he asked, ignoring my questions.

"Yes, but there was no note."

120

"Which would you prefer? For me to tell you how much I'm diggin' you or for me to *show* you how much I'm diggin' you?"

"Why have someone deliver flowers only to show up five minutes later?"

"I was going to deliver them myself, but a crackhead up the block approached me for money, so I paid him five-dollars to bring them to your door."

"Oh. That was classy," I said with a hint of sarcasm.

"Hey, I try," he answered, his eyes roaming the length of my body, stopping at my shapely thighs that my faux jersey teasingly revealed.

When I noticed him gawking, I stepped back behind my door and tilted my head to continue talking to him.

"Well, thank you for the flowers, but I was just about to call it a night," I said, starting to close the door.

He glanced at his watch, then put his hand against the door to stop me. "It's just nine o'clock, sweetie."

"Yeah, but it takes me a long time to fall asleep."

"I can help you with that." He said, taking a step up so that he was now standing just outside my foyer.

"I hope you don't think a bouquet of flowers entitles you to anything."

His face became darkly serious. "Let me in!" he demanded softly.

"I don't want to."

"No, you're afraid to."

"Hey, I got nine in the chamber and one in the clip. Try me if you want to!" I fired back, despite being weaken by his good-smelling cologne.

"I'm not talking about that kind of fear," he said, taking a step closer.

"Then what it is that you think I fear?" I bit my bottom lip in anticipation of his answer.

"Getting hurt."

I gulped as his response sliced at my heart.

"Goodnight, Dontae. And thanks for the flowers."

Before I could close the door, he turned sideways and slipped inside. "Now you can close your door."

"You're invading my space, young man!" I retorted, still clutching the knob of my cracked-open door.

"Oh, you're going to know when I'm invading your space."

"You just don't know when enough is enough, do you?"

"*Trust me*," he uttered, barely above a whisper, slowly approaching me.

"Dude, you're like young enough to be my son if I was a preteen mom." I tried not to be captivated, but he smelled so good, always like fresh coconuts, almonds and something sweet.

"*Trust me*." His warm, moist breath whispered in my ear.

"Why should I?" I tried keeping up my defenses, but my knees were weakening.

"I gave your girl her money back."

I quivered at that revelation. "She didn't tell me that."

"I asked her not to."

"Why?"

"Because I want you to sleep with me...*for free*," he leaned over to whisper in my ear. "*Trust me*," he murmured again, nibbling my earlobe and swirling his tongue in my canal.

My entire body was ablaze and simmering in desire despite my best efforts to control my emotions.

He closed the door behind us, licked my cheeks, bit at my nose and kissed my eyelids with warm, sensuous lips.

His mouth met mine. We kissed each other hungrily. I was fully aware of what was happening to me, but I felt as if I were drifting and had no control over where the moment was taking me. He lifted me from my feet and carried me over to my sofa before laying me on it and straddling me.

I placed my hand against his hard chest in a hopeless attempt to stop him, but he brought it to his mouth and inserted his tongue between my splayed fingers.

That's so unfair, I thought.

D.D. Sherman   Rare Orchids

He slipped off his jacket and flung it across my naked lady coffee table. He loosened his tie and lifted it over his head, unbuttoned his shirt and tossed that on top of his suit jacket, then pulled his wife beater over his head to reveal a set of tight, caramel-hued abs. He stood up to step out of his boxers and slacks, and about eight inches of stiffness poked out at me.

I'm done! I surrendered silently.

He reached under my jersey and pulled down my lace thongs, and then lifted my shirt over my head. My nipple were erect; standing at attention.

"Ahem," I started, clearing my throat. "Condom, please." I couldn't believe I was giving in so easily, but it was useless to fight. In that moment I wanted him just as much as he wanted me.

He smiled seductively before leaning over to reach for his pants. He extracted a condom from his front pocket and pulled it on, eyeing me savagely.

I felt him enter me. He struggled a bit. It *had* been a good minute. And then...and then...I felt him fill my insides as I got caught in a rapture of bliss. He leaned over to kiss me and our tongues met in unbridled ecstasy. He thrusted against me rhythmically and relentlessly as I bit my bottom lip to keep from screaming out in sheer carnal pleasure.

"*You trust me?*" he whispered, as we grinded in synchronized harmony.

I didn't reply, but just held on to his contoured waist as I tried to keep the height of ecstasy at bay.

"*Do you trust me?*" he persisted, leaning over to trace my areolas with the tip of his tongue, and then taking my stiff nipple into his warm, sumptuous mouth.

All I could manage was a faint nod of my head.

"*Good*," he responded as he lowered his head to the spot between my thighs and allowed his warm tongue to explore my love canal. He lifted himself to enter me again, and then lowered his head to taste me, and then lifted himself to thrust me, and then allowed his sweet kisses to run the length of my inner thighs stopping at my sweetest spot to pleasure me once more, before entering me a final time.

"Ugh! Ugh! Come on baby!" he coaxed as I groaned and moaned from a state of bliss I'd never experienced before.

I could no longer contain myself and neither could he. I shouted his name as I released and his body twitched and convulsed before his short, unruly afro collapsed against my pounding chest.

I was breathing like I had just ran a marathon.

Dontae lifted his neck to look at me. "Damn!" he panted. "I should be paying *you*."

I giggled as my thoughts raced, wondering how the hell I allowed myself to become so vulnerable.

"Can I get up?" he asked.

"Oh, I'm sorry." My cheeks burned with embarrassment as I released my hands, which still gripped his slender waist.

"I have to use your bathroom," he said with a grunt as he lifted himself up.

"Sure," I said, feeling a bit slippery between my thighs and thinking how desperately I needed a very long and very hot shower.

I watched his slightly hairy butt cheeks saunter out of sight.

I listened to water running in the sink and after about ten minutes, Dontae returned to the living room and started getting dressed which saddened me.

"Can I call you tomorrow?"

"You don't have to," I said, lifting myself up from the sofa.

"What if I want to?"

I released a puff of air through my flared nostrils. "Look, I know what this was all about."

"Oh yeah?" he questioned, refastening his ruby-like cuff links. "Then tell me, what do you think this is all about?" he stepped into his slacks, then slipped them up.

"You think I don't get that I'm just another notch in your mile-long belt?"

Dontae chuckled, then shook his head. "I thought you said you trust me."

"I did in the moment," I said, reaching for my nightgown and slipping it back on.

He tittered again.

"I don't see what's so funny."

"Tell me, Symone. Who is your ideal mate?"

"Oh geez! This is a nice time to ask me that."

"This is the best time to ask you that."

I shrugged. "I guess he would be smart, and *gainfully* employed."

Dontae smirked as he slipped his tie over his head and adjusted it to his neck.

"He would be from a close-knit and successful family. He'd probably drive a Benz or a Rover. He'd have a couple of degrees under his belt and be in a supervisory position at work."

Dontae stuck his arms through his suit jacket, pulled at his lapels, and rolled his shoulders.

"He'd be altruistic with exceptional hygiene. And if he was rich, he'd definitely be a philanthropist and a globe trotter. He'd be tall—at least six feet or better—average to good looking, clean, monogamous-minded, God-fearing, and definitely over the age of thirty-five."

He slipped into his patent leather shoes and walked to the door.

"Why did you ask me that?" I asked, following him.

He turned to face me. "Oh, I just wanted to know what your alternate reality was."

"Huh? Alternate reality? What do you mean by, *alternate reality*?"

"In my short twenty-nine years on earth, I've come to realize that humans exist in two simultaneous realities. The one that's going on inside their heads and the one that's going on for real. Sadly, a lot of us can't see the difference."

He turned to open the door as I reflected on his words. *Was I living in two realities?* I quickly dismissed the thought and refocused on the reality I was dealing with at that moment.

"I guess you're heading off to your next rendezvous? Let me guess. The Ducati lady?"

"There's some kind of small gathering at her house tonight. I don't know, something about a business acquaintance being promoted to some sort of chief strategist officer at some Fortune 500 company." He glanced at his Rolex Presidential. "And I'm late."

His blatant response jolted me. *What the hell did I just do?* I admonished myself.

"She gets a kick out of dressing me up and parading me around her filthy rich compadres," Dontae continued, despite my apparent dismay. "Though they're all pretty much used to me by now. I've been seeing her for three years, not long after her tycoon husband died."

"Thanks a lot, dude. You've just reminded me of how disgusting you are! Please get out!" I exclaimed, swinging open my front door.

"Oh come on, sweetie. There's no need for all this animosity. My friend is fifty-five years old. Most of the time, she's not even in the mood. I'm more or less a companion," Dontae said, stepping through the door. He turned to face me. "Look, I'm really feeling you. Especially after what just happened between us. Trust me, there's no need for jealousy."

"I wish I can take back what I just did."

Dontae chuckled. "No you don't."

"More than anything in the world."

"Come on. Don't act like you don't know what it is that I do for a living." His face inched up to mine, so close that the tips of our noses touched. "You need a reminder?" he asked as his tongue swiped my pouty lips.

I recoiled. "Actually, you will never have to remind me again. Trust me!"

"It's a job! It's not about love, feelings, or emotions. It's a *job*!"

I flared my nose and sucked my teeth. But Dontae had a point. He had been honest about his line of work from the beginning so if I were to be angry I had only to be angry with myself.

He gave me a peck on the lips. "Trust me," he uttered again, before turning to leave and racing down the flight of steps. He kissed at me from the landing. I watched him stroll up the block then turn a corner out of sight.

A stray black cat sidled up to me and comfortingly rubbed its head against my leg. I needed a shower; a steaming-hot shower.

CHAPTER 12

When I opened my eyes at the crack of dawn—Dontae. On line at the local coffee shop, awaiting a caramel iced latte—Dontae. Every time my cell phone rang—Dontae. At work—Dontae. At lunch—Dontae. In the midst of conversations with other people—Dontae. When I prayed— Dontae. When I dreamed—Dontae. On the elliptical—Dontae.

Dontae had become an addiction since our sexual encounter three days prior, and it seemed no matter how hard I tried I couldn't stop visions of him from high jacking my every waking thought. His sending me texts morning and evening of a different kind of flower along with brief poems demonstrative of his feelings for me weren't making things any easier.

That following Tuesday after our encounter he sent an image of a fuchsia colored rose accompanied by a short poem written in fancy text that read:

> 'I was offered the world's gold
> or a single wish in lieu.
> I wished for this Wild Prairie Rose,
> And am surrendering it unto you.'

The following Wednesday my phone vibrated, jolting me from a deep sleep; I scrambled for it beneath the covers. Dontae had sent me a picture of a single chrysanthemum with white, daisy-like petals and a golden-hued crown, bending in the wind. The colorful text read:

> 'You've kidnapped my heart
> and are holding it at ransom.
> In exchange for your love
> I submit this chrysanthemum.'

D.D. Sherman   Rare Orchids

On Thursday he sent photos of vibrant green bushes with sprouting white flowers and another poem that read:

> *'I long to caress your body.*
> *I long for you for good.*
> *I long to make love to you*
> *In fields of Arrowwood.'*

"I think he's *adorable*," Phil said, handing my phone back to me after having read all three of Dontae's poems. We were standing on a packed line at the movie theatre. "Where's Friday's poem?"

"He's a bit more random with the poetry. He either sends it in the morning or late evening—but trust me—he'll be sending one soon."

"I say he's a keeper."

"Huh!" I interjected, with a quick shake of my head.

"What do you mean, 'huh'? Can't be any worse than the loser palooza you've already got going on."

"He's a kid!"

"But he's a grown man in bed from what I hear," Phil stated too loudly.

A white-haired man with glasses standing directly behind us and holding hands with who I assumed was his flabbergasted wife, grunted then cleared his throat.

"I really need to learn to keep some things to myself," I sighed.

After a fifteen-minute wait, it was finally our turn at the window.

"May I help you?" The slumped over, scruffy young man at the ticket counter asked.

"Just a minute," Phil said to him, then looked at me. "Okay, so what's it going to be? *Blade Runner*, *It*, or *my My Little Pony?*"

"*My Little Pony?*" I questioned in disbelief.

"I love animated movies. Besides, I still have my, My Little Pony from when I was a kid."

The white-haired man grunted again before being waved on to counter #2.

"Excuse me!" he sounded frustrated as he brushed past us.

"Seriously?" I stated. "What about, *The Mountain Between Us*?"

"What's that about?" Phil asked, as customers behind us groaned and shifted with impatience.

"Hell, I don't know. I think it's something about a couple being lost in the Artic. Look, Idris Elba is starring in it so who gives a damn what it's about."

"So true." Phil turned to face the ticket window. "Two adult tickets for The Mountain Between Us."

"The nine-twenty or twelve o'five show?" the boy asked lazily as if every word he spoke took monumental effort.

Phil glanced at his watch then looked up at me. "It's just eight. Do you really want to wait that long just to gawk at Idris Elba on a picture screen?"

"So what's playing now?"

"*It* starts in fifteen minutes."

"*It*, it is." I said exhaustingly.

Phil paid for the tickets.

"I've got soda and popcorn," I said, as he handed me my ticket.

"'Sheesh!'" I heard a lady exclaim as she approached the window after us.

I sprayed the seat with my travel-sized can of Lysol and wiped down the arm rests before sitting. People to the left and right of us sucked their teeth, fanned the air, or grunted their disapproval.

"She has an airborne disease and just doesn't want any of you good folks to catch it," Phil explained.

People's eyebrows shot up and some of their mouths fell open.

"What did he say she has?" a frowning lady asked a man sitting beside her.

The man shook his head half-confused. "Something about an airborne disease."

The woman gasped and scooted away from Phil and me.

Phil pressed his fist to his mouth and snickered while I shook my head. "You're going to start a riot in here," I whispered to him as I sat down.

About a half hour into the movie, my phone buzzed, illuminating me in translucent blue to the chagrin of a mother and her three boys behind us.

"Mommy, that lady's phone's hurting my eyes." One of the boys who looked no more than nine or ten years old squirmed in his seat.

"Let me guess," Phil started. "Shakespeare?" he said, obviously referring to Dontae.

I nodded and shaded the light of the phone with my hand. A vivid image of an orange flower with rain-speckled petals popped onto the screen accompanied by these words.

> *'I can't help but think of you*
> *every minute of the hour.*
> *Please accept in my absence*
> *this Mexican Sunflower.'*

I handed Phil the phone and bit my bottom lip to keep from blushing. His eyes quickly scanned Dontae's message before he handed it back to me.

"Okay, at this point, *I'm* willing to date him if you don't."

I chuckled, wondering if Phil's statement was as close to a confession as I would ever get.

"The nerve of him to think that he can just woo me with a few lines of poetry?" I said, dropping my phone into my handbag before cozying back against my seat.

"Shhhh!"

I whipped my head around. The mother, wearing a Yankees baseball cap, had a finger pressed to her pursed lips.

I started to say something about reporting her for having smuggled her under-aged sons into an R-rated movie but thought better of it. Besides, I was secretly floating on a natural high and in that moment nothing or no one was bringing me down.

***

It was early Saturday morning. The sound of crackling bacon, the smell of fresh biscuits, and a melodious instrumental that I recognized as Damien Escobar's "Forbidden Love" song, startled me awake. I leapt out of bed and stumbled sleepily to my closet. I yanked opened the door and reached for the safe. My fingers fumbled over the keypad as I struggled to remember the combination. *Thirty-three, seventy—no, it's seventy-thirty-three—I mean, thirty-seventy-three*. Finally, the door to the safe popped opened, and I grabbed for my gun.

I held it close to my chest with the barrel pointed upward. I tip-toed from the bedroom, stealthily sliding my back against the wall, steeling for a deadly confrontation. I could hear the intruder moving around, rattling dishes and silverware. My heart slammed against my chest as my moist palms tightly gripped the butt of the gun.

The soft glow from the kitchen light poured into my shaded hallway. *This is it*, I thought, trying to recall my firearms training. I sprung into the doorway with a barbaric scream and fired away at the tall stranger—clad in nothing but a black apron that split in the rear to reveal a tight, muscular, mocha-colored ass—and heard the clicking sound of an empty chamber.

The man yanked around to face me. "Hey! It's me!" Dontae yelled, throwing his hands up.

"Wha-what the hell?" I stammered, waiting for my adrenaline-spiked heart to slow to a normal rhythm. "I mean—I mean, how in the name of all that's righteous did you slip your ass in here?"

Dontae walked over to me and unfurled my fingers from the grip of the gun, gently prying it from my hands. "Luckily, I had the presence of mind to unload this last night." he said, placing it on the counter.

"Last night? What do you mean, *last night*?" I asked, totally flabbergasted.

"I didn't have the heart to wake you, so I slept on the sofa. Besides woman, you snore!"

"Snore? Huh?" I felt like I was caught up in some bizarre dream, as if I were watching everything through those spooky fish lenses cinematographers use.

"…and talk in your sleep."

"I do?" I frowned confused, then raked my fingers through my bushy hair.

"Yep. How do you think I got the combination to the safe?"

"I told you the combination to my safe?" My voice sounded laden with disbelief.

"Well, after I asked you for it."

"I don't remember that," I said, trying to recall how many drinks I had after seeing the movie with Phil. I remembered. I had two glasses of wine. That was my limit and certainly not enough to induce a near-comatose state like the one Dontae alluded to.

He placed his hands on my shoulders and walked me over to the kitchen table where he had set a centerpiece of pink tulips.

"Thanks for the flowers," I said, plopping into the chair. "I feel bad. If that gun had been loaded, I could've killed you."

"And rightfully so," Dontae replied, walking back over to the counter. He scooped up a plate and then walked over to the stove to fix my breakfast.

"Wait! Wait a damn second!" I darted up from the table. "How did you get in here in the first place?" I asked, feeling a tsunami of heat wash over me. "How did you get past my alarm system? The two locks on the front door? The bars on my windows? I mean, what is it with you and slipping into people's homes uninvited?"

Dontae walked over to the table and set a plate of bacon, poached eggs, a fresh medley of fruit and two golden brown and flaky biscuits before me. He pushed at my shoulder for me to sit down, but I resisted.

"Come on, eat up!" he urged, pushing at my shoulder again.

"As soon as you answer my questions."

"I came through the front door, sweetie. I don't do windows." Dontae smirked at his joke, then seductively sucked the raw honey he had ladled over my biscuits from the tips of his fingers. He walked back over to the stove to prepare his own plate.

I frowned and squinted.

"I started to ring the bell, but it was late, and I wanted to surprise you with breakfast. I had a few paper clips on me, so I just used them to pick the lock open. By the way, only one of the two was actually locked."

I dropped in the chair, the shock gradually wearing off. "What about the alarm system?" I asked fearing his answer. "Did I tell you the password *to that* in my sleep?"

"Actually, you did me one better."

"How so?" I was disgusted with my lack of security conscientiousness by then.

"You wrote it down. *Rita Margarita*. It's written on the door of your safe."

"But it's written backwards."

"Hmm...kind of clever, but no cigar. I mean, what's an Atir Atiragram? Not English, or any language that I know of."

"How do you know? There are thousands of languages in this world," I questioned, fed up with him making a fool of me.

"I Googled it," he said, taking a seat at the table opposite me. "Eat your breakfast, baby."

"And my BS alarm company didn't even bother to call me." I took a bite of biscuit and was surprised that they were actually homemade.

"They did. They called you on your cell. I took the call in the bathroom." Dontae flashed his prized smile. "Like I said, didn't want to wake you." He forked up some fruit and stuck it between his sumptuous lips.

"Look, I appreciate the breakfast and the gorgeous flowers, but this is too much. I mean this is crazy. This is really off-the-chain. You breaking into my house and into my safe, and—"

"Into your heart."

My eyes darted downward. Unexpectedly silenced, I lowered my head and started on my poached eggs.

"Look at me, Symone," Dontae softly urged.

Blood rushed to my cheeks as a thrill surged through me, but I refused to heed his request.

"Look at me, baby." His gentle voice was reassuring, but I still hung my head.

I heard him get up from the table and his bare footsteps nearing me. He gently placed his fingers under my chin and lifted my head so that we were eye to eye. I chewed, then swallowed. I couldn't help but notice the hard bulge poking through his apron.

"Suppose I was someone looking to harm you?"

I averted his gaze.

"I'm going to protect you and I'm going to show you how to protect yourself."

What about my heart, youngan? Can you help me protect that? I wondered as his soft hand coaxed my face until we were staring in each other's eyes again.

"What could you possibly want from me?"

"Trust me," he whispered. Dontae kneeled down and began to push my nightgown above my thighs. He pulled at my panties and I lifted my rear so that he could ease them off. His strong but gentle hands parted my knees. He pressed his face between my thighs and begin to pleasure me. I spiraled into bliss as my heart now raced for a different reason.

CHAPTER 13

Dontae left that evening and returned a couple hours later, cradling white boxes tied with red satin bows in his arms.

"What in the world?" I asked, as he walked through the door.

He dropped the two boxes on my sofa, then looked at me. "Get dress. We're gonna have us some fun."

"Fun?" I scanned myself over. I was wearing a pair of low-rise jeans that accentuated my round bottom and a mid-drift Giant's jersey. "What kind of fun?"

"The kind of fun that you're probably not used to." He smiled warmly.

My eyes darted to the boxes. "What are those?"

"We're playing dress up."

I checked out Dontae's get-up. He was wearing black jeans, a plain, black T-shirt and a leather jacket reminiscent of the bombers that were so popular in the early eighties.

"But you're dressed *down*. Besides, I think what I have on is fine."

"I'm going home to change, but *I'll be back*, he said in a decent imitation of the Terminator.

I felt a little queasy. I had no idea what Dontae was cooking up and him breaking into my home earlier—though, to cook me a fabulous breakfast—still made him seem a bit suspect.

I glanced over at the two boxes again. "So, I'm guessing those are my dress-up clothes?"

"That would be accurate." He looked down at his Chopard. It was joltingly impressive with an onyx face and several flawless diamonds floating below the pristine crystal. "It's five o'clock. Be ready by six-thirty...the latest."

I inhaled deeply, trying to decide if I was up to whatever Dontae had planned.

I took a shower even though I had bathed just a couple of hours ago. New clothes on old skin would've left me feeling slimy.

After moisturizing myself from head to toe, I took in another deep breath and grabbed for the larger box that was now sitting on my bed. I undid the bow, lifted the top off, pushed the white tissue paper aside, and pulled out the loveliest, fiery red dress I had ever seen. It was meticulously woven and I imagined that it was spun from the finest silkworms money could buy. The soft material felt so smooth and sleek in my hands.

    I slipped the dress over my head and pulled at the hem until it clung to every contour of my curvaceous body, highlighting my full bosom and plump bottom. I twirled before my full-length mirror. The back of the dress—from my waist up—was held together with fine, gold chains that shimmered and dangled, and allowed a good portion of my smooth back to be seen.

    "O...M...Geeee!" I stated, admiring my rear profile in the mirror. "This is fitting me like a like a second skin. What—I mean—how on God's green earth could he have known my size?"

    I charged over to the bed and tore into the second box. Inside was another gold box with the name "Louboutin" scrolled across the lid. I snatched it off to find a pair of black patent leather needle-point heels with gold metal straps to wrap the ankles. I turned them over, stunned at the red soles. I fell back onto my bed with outstretched arms. "Now, I know I'm in love!" I shouted, then laughed wickedly.

    My cellphone played, "Hey," by a new group I was digging called KING. I grabbed it from my nightstand and pressed it to my ear.

    "Hey, Momma!"

    "Wassup, Amb!" I exclaimed. "Miss you!"

    "Alright now! You soundin' all upbeat. What's been going on? Am I missing any tea?"

    "Nothing really," I replied, instantly deciding not to mention that I'd been seeing Dontae. "How's the honeymoon goin'?"

    "Chile, I'm wore out in more ways than one. If you get my drift." Amber laughed. Her laugh sounded as pretty as she was.

"That's a good thing."

"Hey, I'm not complaining. So have you heard from Hot Mocha Latte?"

"Hot Mocha Latte?"

"Girl, don't start acting like you don't know who I'm talking 'bout. He's a little too fine to forget that easily."

"Oh, you mean what's-his-name?"

"Dontae," Amber said with a suck of her teeth.

"Yeah, that's it," I said, trying my best to sound convincing.

"Uh-huh. You know who I meant."

That was the thing about Amber, it was as if she were hard-wired to me. Sometimes I felt like I was unwittingly transporting all my business to her through some unknown telepathy. She was the only person in my life who could read me like a book.

"I heard from him a couple times after the wedding, but that was it."

"Okay, whatever. Guess you'll tell me the *real deal* when you're ready to. I just called to holla at you for a minute."

"Thanks, girlie," I replied, happy she didn't push the Dontae issue. "Can't wait to see you."

"Okay, peach pie! Au Revoir!" Amber kissed at the phone three times before hanging up.

I stood before the mirror, adding the finishing touches to my impeccably applied makeup. I raked my fingers through my voluminous hair which was light, bouncy and fell to my mid back in a bunch of dark auburn spirals. I remained there an additional fifteen minutes, prancing and admiring my reflection. I had never looked or felt more beautiful.

About a half hour later, my phone played, "Hey," again. I pushed the phone symbol and pressed it to my ear.

"You're ready?" Dontae asked.

"As ready as I'm going to be. Why? Where are you?"

"I'm outside."

"Okay. I'm coming out."

D.D. Sherman   Rare Orchids

I rushed over to my hall closet, swung open the door and searched my wardrobe for the perfect overcoat. There was a long wool coat that wouldn't have looked so bad, except it was too warm for it. I had a black leather trench, but it wouldn't have done my stunning dress justice. I threw a scarlet-red shawl over my shoulders, then thought better of it. Finally, I settled on a short nylon swing coat. It still was a little too dressed-down for my fancy outfit, but it was the best I had to work with.

I swung open the front door, sprinted down the flight of steps and halted mid-way. There, parked in front of my house, was a shiny black Mercedes stretch limousine; even passing cars slowed to take a look.

"Oh...my...word. What has this boy gone and done?" I murmured as I continued down the steps. I squinted and craned my neck forward, trying to see through the tinted glass.

A chauffeur popped out and held the rear door open for me. "Good evening," he stated with a nod as I approached the vehicle.

Too stunned to speak, I nodded in reply and slipped onto the supple leather sofa next to Dontae. He was wearing a single-button blazer, black with satin lapels. Underneath, he wore a black T-shirt with the continent of Africa depicted in red, black and green. He had on black jeans with green and black leather knee patches, a pair of black leather Gucci shoes and a black Gucci watch that complimented his overall color theme.

"Don't you think this is a bit much?" I asked him as the chauffeur closed the door after me.

"I started to bring the Phantom. *Now that* would've been too much," he said turning to face me so he could scrutinize me from head to toe. "Hot damn! I never cease to amaze myself!"

"I do have to give you that much." I looked myself over. "This outfit—I mean these shoes—" I broke off to stick my feet out before me and twirl my ankles. "Are *everything*!"

"Everett!" Dontae pressed a button on a wall and spoke into what looked like a speaker.

"Yes, sir?" the chauffeur's Caribbean accent came through the same speaker.

"Westchester."

"Oh, me see where you wan' go." the chauffeur stated with a chuckle.

"And where are we heading to?" I asked, still looking around with astonishment.

"Westchester County."

"I heard that. Where in Westchester County?"

"The airport."

"The airport? Why are we going to the airport? I need to pack a bag if we're going on vacation."

"Hey, you're asking too many questions. Just sit back and enjoy the ride."

And what a smooth ride it was. "Who are you? Some undercover multi-millionaire or something?"

"In a way," he replied, reaching for two crystal glasses and a bottle of chilled champagne from the illuminated bar across from us. "I guess you can say I'm well-paid."

"I mean you *are* good, but not this good." My eyes wandered, still taking in my opulent surroundings.

I looked up at the glass ceiling that allowed us a view of the transitioning sky. The interior lighting alternated in soothing shades of yellow, red, blue, and violet. Daley's, "Look Up," was coming from the speakers in crisp melodic tones. The sound of his voice was so life-like that it was as if he were there singing in my ear.

Dontae offered me the glass of champagne that he poured, then poured a glass for himself before replacing the bottle in a stainless steel-sink brimming witch ice.

"See, you're just thinking sex," Dontae said, then took a sip of champagne.

So did I, and oh my word, was it good.

"What I offer women is priceless and more than just sex." He smacked his lips and placed his glass in a cup holder beside him. "I fulfill fantasies. I can make a woman feel as if she's the only woman in the entire world—even if for a few moments in time."

I couldn't argue with that especially since I *was* feeling like the only woman in the world that night.

Dontae cued the audio system to play John Legend's, "You and I," and I melted into the warmth of his intoxicating embrace. It was useless to fight. It was hopeless to resist. All my defenses had been brought down and I found myself surrendering even knowing that might have been just another fantasy Dontae was providing. What perplexed me was why? I had nothing to give him—at least not on a material level.

After an hour's drive, the limo pulled up to an airplane hangar. A dark-haired, blue-eyed man in a flight suit greeted us as we exited the vehicle.

"Wassup, Preston?" Dontae and the man clasped hands, then bumped shoulders.

"Oh, nothing much," Preston answered with a British accent. "What 'bout you, mate?" Preston cut his eyes to look at me.

Dontae looked at me and smiled. "Life's good. No complaints."

"I bet." Preston glanced at me again. "You're taking her up?" he asked, running his hand over his hair against a slight wind that whipped it up.

"For about a half hour."

"Okay. I'll bring her out." Preston sprinted back inside the hanger.

"You have *got* to be kidding me," I managed to say after coaxing my jaw shut.

"What's the matter? You're not having fun?"

"Jury's still out on that." And it was. The day's events moved on fast forward and it was as if I couldn't readily process all that was happening. "I guess I'm floored."

"Good. I like floored." Dontae's luminous teeth gleamed.

A few moments later, a red and black Cessna, piloted by Preston, rolled out of the hanger and stopped in front of us. The word YOLO was painted across it in large white lettering.

"Don't tell me that belongs to you?"

"And you thought the Ducati was something."

"And where are we supposed to be going?"

"A quick ride over the harbor."

"Boy you done lost your mind!" I felt my eyes bulge. "I'm not getting in that thing. I only do large commercial aircrafts? They're safer."

"Boeings are not for sight-seeing. Unless you find looking at clouds exciting."

Preston jumped out of the small plane.

I whipped my head in his direction, then whipped back around to look at Dontae. "Isn't he supposed to be flying this thing?" My eyes pleaded to Preston as if he could save me from some impending disaster.

Preston walked around to where I stood. "No worries. You're in good hands."

I gasped and looked at Dontae again. "*You're* flying us?"

"I know. I'm just full of surprises," he smirked, then winked at me.

"I thought you were into growing plants. Do you even have a license to fly planes?" I swallowed a knot in my throat.

Dontae reached inside the back pocket of his jeans, extracted his wallet, flipped it open and held it up detective style.

I squinted at it. "Can't make out what it says. Getting dark out here."

He folded his wallet and slipped it back into his rear pocket. "Come on! Trust me. You'll thank me when it's over," Dontae prodded.

"*If* I'm alive when it's over."

"Come on." He grabbed my hand and led me to the pimped-out plane with its high-glossed wings and shiny windows. "Hop in."

"Hop in? Just like that?"

"Just like that."

"Oh my Lord! This is insane! I'm deathly afraid of heights, you know? Even standing on a ladder gives me vertigo. Why did I ever agree to you taking me anywhere?" I said, trembling.

Preston grabbed me by my upper arm and helped Dontae lift me up and into the aircraft all the while I continued fussing and protesting.

"I'm wearing a dress. This is so awkward. I could've left my jeans on!"

"I wanted to see you in a dress and I *always* get what I want."

"He really does." Preston affirmed with a grin.

Moments later I was fastened in my seat, given a headset and sitting next to Pilot Dontae—wait a minute! I realized that I didn't even know his last name. I should at least have known the last name of the man who literally held my life in his hands.

"You know I-I-I don't even know your last name," I said, wringing my hands.

Dontae chuckled. "I was wondering when you was going to ask me. It's Cum—"

"What!"

"…mings. Dontae Cummings."

"Oh." I sat so rigid I felt I would shatter at the slightest movement.

Dontae pressed a few buttons and flicked levers. The colorful flight deck lit up. He adjusted his headset and spoke into the microphone. I made out some of what he said.

"Bravo 423 to tower control, preparing for takeoff from runway two A…" He started the engine and the rest of what he said was drowned out. The propeller thundered on, its blades a spinning blur.

A static-laden voice coming from the control panel greenlighted his transmissions. It said something about the weather, the wind direction and other pilot jargon that was foreign to me. Dontae checked the fuel level and some other dials, then scribbled numbers on a pad.

D.D. Sherman   Rare Orchids

    We began to bump around as we taxied up the runway. We started slow, but quickly accelerated to a speed that forced me back into my seat.

    I prayed fervently, asking God to forgive me for lustful thoughts; acts of fornication; fits of anger; the crackhead I told to "kick rocks"; the five-dollar-bill I took from my mother's purse; putting salt instead of sugar in my stepdad's coffee; lighting a row of firecrackers and tossing it in Mr. Lou's window and any other transgression from child to adulthood I could think of.

    "You okay, baby?" Dontae's voice vibrated through my headset.

    I wanted to look at him, but I was too afraid. It was hard enough trying to digest the image of this twenty-nine-year-old call-guy flying an aircraft, let alone coming to terms with the reality of how I got there in the first place.

    Dontae pulled back on the throttle and manipulated the control wheel between his legs. I clamped my eyes shut as the aircraft lifted off the ground and nosed up into the air. I could feel us making a gradual ascension and heard the wind lashing the wings. Dontae went full-throttle. We soared toward a purplish sky and waxing gibbous.

    "We are now flying at an altitude of three thousand feet, baby. Stewardess, please report to the cock…pit," Dontae joked in his official pilot's voice. But I was too busy grappling with thoughts of plunging from the sky to appreciate his attempt at being humorous.

    "You okay, sweetie?" he asked, placing his warm and soft hand on top of mine, which gripped the seat.

    I pulled my eyelids apart to look at him.

    "Huh?" I asked, dumbfounded.

    He twisted his neck to the right and looked past me. "Wow. Just look at that view. I love it! Nothing on earth like seeing the world through God's eyes."

    "Keep your eyes on the road—I mean the sky!" I ordered. "We may crash into something!"

Dontae chuckled at my ignorance. "Yeah, like a fallen star. Look!" his nod indicated Manhattan Island to the right of me. "Isn't it amazing how condensed and simplistic everything appears when surrounded by all this water?"

I mustered up enough courage to glance out the window.

We were angling over an enclave of megastructures. Toy-like cars lit up the streets between them in glowing dots of red and white, and people were no more than bustling specks.

"Oh, it's Manhattan!" I exclaimed, trading in sheer terror for astonishment. Besides, Dontae was professional and confident and his behavior was beginning to reassure me.

"The city of lights."

"I thought Paris was the city of lights." The tone of my voice sounded thin and high through my headset.

"Nah! They stole that moniker from us."

We swooped down near the Empire State Building and angled up and over towards the Freedom Tower. *If only my friends could see me now…sitting next to this self-made gigolo…thirty-five hundred feet above the city scape...like I ain't got a care in the world.* Dontae pulled left on the yoke guiding the small aircraft in the direction of Ellis Island, reducing Manhattan to a mere island of Monopoly-sized objects.

The murky river eddied below us as we approached Lady Liberty. She held her flaming torch with conviction and her joltingly enormous face wore an expression of humble resilience.

"Do you know what her tablet says, baby?"

"July 4, 1776."

He winked at me. My girl has a brain."

My girl? I repeated his declaration in my head. *Is that who I am?*

Right there in that moment, in that space, I fell in love. I tumbled helplessly into the strong pull of rapture, the glorious melding of two hearts, the sweet bliss of ecstasy and the kind of love that money and every fine thing in the world could never equal. He stood out in a field of a trillion orchids. Perhaps his stem was a bit longer, his petals a bit softer or brighter, but I took notice.

He demanded that I take notice and there wasn't a damn thing I could do about it except to embrace the fall and hope to grasp onto a ledge before striking bottom.

We encircled the colossal woman a few times before hovering above her. I was so fascinated by all I had seen that I almost forgot how frightened I had been fifteen minutes before. I even snapped a few selfies and took pictures of Dontae throwing up the peace sign from the cockpit as we hovered above the statue's spiked crown.

After a few more three-sixties, a couple of swoops, and angles upward, the tricked-out red and black Cessna headed back toward Westchester.

We came in with a smooth landing. We might have been on the ground, but in my heart and soul, I was still soaring on a love-induced high.

"You're hungry?" Dontae asked, yanking his headset from his head.

I was almost afraid to answer him. I pulled mine off as well. "Yes. Why? Are we dining underwater? Should I go purchase a wet suit?"

His eyes wandered upward as if considering my question. "You know, if it wasn't so late that wouldn't be such a bad idea."

"Please! I'm joking. I'm just happy to be on terra firma in one piece."

Dontae exited the plane, walked around to my side and held his hand out to me. I took it and jumped down.

Preston jogged up to us. "Did you like it?" his eyes sparkled with enthusiasm as if he vicariously derived some pleasure from hearing about the pleasurable experiences of others.

"Yes!" I exclaimed. "It's definitely at the top of my best-things-I-ever-did-in-life, list."

"Good! I knew you'd love it!" he said while rubbing my upper arm in a way that implied he congratulated my bravery.

Dontae and Preston bade each other farewell, clasped hands and exchanged a manly hug before we were back in the limo with me wondering when I was going to get the opportunity to show off my fiery red dress.

"Everett!" Dontae pressed the speaker button again.

"Yes, sir?"

"Home."

"For sure, mon."

"Home?" I asked, a bit disappointed. I wanted high-end restaurant, with maître d' and leather-bound menus in French.

"One of them?"

"What do you mean by, 'one of them'?"

"You're asking too many questions again," Dontae teased before giving me a peck on the lips.

He dialed a number on his phone and pressed the speaker button. "Sir?" The voice on the other end said.

"Wassup, Yamaguchi?"

"Nothing much, sir."

"I'm on my way." Dontae rubbed his stomach. "And I'm starving."

"Yes, sir. What do you have a yen for, sir?"

"Seafood. What do you recommend?"

"Madame received an order of Lobster today. Fresh from Maine."

"Yeah, baby. That's what I'm talking 'bout."

Yamaguchi chuckled on the other end. "How would you like that prepared, sir?"

"Give me some options, Yama."

"Is someone joining you, sir?"

Dontae cut his eyes at me. "Yeah, I'm with someone," he answered, placing his hand on my thigh.

"For the lady, I can prepare Lobster Newburg."

"That sounds wonderful!" I interjected.

"What's Newburg?" Dontae asked.

"A cream sauce, sir."

"No, I'll pass."

"For you, sir, I can prepare a lobster mac 'n cheese made with aged white cheddar and smoked Gouda.

"Yes! Now, we're talking my language. Add some grilled broccoli to that and we'll be in business, Yama."

My stomach growled listening to the two go back and forth about dinner. I placed my hands over my belly, hoping to muffle the sound.

"Very well, sir. I'll go prepare for you now."

"See you in a bit, Yama!" Dontae disconnected the call and looked at me. "Learning to trust me yet?"

"I'm getting there, but I'm still a little unsettled with all of this posh living."

"Why?"

"Usually, people with this much bling are involved in some kind of illegal activity."

"Oh please don't go playing cop on me. You're blowing my high." Dontae smiled and took my hand in his. His expression was serious as his eyes studied mine. "Listen, I'm doing all this because I'm trying to show you that I really, really, dig you."

"Oh really?" I asked, studying his pretty, hazel eyes.

"Yes, really."

"Why me? What's so special about Symone Alexander? How am I so different from the other hundred women you probably bed on a regular basis?"

Dontae chuckled. "First off, I'm not sleeping with a hundred women. Don't go startin' false rumors. Second, I find you a bit of a challenge and I like that." His smile melted my insides.

"Okay, I'll buy that."

"You'll buy that?" he smirked.

"For now. I mean *I am* hot."

Dontae eyes scanned me over. "You damn sure are."

"Smart."

"I ain't gonna argue with that."

"Independent."

"Fiercely so."

"And—"

"*And*, a cougar I'm just dying to tame."

"Listen, youngan. You will not be addressing me by cou—"

"Shut up!" he said jokingly, his face inching up to mine.

"*Excuse* me?"

"I said shut up so you can kiss me."

Before I could utter another word, his lips pressed against mine and his tongue snaked its way into my mouth. I sucked it for a moment or two and then gave him mine in exchange. We spent the remainder of the hour-long ride exploring every inch of each other's love palette.

Chapter 14

The curved driveway of stone pavers and glowing lights directed us toward bronze gates, which opened to reveal a Tudor-style mansion. The sprawling edifice sat atop a compound of lush evergreens and reminded me of a castle with its tower-like appendages and arch windows with balconies. I had never seen a home that grand up close and personal. All I could do was marvel while struggling to discern Dontae's affiliation with such grandeur. The Mercedes stopped before the elegant entrance of marble columns, stone plinths and embellished redwood doors with gleaming brass fixtures.

 Everett darted out of the driver's seat and over to my side to assist me exiting the vehicle, but I was halfway out of the car by then. He awkwardly nodded at Dontae who stood on the opposite side. Dontae extended his hand and I walked around the limo to accept it. My heels clicked against the slick marble as he led me up a tier of steps. He lifted a metal door to a keypad inconspicuous behind a huge planter which was a limestone sculpture of a sad-faced woman in a toga with one of her breasts exposed. He pressed a few numbers. The elegant front doors sprung open, inviting us inside the grand foyer. Calacatta tiles, French hand-cut crystal chandeliers, and spiraling staircases of wrought iron and glossy African Black wood, were joltingly impressive.

 An older Mexican woman in a plain gray dress and black orthopedic shoes that gaped around her ankles, scurried crookedly over to greet us and take our jackets.

 "Alda!" Dontae sang her name, spreading his arms then leaning in to kiss her droopy cheek.

 "Como esta, mi amor?" Alda responded, reaching up to grab Dontae into a motherly embrace.

 "Ah, bien! Bien! Y tu?"

 "Asi. Asi," Alda replied, fumbling with the neckline of her dress and brushing loose strands of hair from her aged eyes. She nodded at me then scuttled away with our jackets flung across her arm.

Dontae turned to face me. "Ready for the best part of the night?"

"I'm so overwhelmed right now. It's like I keep waiting for someone to dash me with a cold bucket of water so I can wake up and find out that all this was just an exquisite dream." I wasn't the fawning type, but it would've been fruitless to try and hide how enamored I was.

"Let's eat!" Dontae grabbed my hand and led me down a corridor of Oriental rugs, Venetian sconces and oil paintings of ships being jostled in turbulent waters, old cottages hidden in thickets of colorful forest trees, and Chinese geese flapping their wings over serene lakes.

I began to worry, borderline-panic worry. None of this unapologetic display of obscene wealth was representative of the Dontae I was getting to know. The tricked-out Ducati and Cessna—absolutely—but definitely not the over-stated elegance and feminine aesthetics.

We entered the formal dining room. Maroon and gold silk drapes cascaded from huge arched windows. We sat at a large table that Dontae said was made of pricey Agar wood in what he referred to as 'eighteenth-century Louis the XVI', floral printed chairs. Three massive chandeliers hovered above the elongated table.

Yamaguchi, a slim, subservient looking middle-aged Japanese man, appeared toting a silver tray of warm hand towels.

He walked over to me. "Madame?" he offered.

"Thank you," I replied taking one of the towels, extremely grateful for the opportunity to clean my hands.

He walked over to Dontae. "Thanks, Yama." Dontae wiped his hands on the towel then tossed it back onto the tray. Yamaguchi walked over to collect mine.

"Dinner in another fifteen minutes, sir."

"We good," Dontae replied.

Yamaguchi nodded, apparently understanding what Dontae meant before disappearing into the kitchen again.

"What's all of this?" I asked Dontae throwing my hands up with a shake of my head.

"*All of this* is my home." Dontae, who had been sitting back, sat up in his chair and leaned into the table.

"I guess what I'm asking is—who does all of this stuff belong to?"

He tilted his head and clasped his hands on the table. "All of this *stuff* belongs to me."

I shook my head in disagreement. "Oil paintings of birds and trees, floral printed Louis the XVI chairs? I'm sorry, but this just doesn't seem like your style."

"Why? Because I'm a young, African American man who fulfills the wishes of lonely, older women for a living?"

I nodded. "Exactly."

He tittered. "You've met my personal driver, flew in my private plane, met my maid, my cook, and you mean to tell me that you're still not convinced?"

All the "Snapped" and "Fatal Attraction" episodes I had been binging on instantly rushed to the forefront of my mind like a horror movie on fast forward. Could Dontae have killed his benefactor, the owner of that posh home, and with the help of Yamaguchi, Everett—or hell even sweet old lady Alda—hidden her body in the cellar? And now were they all there just burning through her millions like paper being tossed in a fire? His staff did appear a bit more personable toward him than one would expect for such monetary disparity between employer and employee. But then again, Dontae was very down-to-earth and, thus far, a likeable guy, so that observation didn't hold water.

"Hey!"

"Huh?" I asked, hitting the pause button on the blood and gore flick starring Dontae Cummings playing unedited in my head.

"Are you still not convinced?"

"Honestly?"

"Of course honestly. I don't want you to lie to me."

"Not quite."

Yamaguchi appeared with our steaming plates in hand. He served my food first and then scuttled over to Dontae. He poured two glasses of chilled champagne, instructed us to, 'enjoy' and nodded at each of us before disappearing into the kitchen.

"There's seven bedrooms in this house," Dontae started, picking up his fork and stabbing at his lobster mac n' cheese. "Each one has its own theme. Each one represents a region in the world. I'll let you pick the one you want to make love to me in. Though I'd like to have you in the Serengeti. The zebra-printed rugs, life-like replicas of lions and tigers, spears and tribal masks, and oh..." Dontae broke off to shake his head. "Those blood red walls bring out the warrior in me."

Making love to Dontae in a room made to look an untamed safari did sound like an interesting idea, but I wasn't yet comfortable with the whole sleeping-in-someone-else's-bed proposal.

"Even though you're a cop, you're still a bit refined. I bet you'd probably like the Versailles room."

"After the Palace of Versailles?" I sat erect in my chair and was sure my eyes lit up. There I was again, acting like an impressionable child.

"Of course."

Remembering myself, I calmly reached for my fork. "I don't think I'll be staying," I said, then plunged a forkful of Lobster Newburg into my mouth. The succulent, sweet meat bathing in that flavorful and decadent cream sauce was up there with one of the best things—no, it *was* the best thing I'd ever tasted. The bold spices and buttery undertones played on my palette like musical notes. I wanted to plow through my dinner bread and fingers style, but I was determined to remain a lady and forced myself to take my meal in conservative forkfuls.

"Oh?" Dontae glanced at his watch and raised his brows. "It's almost ten o'clock. Sorry, my driver's off-duty."

"I'm sure you can pull out the Bentley or Rolls to drive me home yourself." The censure was evident in my voice.

"Yeah...well." Dontae started, but paused to scratch at the back of his neck. "Remember I told you that I turned twenty-nine the other day?"

"Uh-huh, but what's that got to do with anything?"

"My driver's license expired on my birthday and I haven't had the chance to renew it."

"Am I to believe that you have a license to fly a plane, but none to drive a car?"

Dontae shrugged. "Why else do you think I would show up at a wedding reception on a motorcycle wearing a tux?"

"Because you're the most eccentric person I've ever met. After what I've witnessed, you showing up at Amber's wedding on a motorcycle wearing a tux is merely a show of your more conservative side."

"Then you must lead a very dull life, sweetie." Dontae took another bite of his lobster mac n' cheese and flashed his blue-ribbon smile.

At a momentarily loss for words, I stuck a crown of broccoli into my mouth and even that lowly vegetable was bursting with flavor.

"So what's it going to be...the Serengeti or Versailles?"

I don't remember how or when—perhaps it was after we'd kilt that third bottle of Louis Roederer—that I found myself engaged in unbridled sex with my young, charismatic lover. Our naked bodies entwined in a room of statuettes toting trays of gold candelabras in a space made to mimic the Hall of Mirrors in the Palace of Versailles; he'd yanked my hair and straddled me from behind in the Brazilian jungle while painted birds with their rich and colorful plumages spied from a domed ceiling; he thrusted me amongst the wild beasts of the Serengeti as I yelled and bit my bottom lip in ecstasy; we soared on a climatic high over the pyramids of Egypt and after what seemed like hours of intense love making, caressed and fell asleep amid the cherry blossoms of Mount Fiji.

D.D. Sherman   Rare Orchids

    I dreamt of Dontae that night. He was in bed with multiple women who were taking turns serving him. I looked on from afar, both with lust and utter sadness.

Chapter 15

The flat iron steamed as my cousin Felicia drug it along a swath of my long hair. It was the Wednesday following my glorious weekend with Dontae. I sat in her salon chair recounting all the events of that past Saturday, moment by moment, careful not to leave out a morsel of detail. Maybe my braggadocios ramblings were premature and telling of my naiveté, but I was brimming with excitement and I couldn't help but share my dream love affair with almost everyone I knew. Amber was probably the only one still unaware of my tête-à-têtes with the man she hired to sleep with me and the one I was most afraid of sharing them with. She could be a little judgmental and if the other shoe had dropped in my fairytale romance, she'd have been the first 'I told you so.'

I heard her voice in my head. *Hiring Dontae was sort of a joke, honeycakes. I just wanted you to have a little fun. How you gon' jump into the deep side of the pool and you can't even swim?* Or something like that.

"If you hadn't showed me the pictures of Dontae in that airplane, I'da never believed it!" Felicia said as she parted another section of my hair and clamped it in the flat iron.

"And that house. I wish I had taken pictures of it. But I didn't want to make it look as if I'm not accustomed to the finer things in life. I mean, picture me lookin' like a groupie or something."

"Aww...don't be so hard on yourself. He knows you're *that girl*. The girl he has to work to impress."

"You're being too kind, Felicia."

"No, seriously. You're educated." She broke off to spin me around in the salon chair so I was facing a huge mirror that reflected my entire body. "Cute as hell."

I whipped my head aside, pushed my torso out, pursed my lips and struck an exaggerated pose.

Felicia laughed. "And a damn riot when you want to be."

My shoulders dropped, and I sat back in my seat as a frightening thought sent a shiver through me.

"What if all this really is too good to be true, just like that crazy dream I told you I had? What if I really am just another notch in his belt?"

"And what if you're not?" Felicia countered with a reassuring smile.

What I loved about Felicia—besides the fact that she was my favorite first cousin—was that she was not a hater. She was genuinely happy for me.

"Well, he did drop by my house the next day with a fresh bushel of orchids. And he's coming by tonight to beef up my security."

"Beef up your security?" Felicia repeated, the smoke from the flat iron billowing up to her face.

"He broke into my apartment the other day."

She sat the iron down on the counter and placed her free hand on her hip while her other hand held onto a section of my hair. "What do you mean, he broke into your apartment?" The skin between her brows creased.

I chuckled. "Girl, it's a really long story, but he says I'm not secure enough in my house so he's installing some new—supposedly—tamper-proof locks on the door."

"Oh." Felicia nodded then reached for the flat iron. "See, I told you he's the bomb. Just lay back and enjoy the ride he's taking you on. Right now, you're happy. That's all that matters."

***

"Wow, look at that beautiful hair!" Dontae greeted me at the door in robe and slippers after I rang the bell.

It was a nice surprise. It was rare that he stayed. "Hey!" I replied, the skepticism obvious in my tone.

"Did you notice your new lock?"

"Sure did. It looks great, 'cept it would be nice if I had the code."

"Oh, it's," still standing in the doorway, Dontae looked around, then lowered his voice to a whisper. "Three eight two nine."

"I should've guessed that," I replied, stepping inside.

"Yeah, I kind of thought you would have. I want you to change the code every three months," he said, closing the door after me. He grabbed me from behind and wrapped his strong arms around my waist, pulling me into him.

It felt good. *He* felt good; kind of like something I could get used to coming home to everyday. It was foolish of me to entertain such a far-fetched thought, so I quickly put it out of my mind.

"You're hungry?" he inquired, releasing me to retrieve his phone from my naked lady coffee table.

"I feel yucky. I need a long, hot shower before even thinking about food." I walked to the hall closet to hang up my jacket and started for my bedroom. I scrambled through a top drawer looking for something sexy to wow Dontae with after I came out of the shower, but all I seemed to come across were boy shorts and tank tops. After a deeper excavation of tiny mountains of nightclothes, I finally retrieved a lacey black negligee that still had the tags on it.

"Well, don't be too long."

I spun around and jolted at the sight of Dontae standing in the doorway, eyeing me lustfully.

"I ordered Mexican food."

"That sounds good," I replied, trying to conceal the skimpy article of clothing in my hands.

Dontae studied them, leaning his head to one side. "Is that for me?"

"Just go!"

The whites of his teeth flashed in the dimly lit room.

"Go on! Get out of here!" I started toward him. "You're going to ruin the surprise."

He threw his palms up, kissed at me then disappeared from the doorway.

D.D. Sherman   Rare Orchids

    I stood under the showerhead head allowing the hot water to sluice over my shoulders and glide down my back and legs as I scrubbed my skin with a soap-infused loofah. I had wrapped my hair with pins to keep it from getting wet but planned to take it back down once I was out of the shower. I wanted Dontae to crave me as much as I craved him, to love me as much as I was starting to love him, but there was always that little voice in my head reminding that he was a man who sold himself for money. It sounded ugly when I thought of it in that way, but that was the bare bones truth of the matter. No euphemism—male escort, personal assistant, gentlemen caller—made it sound any nicer. He was who he was, but that didn't settle the murky emotions ebbing and flowing in the depths of my being. There was a burning question I needed to ask him.

    "Dontae?" I started, leaning my head against his chest as we watched the Nets play the Utah Jazz. We had finished our dinner followed by a few rounds of steamy lovemaking.

    "Yes, baby?"

    I sat up to face him. "How come you never call me by my name? Do you even know my name?"

    Dontae laughed. "What's it going to take to get you to trust me, Symone?"

    I bit the inside of my bottom lip feeling a bit foolish. "I want to ask you something."

    "Okay," he replied with a shrug. "Ask me something."

    "Would you be willing to give up your lifestyle?"

    He furrowed his brows and whipped his head aside as if to hear me clearer. "Give up my lifestyle?" he chuckled. "I'm not sure I know what you mean by that."

    I took in a deep breath then sighed while mustering the courage to clarify my question. "Would you give up this profession of sleeping with other women to be with me and only me?" That was it. The words were out there, floating around in the universe. I was moving full-steam-ahead, ripping my heart out my chest, and tacking it to my sleeve for everybody and their momma to see.

Dontae rested his back against the sofa. Dinwiddie had scored for the Brooklyn Nets, but he didn't seem to notice. Instead, he seemed to be tossing the question around in his head a few times if the side to side movement of his eyes was any indication.

"Welp, I guess no answer *is* the answer," I said collapsing back onto the sofa.

Dontae placed his warm hand on my naked thigh. "I am caught a little off-guard, to be frank with you. I've never been asked to make a decision like this. I mean, if it wasn't for my line of work you and I would never have met."

I sat up to look him square in the eyes. "Dontae you are one of the smartest people I know. You can get a legitimate job doing anything you like. There are plenty of things you can do to earn a good living. I'll help you. And I'm not going to lie, I'd like to have a couple of babies before my clock ticks out. Remember, you're dating a middle-aged woman. It's not like a got a lot of time."

Dontae chuckled. "Trust me, you've got more time than you think. Look at Janet Jackson."

"Yeah, but I ain't got Janet's money. But look, I've got this big ole house. A great job and no baby daddies you have to be concerned with. It'll be just us doing us."

Dontae slapped his hands to his face as if feeling overwhelmed. I felt a sinking sensation drop to the pit of my churning stomach and inwardly admonished myself for sounding so desperate for a relationship with him.

"I'm sorry," I said, collapsing back against the sofa. "You were hired to have sex with me, and that's what you've done. Several times over. I don't know why I even entertained the thought of being more than a client to you."

Dontae slid his hands from his face and twisted his neck to look at me. "Because you are more than just a client to me, Symone." He darted up from the sofa. "These women that I spend time with are not just looking to jump my bones every time they see me. Sometimes they just want to be held, to be heard, to be noticed. And I've gained from these experiences in more ways than I can tell you. I've dined over the Aegean at sunset. I've had suits tailored in Abu Dhabi. I've shook hands with the leaders of small nations and talked sports with heads of Fortune 500 companies. I've been mentored; I've been educated; I've been cultivated; but most of all, I've been loved. I've received much more love than I've had to give. I'm sure it sounds selfish, but if I'm being honest here. I was just a dude from the projects doing whatever I had to do. Tryin' to get my hustle on. Then one day—purely by happenstance or God's intervention one, I'm not exactly sure, but I stumbled into something that changed my life forever."

I bolted up from the sofa. "Then that's it. You've spoken your piece. There's no separating love and work in your mind. They're one in the same, or maybe not—or maybe so. You've crossed lines that some people would never cross no matter what they stood to gain. Now those lines are blurred, and you can't tell love from lust; what's real from what's pretend."

"Repeat your question to me?" Dontae ordered.

"Which question—?"

"The question you asked me earlier. The question that initiated this whole diatribe."

I gasped and felt my nostrils flare as they often did when I was angry. "I wanted to know if you're willing to give up sleeping with other women to be with me exclusively. Or something like that." I inhaled, then crossed my arms over my chest to brace myself.

Dontae pressed his palms together and lowered his nose to his fingertips as if in deep contemplation. After a while, he lifted his head to look at me. "Yes, Symone. I would give up sleeping with other women to be with you exclusively."

I was pleasantly stupefied. I just stood there looking dumbfounded, I'm sure. I wanted to ask him to repeat his answer for fear I might've heard him wrong.

He clasped my hands in his. "Look, Symone. You're the only thing in my life that reminds me of who Dontae Cummings *really* is. With you, I can simply be my grungy, ill-mannered, manly self."

We laughed, pressing our foreheads together.

"Eat a spam sandwich and not be judged." Dontae said, gobbling his fingers.

"Spam? Oh, I'm judging you on that."

"Shovel up remnants of leftover spaghetti dinner with my bread and then pack it in my mouth without being looked at sideways.

"Now come on babe, that's just bad manners," I said laughing.

"Fart, belch."

"Let's not get carried away."

Dontae pulled me close to him. "So glad I met you, Symone. You truly keep me grounded."

In all my momentary glee, something heavy tugged at my heart. "Dontae, what about that fancy house? The cars and plane? Clothes and jewelry and God knows what else I don't know about?"

"What about them?"

"It'll all be taken away once your...*benefactors* learn of your decision to be monogamous."

"Those things can't be taken away because they're mine. I've *earned* them."

Oh, I bet, I thought to myself.

"Besides, you're jumping waaaay ahead. I said I'm willing to give sleeping with other women up. These people are my friends and I plan to maintain at least an amicable relationship with them. What I want you to do in return is to learn to trust me. Put your damn guards down,
woman!"

"But I'm just afraid of—" *Damn was I being vulnerable.*

Dontae pulled me to him and held me close. We must've stood there for fifteen minutes or so. Hell, I don't remember. I never had any real concept of time whenever I was with Dontae because the hours always seemed to fly by. He took me by the hand.

"Come on baby, let's go to bed," he said, leading me to the bedroom.

I slept comfortably in his arms that evening, lulled by the easy rhythm of his heartbeat. There were no licentious dreams invading my peaceful slumber, just him and me and in that moment, all that I thought I've ever wanted.

Chapter 16

Amber stared at the white thermometer-like stick in her hand, wearing a crooked smile that broke her otherwise stoic expression.

"Well, what does it say?" I asked, then took a sip of white chocolate Irish cream. I sat at her dining room table while she disappeared into the bathroom to take a store-bought pregnancy test. This was actually the third test she had taken in the last two days.

"It's a plus again," Amber grumbled wearily, plodding from the bathroom then dropping into one of the dining room chairs beside me.

I darted up from the table and threw my arms around her neck for the second time that day. "I'm so happy for you. You're going to be someone's *hot* momma!"

"God help him...or her."

"What do you mean?" I asked, plopping back into my chair. "You're going to make a super-fantastic-stupendous-mommy." Clearly, the liquor was starting to seep into my brain cells. I picked up my glass and took another sip of my drink. "Aren't you excited?"

"No! I mean, yeah. I mean no and yeah."

I shook my head, confused.

"It's just that Antoine and I were looking to buy a house, and this is all kind of happening out of sync."

"Why weren't you using birth control then?"

"I am. I mean I *was*. Obviously something got miscalculated."

"Does Antoine know?"

"He doesn't have a clue."

"Whyyyyy?" I practically sang.

"Because he probably thinks I'm on top of things."

"I'm sure he'll be happy to know that he's going to be a father."

Amber inhaled apprehensively and shook her head. "I don't know. I mean, of course we've talked about having children, but were planning to put it off for at least a couple of years to just do us."

"Oh," I said, sipping the last bit of liquor in my glass. I wanted to tell Amber about Dontae and me. I wanted her to know that I had fallen in love with him and that he was the only man I saw when I thought about my future, but Amber was—understandably—wrapped up in her own affairs. Unloading my complex relationship issues on her felt a bit selfish, until she said,

"Okay, so I need to know what's going on with you and mocha hotté."

I was shocked that she was even interested in my love life shenanigans with her own plate running over.

"Listen, Amber, I don't want to bog you down with my stuff. You've got enough to deal with."

Amber squinted one eye. "I'm pregnant, sugar dumplings, not terminal. I'll figure things out. Besides, I need to focus on *your drama* to get my mind off of mine."

I inhaled deeply, then pushed a quick breath out through my nose. "Well...I think I'm in love with him." A wide smile stretched across my face and I was sure that my eyes sparkled the way they always did whenever I talked about Dontae.

Amber stared at me straight-faced then burst into a laughter so hard it made her shoulders quake.

I wrinkled my forehead. I was both perplexed and insulted at Amber's reaction. I would have felt better if she'd chastised me for acting like a love-struck schoolgirl rather than to guffaw at my statement like it was part of a stand-up routine. I crossed my arms over my chest and tapped my toes against the floor, waiting for her to pull it together. She placed her soft and always manicured hand on my forearm to brace herself.

"I'm sorry, Symone. I just wasn't expecting you to say that."

"I don't understand what I said that was so funny," I retorted, clearly perturbed.

"Listen," she started, her lips quivered as she apparently struggled to control an urge to laugh. "I just can't see how *you*, Miss Neurotically Afraid of Everything, let someone like Dontae convince you to take him serious."

"That's because *we are* serious."

"He's a GIG...O...LO!" Amber raised her voice an octave. "He sleeps with rich women *for* money. He's not boyfriend, husband, or even baby daddy material."

"He's agreed to stop."

"Stop what?"

"Sleeping with other women."

Amber giggled, a deep-from-the-gut-giggle, the kind that—try as hard as you may—you cannot suppress.

"You can laugh all you want, but whatever happens between us will be all your fault. You brought—or should I say, *bought*—him into my world."

She finally composed herself, clearing her throat. "You're going to blame me because I treated you to an orgasm?"

"He returned your money."

"I actually demanded it back because you were refusing to make good on it."

"That's not how it was told to me."

"Look, Symone, I'm not saying that Dontae doesn't genuinely like you—or possibly love you. All I'm saying is that I cannot see him giving up the very lucrative lifestyle he's come to know just to settle down with one chick. I mean, I hear he's sleeping with the daughter of some heiress whose net worth is somewhere in the hundreds of millions. Some rich white woman who's heavily into young, black men. Dontae's not the only one. I hear Ebony's little's brother's trying to get into that filthy rich circle." Amber broke off to flick her illustrious weave behind her shoulders. "Cept he's not as debonair or as good looking as your friend is."

I couldn't blame Amber for reacting the way she did. I guess I was wrong to expect her to go shaking her poms-poms in the air, cheering me on like my cousin Felicia did.

D.D. Sherman   Rare Orchids

My thoughts were invaded by the sound of rattling keys in a lock, a door being pushed open and Antoine appearing in the kitchen doorway of their small two-bedroom apartment in Clinton Hills.

Amber bit her bottom lip and cut me a quick side-eye glance before springing up from the table. She grabbed him around the neck and his large hands cupped her voluptuous butt cheeks.

Antoine was classic fine with a low-cut hair, styled in rows of waves, a neatly trimmed mustache and sideburns against skin the color of warm fudge.

"Hey, baby! Something smells damn good," he said, giving Amber a peck on the lips, then looked over at me. "Hey, stranger!"

I wiggled my fingers. "Hey, Antoine! Oh my! Don't we look all tanned and rested?"

Amber unwrapped her arms from around his neck. "Hungry, baby?"

"You know I am," he replied, turning away to hang his overcoat in the hall closet.

Amber's eyes widened at the pregnancy kit sitting on the table with the positive dipstick laying on top of it. She waved her hand quickly gesturing for me to hide it. I snatched it from the table and dropped in into my handbag just as Antoine turned from the closet.

"I made spaghetti with meatballs and a Caesar salad," Amber said with a little shake in her voice, clasping her fidgety hands behind her back.

"Nice. Let me go wash up," Antoine said, wringing his hands. He turned his attention to me again. "You eating with us, Symone? We'd love to have you stay for dinner."

"I wish I could," I replied, getting up from the table. "I just got an urgent text message from the 79th. I'm sure it has something to do with one of my wayward clients. Grown men and women who didn't get the memo that they're grown men and women."

Antoine tittered. "Well, some other time."

"Yeah, I guess," I replied wearily.

"Don't let 'em work you too hard," he added, starting up the hallway toward the bathroom.

"Oh, they're beyond that." I gathered my things and started for the front door.

Amber held her hand out. I dug through the contents of my handbag and handed her the opened box with the test stick inside. She discreetly stuck it in the pocket of her sweatpants and pulled the hem of her hoodie over it.

I leaned in and whispered. "When are you going to tell him?"

"Probably tonight. I don't know. Soon," she whispered back.

"I don't see why you don't just get it over with. I'm sure you're making too much of a big deal out of this."

"I *said* I'm going to tell him. Just have to wait for the right time," Amber snapped.

I backed off, nodding and giving her a thumbs up.

"Hey, why don't we all go out for dinner one day?" Antoine appeared over Amber's shoulders, which startled me and made Amber flinch, though he didn't seem to notice our apparent discomfort.

"We all?" I asked.

"Yeah. Me and Amber and you and your new boyfriend. He seems like a cool dude."

"You mean her *friend*, Dontae," Amber clarified.

"Yeah. He's a diehard Nets and Giants fan like me. And I got the chance to talk to him a couple of times. He seems like a real smart brother."

I looked at Amber. *See, even your husband realizes Dontae's potential*, I thought then stuck my tongue out at her in my mind's eye.

"He would love to, I'm sure," I said with a smirk that probably irritated Amber.

"Cool," Antoine replied before disappearing from the doorway.

"Well, let me see you downstairs," Amber said, stepping out into the hallway.

Amber walked down the three flights of steps with me even though there was an elevator. We always took the elevator up, but never down since she lived on the third floor of a six-story building. We entered the lobby which was decorated with paper cornucopias spilling its contents of fruits and vegetables that dotted the walls, a lit string of red, brown, and yellow leaves running the length and sides of a coffered ceiling, and mason jars of candy corn set out on the counter of a security desk.

"Okay, sugah dumplings. Let me go feed my man." Amber reached out to me for a hug. We pressed our cheeks together and kissed the air.

"And don't go giving your heart away to just anybody. Make him work for it!" She winked and turned from me with a wave goodbye.

"Oh, he's working for it," I yelled after her. "Got a pair of Loboutins."

Amber halted in her tracks with one hand pressed against the stairwell door, and the other grasping the knob. She snatched around to look at me. "Did you say Louboutins as in Christian Louboutins?"

"Yep. Even Christian understands that love is everything. That's why he makes his soles red."

"Love?" Amber furrowed her immaculately arched eyebrows.

"And he brings me fresh orchids almost every day."

"Hmmm..." Amber interjected thoughtfully, then waved goodbye a final time.

I knew that by appealing to her penchant for expensive things, I'd start to chisel away at her hard, judgmental exterior.

***

Lance stood up as I walked in the precinct and pulled at the waist of his uniform pants as if trying too hard to look official. I hadn't seen him since that date debacle, much less thought of him. Dontae had put any relationship ideations with Lance completely out of my mind.

I found his feigned rigidness odd and pretentious and got a serious kick out of seeing him struggling to keep it professional.

"We've got one of yours back there," he said, thumbing over his shoulder as I approached his elevated desk. I always hated visiting him at the precinct for that reason alone. He got to sit above me, and I often wondered if that was a metaphoric representation of how he viewed his role in our pseudo relationship. "Here's the arrest report."

I took the paper from him and scanned it briefly.

"By the way," he started, thrusting his hands down in his pockets. "I'd like to apologize for that last time we saw each other. I didn't mean for it to come off as if that's all I invited you over for."

"Tell you the truth, I hadn't even thought about it," I said, waving my hand.

"Look, I've got a nice bottle of Cabernet Sauvignon on ice. I'd like to make it up to you."

"Nah, I'd rather we keep things professional," I replied nonchalantly.

"Whatever, Symone!" he retorted, reaching to answer the phone after the fifth ring.

"Why so salty?" I asked, reveling in the sudden shift in power.

"Your client's in room two," he said bitterly, pressing the handset to his ear. "Lieutenant McMillian."

"Thanks," I replied with a smirk before an officer escorted me to the rear of the precinct where my client awaited my arrival.

Trina Murrow guiltily looked up at me, chewing her acrylic nail. The tracks of her weave were insultingly visible and at least two faux fingernails were missing from each hand. Her batty eyelashes adhered to her lids with gobs of black glue and piercings that ran the length of both ears went mostly without earrings.

"Hey, Officer Alexander." She sounded like a child bracing for admonishment after having been naughty. At just twenty-two years old, she might as well have been a child as far as I was concerned.

"Lord, can I just get through one week without getting an emergency text concerning one of my clients?" I flung my attaché case on top of the clunky metal desk and dropped in an armless wooden chair opposite her.

"But I didn't do nothin'. I swear!"

"You'd better be thankful I have a good rapport with everyone here and that they give me the heads up on all of my clients or you're behind would've been spending the night in Central Booking."

"But I swear I didn't do nothin'." Trina kept flicking her pierced tongue and her ocean blue contacts looked odd against her very dark skin.

I wearily snatched up the arrest report. "Says here you solicited an undercover cop."

"They're lyin' on me, Officer Alexander. I swear on everything I love. I wasn't tryna to get with no cop 'cause I kinda suspected he *was* one." Trina sat up in her chair and pushed her augmented torso out, a gift from one of her regulars, I surmised. "Dude solicited me!"

"I'm trying to help you, Trina, but you've got to work with me." I sat, studying her pocked skin that no amount of makeup could remedy. At twenty-two, Trina was already the mother of two children, a five-year-old boy and three-year-old girl, who she unloaded on her sickly grandmother whose sole income was a monthly social security check less than nine-hundred-dollars a month. Trina's alcoholic mother died of liver cirrhosis when Trina was just fourteen. I'd revoked Trina's probation myriad times for dirty urine, finding everything from cocaine to methamphetamines to marijuana. Unfortunately, the disease of addiction did not overlook her.

"With three prior convictions for sexual solicitation, I find that hard to believe," I said, folding my arms over my chest.

"I was just on the block kickin' it with my girl Lakeesha. Nig rolled up in his corny Nissan Sentra and asked me if I can blow him off. I told him I don't be doin' no blow jobs, but I know a girl name Kendra who could get him off right there in the back seat of his car for a buck fifty. Then dude jumped out and told me I was under arrest. How you gonna arrest me for *tellin'* you where you can go get your dick sucked?"

I chuckled for a lack of anything else to do or say.

"Please, Officer Alexander. I can't do no mo' time. I swear! If I have to go back to jail, I'm just gonna kill myself."

"Spare me the dramatics and go try your psychology on someone who doesn't know any better."

Trina folded her arms across her chest and shook her head.

"Now, if you want me to be straight with you, then you have to be straight with me. These little mind games you're playing will hurt you more than help you."

Trina sucked her teeth and swung her crossed leg. She wore five-inch patent leather platform heels. I secretly admired how she could walk the broken concrete streets of Brooklyn in those stilts.

"Alright, I'm sorry, but I'm trying, Officer Alexander. I swear. I gotta a job interview the Friday after Thanksgiving."

"To work where?"

"A hostess at Applebees."

"Applebees is good.

"Yeah, I used to be a waitress at the Olive Garden."

"If I drop you, will you test positive?"

Trina dropped her arms and threw up her palms. "Absolutely not. I've been attending the drug program you got me in on a regular basis. Haven't missed not one session. I promise you I'm tryna to do the right thing."

It seemed the courts were all too ready to incarcerate rather than to rehabilitate clients who violated probation for minor offenses. Sending Trina back to jail for another year or two would've just fed the insatiable recidivism beast and wouldn't have benefited her, me, or the taxpayers of New York City one iota.

"Look, I'm giving you one more shot," I said, pointing my finger at her.

Trina drooped her shoulders and slapped a palm to her chest. "Thank you, Officer Alexander. I swear I'm gonna—"

"But!" I held a finger up. "Your drug test *has* to come back clean."

"Not a problem, Officer Alexander."

"I'm going to have them release you, but I want to see you in my office first thing tomorrow morning." I took out my phone and looked at my calendar. "Let's meet at nine."

"You got it, Officer Alexander," she said, clasping her hands while her fake blue eyes wandered up to the fluorescent lighting. "*Thank you*, God!" she exclaimed. "And thank you too, Officer Alexander."

I got up from the table. "Remember, tomorrow morning, no later than nine. A minute later and I'm violating you."

"Don't worry. I'll be there."

The officer escorted Trina away to be processed for release.

"So, Trina Murrow gets to walk," Lance said with a shake of his head as I approached his desk.

"I appreciate you contacting me first. I've been trying to help her get going in the right direction, but it's so hard when you don't have any real role models in your life."

"Aren't you a role model?"

"I think she just views me as the law," I sighed.

"You're too soft on these crooks," Lance said with a snarl.

"Maybe, but sometimes I'm all the hope they have."

"Well, it's not like they appreciate it. You see how they keep messing up."

"There's no limit to how many times God forgives us for *messing* up?"

"You're not God!" Lance spat.

"To some of these clients I am."

Lance shook his head and locked his eyes on my endowed bosom.

"Ahem!" I grunted, zipping up my jacket.

His eyes wandered back up to my face. "Interested in a nightcap? I'm getting off in a half hour."

"You know, that used to sound like fun but somehow it's not as tempting as it once was. Thanks for the offer, but I think I'll just head home."

"Must have somebody keeping you entertained." Lance's statement sounded more like a covert question.

"That would be none of your business."

"Gotchu!" he said with a slow nod.

"Too-da-loo!" I said, wriggling my fingers as I turned to leave.

Chapter 17

Antoine, clad in his Odell Beckham Giants Jersey, stood at the bar inside of the luxury suite watching the skillful bartender execute a perfect margarita. Amber and I sat in leather recliners sampling an assortment of canapés—salmon and cream cheese on pumpernickel toast, prosciutto and roasted asparagus atop a slice of cheese and white toast, and cherry tomatoes with black olives lying on dollops of vegetable cream cheese. Succulent shrimp cocktail rested on a platter of ice and every variety of sushi was there for the taking.

Dontae re-entered the room after having left to chat it up with some important looking men in business suits and windbreakers with the Giants' logo printed across them. He crept up behind me and wrapped his arms around my shoulders. I titled my head to kiss his lips, and Amber shot us a curt smile.

Antoine rushed over to Dontae, careful not to spill his brimming cocktail.

"Damn, bro. I never imagined I'd be watching the Giants game from a luxury suite. I can't thank you enough for inviting me and my lady," he said, rigorously shaking Dontae's hand.

"Not a problem, my man. Hey, y'all are good to Symone. It's only right."

"But damn, man! I'm in complete awe," Antoine exclaimed, finally releasing Dontae's hand. "I knew you were a cool dude when I met you, but this is a whole 'nother level of cool."

I had never seen such fawning from Antoine. He was a burgeoning investment banker with a pretty impressive resumé. It was odd viewing him in an inferior role. In my mind, he'd been the paradigm of the perfect gentleman.

The guys chuckled. Dontae patted Antoine's shoulder.

"I just want y'all to relax and have a great time 'cause that's what we came to do, right?"

Antoine heartily agreed, sipping his drink as he strode over to a recliner and gingerly sat down, mindful of his margarita.

The Giants were scheduled to play the Eagles. Dontae was especially anxious since he had a two-thousand-dollar bet on the line. A loss would've been more a blow to his ego than to his pockets. In many ways Dontae was a perfectionist who couldn't stand to lose at anything.

"Hey, listen, if you don't marry this dude, I will," Antoine joked when I had first told him and Amber about the two-thousand-dollar bet and the twenty grand he'd dropped on the suite without so much as a swipe of his eyebrow.

Amber had elbowed Antoine in the ribs, chastising him for co-signing what she felt was a senseless waste of money.

I wasn't too keen on people throwing away money like yesterday's trash either, but I was starting to settle nicely into my new world of opulence. I had been a giver all my life even when I didn't have much to give. My date with karma was long overdue. It was about time I started getting back some of what I had put out into the universe.

"So," Amber started, crossing her legs and looking up at Dontae. "Looks like things are getting *real* serious between you and my girl."

Dontae nodded and dropped into the chair next to me, taking my hand in his. "That would be an accurate observation."

"So how do you plan on maintaining a relationship while working as a gigolo?" Amber blurted.

Antoine's eyebrows shot up as he sat erect in his chair. He slid his hand past his neck signaling for Amber to cut the conversation, but she persisted.

"I mean, what woman wants to be with a man who sleeps with other women for money?"

Antoine's eyes bulged. He darted up from his chair and practically leapt over to Amber, grabbing her by the hand and urging her from her seat.

"Come on, baby. Have you seen the ladies room? Let's take a walk."

Amber snatched her hand away. "Wait a minute!" she fired back at Antoine. "I'm waiting for Dontae to answer my question." She folded her arms over her chest and snapped her neck in Dontae's direction.

Antoine pulled at Amber's upper arm, almost lifting her from her seat. "I said, let's take a walk."

Dontae held a palm up and chuckled.

I shot Amber a wicked side-eye. I understood that she was trying to look out for me, but I was highly offended that she had chosen to confront Dontae head-on rather than trusting me to make good decisions.

Dontae looked up at Antoine. "Your wife has every reason to be concerned about her best friend." He re-directed his attention toward Amber. "Symone and I already had a discussion about my...line of work." Dontae turned his head to face me. "And I'm committed to being intimately exclusive with her." He then looked back at Amber. "Because a wonderful woman like this deserves nothing less."

Amber took a deep breath then let out a sigh of relief, as did Antoine.

The national anthem had begun to play and I rushed over to the glass-paneled window to see if there were any kneeling players.

"Can we just enjoy the game?" Antoine asked. "I mean, this is a once in a lifetime thing." His eyes pleaded with Amber to drop the subject.

"Look, all I want is for my girl to be happy." Amber sat back in her recliner and crossed her legs.

Antoine looked over at me. "Are you happy, Symone?"

I scurried back over to my chair, sat down and looped my arm around Dontae's. "Very," I said with conviction.

"Good. Now let's send them Eagles south for the winter." Antoine said bumping fists with Dontae then retaking his seat before the glass-paneled window.

Antoine remained in good spirits during the limousine ride home despite the Giants dismal loss to the Eagles. He was already making plans for a boy's night out with Dontae in the upcoming weeks. He said he wanted to introduce Dontae to the world of crypto currency and day trading so that he could start making some 'legitimate,' money.

Amber still seemed a little uptight, cutting her eyes suspiciously at Dontae whenever he talked about his private plane and world travels. Dontae was not a braggart. He only spoke of those things because Antoine kept prompting him with statements like,

"Yo, I hear you've got your own plane, my man." Or, "You seem to know a little bit about everything. I know a dude like you has probably seen half the world by now."

"Sorry about your two-thousand-dollar loss, my brother. But I'm sure that's just a drop in the bucket to a baller like you." Antoine slapped his high knees then grinned, nudging Amber in the side.

"Hey, two thousand is still two thousand." Dontae said resignedly as I leaned my head against his prominent chest.

"Can we change the subject, please?" Amber huffed. "We've been talking about trains, planes, and automobiles for the entire half-hour ride."

Antoine placed a hand on Amber's knee. She was wearing a mini-dress and knee-high, high-heeled boots. "So, what you want to talk about, baby?"

"Good that you mentioned it. Let's talk about a baby. How having one would add so much more to our lives. Let's talk about how we should not make plans on when and how to have children and just let God take control."

Antoine's furrowed his brows.

"How there's nothing more precious than the ability to bring another life into the world, especially with the one you love more than any and everything."

I sat up cringing, wondering if Amber was going to tell Antoine that she was expecting right there in the limo in front of me, a man they barely knew and the limo driver in earshot.

"I agree, baby. But you know we wanted to wait a while. Besides, I don't think we should be discussing our personal—"

"I'm five weeks pregnant!" Amber blurted. "There. Now you know."

Antoine gulped while Dontae smirked and reached for a bottle of champagne chilling in a bed of ice. I was compelled to spring from my seat and grab the both of them into a big ole bear hug, but I hesitated, waiting for Antoine's reply.

The car went dead silent except for the sound of a cork being popped. Dontae reached for four glasses and I placed my hand on top of his to stop him.

"Three. She can't have any."

He nodded, put one back in the bar, and began to fill the three remaining flutes. He held one out to Antoine who was so engulfed in shock that he didn't even turn his head to acknowledge him.

"Congratulations, my brother." Dontae said attempting to jolt Antoine from his stupor.

"Oh." Antoine uttered absently before accepting his drink. "Thanks, bro."

"Oh, this is nothing. Anytime, my man."

Antoine refocused on Amber who sat rigid as if afraid to breathe. "I thought—I mean, you told me you were on birth control." Antoine looked at me and Dontae sheepishly as if remembering we were there. "Look y'all. I'm sorry." He swiped his forehead with the heel of his hand. "I'm just a little in shock."

"No, do your thang. We're good over here," Dontae assured him.

"Yeah, you guys are family," I reaffirmed.

Dontae passed me a glass and I decided to propose a toast to try and ease the tension. "Here's to the best future parents any child could ever hope for." Yeah, it was corny, but I was desperate to end the night on a high note.

"I was, baby. But nothing's a hundred percent guaranteed." Amber's usually fiery voice, sounded meek.

Antoine nodded and exhaled, taking Amber into his arms. He kissed her forehead.

She looked up at him. "You happy, baby?" she asked, then seemed to brace herself.

Antoine pulled in a long breath through flared nostrils, then exhaled. "Of course, I'm happy, baby," he replied, pulling her closer to him.

Whew! I exclaimed in my head before propping my head against Dontae's shoulder. He took me in his arms and kissed me deeply. There was nothing else I could ask of life. Everything I ever wanted was sitting right there beside me.

Chapter 18

I squeezed my way through the miniature hordes of restless patrons grasping their hand-held pagers as they gathered about the entrance of Applebees and over to the hostess desk. Trina Murrow was nearly unrecognizable. Her conservative appearance was a sobering contrast to her former "lady-of-the-night," look. Gone were the batty eyelashes and blue contacts that made her look like she was in costume; gone were the tight shirts that clung to her love handles and ample bosom; and her requisite platform heels were replaced with sensible, flat slip-ons. It was if she'd traded in the old, tricked-out model of herself for a newer and more subdued one.

Her natural brown eyes lit up when they spotted me standing to the side of her semi-circled counter.

"Heeeey, Officer Alexander!" she exclaimed proudly, pushing her torso out so I could see her name tag.

I responded with a thumbs up and a 'hi, how's everything?' But I was sure most of it was drowned out in the loud banter. It was senseless to try and communicate amid all the goings-on, so I decided to hang back for a few and simply observe her in action.

I was pleasantly surprised to see how efficiently she coordinated the busy crowd for seating and in the fifteen minutes I stood there, seemed to never miss a beat. It was all I needed to be convinced that Miss Murrow appeared well on her way to solid reformation.

Besides, I didn't have much time to spare. Dontae and I were planning to meet Antoine and Amber at Touché's, a sports bar in the city owned by a friend of his who I heard was both neo-Afrocentric and a former championship fencer. Dontae often bragged about their killer drinks and to-die-for appetizers, so we were all good and anxious to give them a try, especially Antoine who had hung out with Dontae at least three times since the Giants versus Eagles game.

D.D. Sherman   Rare Orchids

    Dontae had already been in the city for business, so I told him that I'd just uber out there when I finished checking in on my last client. Both Antoine and Amber worked in Manhattan, so I imagined they were probably already on their way to the restaurant.

    Everyone in my immediate circle had warmed up to Dontae as he was quickly becoming a consistent presence in my life, and that made me especially happy. He had worked his way into my heart, my soul and every aspect of my being; to have earned the acceptance of my friends and family just made things all the more glorious.

***

Antoine and Amber were a joltingly attractive couple sitting at a VIP table on a charcoal-hued leather sofa in Touché's. They waved me over as if I hadn't noticed them first. Antoine was clad in a navy-blue three-piece—that fitted him to a tee—white dress shirt, and a paisley pink tie. Amber wore a leather dress and leather knee boots with ice-gold accessories. Her weave was always voluminous and wonderfully styled as if she'd just bounced right out of the beautician's chair. I briefly imagined how she'd dress once she started to show. I wondered if she'd trade her cosmopolitan couture in for baggy sweats and oversized hoodies, or try to maintain her fashion savoir faire in high-end maternity wear.

    "Hey there, ray of sunshine!" Amber bolted up from her seat to hug me, reaching over Antoine who had stood up to hug me next.

    I sat across from them and took in the Afrocentric theme which was a tasteful throwback to the sixties and seventies, but not pretentious and overstated like some soul themes. There were supersized portraits of a Marvin Gaye, sweating and crooning away, a shade-wearing Stevie Wonder looking upward as his beaded cornrows dangled past his shoulders, the Four Tops frozen in a synchronized step, a young, and thinner Aretha Franklin bellowing a tune, the Supremes before Diana Ross migrated to forefront of the group, Donnie Hathaway pecking away at piano keys with his wooly sideburns sprouting from a slightly-tilted flat cap, an afro-sporting Nina Simone squatted in militant black, and myriad other great entertainers from that era. There were portraits of Vernon, the restaurant owner and Dontae's friend, highlighting his impressive fencing career including two supersized pictures of him receiving silver medals at the U.S. Olympics. He looked different than the bigger and more muscular person I had imagined him to be.

Drinks were served in repurposed mason jars, and every cocktail on the menu included a blend of some flavor of Kool-Aid.

I sat looking around, expecting Dontae to make an entrance any minute.

"This place is cool," Amber stated over the Temptations's, "Ain't Too Proud to Beg."

Antoine nodded and sipped his drink.

"What are you drinking?" I asked him.

"A merry cherry contemporary." He informed me, raising his voice to be heard over the music. "Vodka, Mountain Dew, and cherry Kool-Aid."

I gave him an a-okay sign and looked around the room for Dontae.

Antoine glanced at his watch. "Where's your man?" he asked. "Thought he'd be here playing the gracious host by now."

I shrugged and glanced at my phone to see if he'd texted me. "I don't know. I spoke to him a couple of hours ago. He told me he was in the city and not too far from here."

"Maybe he just got tied up doing something. Y'all relax. I'm sure lover boy will be here in a few."

It irked me whenever Amber referred to Dontae with monikers that hinted at his past. I shot him another quick text.

Hey, babe. Been here 15 min. Antoine and Amb got here an hour ago. Where are you?

I sat stiff in my seat as Vernon approached our table, half-expecting him to solve the missing Dontae conundrum.

"Wassup, good people?" Vernon was a slim, freckled-faced, light-skinned guy. I'd surmised he was the child of interracial parents. He pointed a finger at me. "Symone, right?"

I nodded.

"I knew it. Dontae talks about you all the time."

I smiled.

Vernon turned his attention to the opposite side of the table. "Amber and Antoine?"

The couple nodded. Antoine stood up to shake Vernon's hand. "Good to meet you, brother. You've got a real cool spot here. Me and my lady are really diggin' it."

"Thanks, brother. I'm trying."

Antoine retook his seat.

"So where's the man of the hour?" Vernon asked me.

"I was hoping maybe you heard something from him?" I said, half embarrassed.

"I did...*earlier*. We spoke about one o'clock. He told me he was dropping by with his girl and a few friends." Vernon looked at his smart watch. "It's near nine."

My phone pinged, and I glanced down at it expecting to see a message from Dontae. Instead my cousin Felicia had sent me a dirty joke; it was a cartoon of a really fat man with a huge, hanging belly and a caption that read, 'I seem to have lost my wee wee. Has anyone seen it?' Under normal circumstances I would have cracked up, but at that moment in time I just couldn't find the humor in it.

"Can I get you guys something?"

"Thanks, but I think I'll just wait for Dontae."

"Well, she can wait. We're hungry," Amber put in. "I'll have the deep fried mac n'cheese bites and the skewered pork medallions with the pickled onion dip. Whatchu having, honey?"

"I'll take the Uncle Nearest ground lamb sliders and the sweet potato chips." Antoine said, rubbing his palms together.

Vernon nodded, while jotting their orders on a pad, then looked at me.

"Can I at least get you a drink?"

"Okay," I acquiesced with a sigh and looked at my cocktail menu. "I'll take the apple berry banga." I said, reaching for my bottle of hand sanitizer in my pocketbook.

"This is all on the house, alright guys?" Vernon said, collecting the menus. "I'll leave a menu for my man."

"Nah I got the bill, brother," Antoine objected.

Vernon smiled. "Thanks, my brother. But that'll be just insulting me. Dontae is a phenomenal friend and generous benefactor. I'da never got this place off the ground had it not been for him. As long as you're cool with Dontae, you'll never pay to eat at Touché's. Now, lemme get these orders in."

I glanced at my phone for the fifth time and looked over at the bar area again. "So, have you thought of any baby names?" I asked Amber trying to suppress the negative voices in my head concerning Dontae's whereabouts.

"Please, dumpling. Hasn't even crossed my mind." Amber took a sip of water.

"She won't be naming our kids. She sucks at names. As I'm sure you know by now." Antoine teased.

I giggled. It was true.

"I was teaching your guy a little bit about crypto currency," Antoine continued. "He's a real smart dude. He seems to catch on quick. I can see us making a ton of money in the near future." Antoine took another sip of his half-drunk merry cherry contemporary.

"That's nice," I replied, half-distracted.

"Yeah, I think we're going to have a lot of fun in the process."

"Uh-huh." I nodded, clasping my hands on the table and rolling my thumbs. Probably sensing my apparent angst, Antoine excused himself to the men's room.

"Geez, it is getting late. Nine o'clock already." Amber said looking at her sleek, gold watch.

"Yeah, I know. I mean, Dontae can be a bit unpredictable at times, but he's usually prompt, or at least makes sure that he keeps me informed if he's running late."

Amber shrugged off what I said. "Or maybe he's *in* to something and can't get to a phone."

"That's not funny!" I shot back at her.

"I'm just sayin'. You act like he's just going to become this overnight saint and cut ties with everything in his past. I think you're being unrealistic, sugah pie."

"He could've been in a car accident, God forbid. Or maybe he's hurt in some other way. Why does your mind tend to go to the worst case scenario?"

"Which would you rather deal with? Him lying between some chick's legs or *lying* in a coma after a car accident?" Amber drummed her fingers on the table, awaiting my response.

"Neither! I'd just rather he be here!" My phone pinged on the table again. I smiled as I glanced down, but frowned to see that it was some random person instant messaging me via Facebook.

"All I'm simply saying is that you shouldn't allow yourself to get all caught up in the hype, Symone. We all know how full of shit these men can be."

A cute waitress in 70s attire—long sleeved shirt, short skirt, and patent leather boots with square heels—brought another round of drinks to the table just as Antoine had returned from the men's room. "These are on the house, okay guys?" she said, sitting drinks before Antoine and me. I'll be right back with your food."

We all thanked her as she strutted off.

I decided to shoot Dontae one last text message and be done with it. *Nine-twenty. Now I'm really concerned. Pray all is well. Call as soon as you can. We're still here.*♥

After another apple berry banga, a serving of hot-buttered cornbread fritters, and an hour of polite, superficial conversation—both Antoine and Amber's attempt at being supportive—I had all but given up on hearing from Dontae that evening.

"That was some good eats," Antoine said, tossing a napkin onto his cleaned plate.

"Yes. I really enjoyed my food, too. Symone you should've at least tried *something*."

"Didn't have much of an appetite," I responded, pushing my almost full cornbread basket away.

"I understand, boo boo." Amber reached her hand across the table to stroke my forearm.

Antoine looked at his watch. "Damn, a quarter to eleven already." He took in a deep breath, exhaled, and looked at Amber as if for a cue on what to do next.

Amber stretched her arms above her head and yawned. "Look, girl. We're about to head out."

"Yeah, I've got to coach in the morning." Antoine was a mentor who coached a neighborhood rugby team that he founded with another guy. His empathetic eyes looked into mine. "I'm sorry about all this. I still think Dontae's a cool dude. Probably just got into a little trouble or something."

"Why don't you try texting him from your number?" Amber suggested.

"I don't think that'll make much of a difference, but okay."

Antoine read his message aloud as he texted it. "Hey, my man? What's good? We missed you today. You've got your girl here all worried—"

Amber elbowed him in the side. "Don't mention Symone. Just act like the text is coming directly from you.

Antoine nodded, erasing the last sentence. "Hit me up as soon as possible, so I can put my mind at ease." He'd hit send, then put the phone on the table to monitor it.

"Thanks," I said, doing a lousy job hiding the disappointment in my voice.

"Of course, Symone. You know we gotchu," Antoine said reassuringly.

***

I ubered back home and started calling area hospitals the moment I got in. There were no patients by the name of Dontae Cummings in any of them. I started to call Ebony to get her little brother's cell phone number, but thought better of it. I was sure Amber had shared every tidbit of information about me and my gigolo boo with her and didn't want her to know that my dreamlike relationship was turning into a nightmare; especially since she and Devin were still going strong.

    I placed my phone on the naked lady coffee table and went into the bathroom to run a hot bath. I always believed that water could wash away everything, even a broken heart. While the tub filled, I inspected my apartment. I noticed that I had not placed a loaf of bread back inside the bread box, and that there were a few dirty dishes and coffee mugs sitting in the sink; a few outdated magazines were still stacked under the nightstand; and the cable box and blue ray player could have used a little dusting. The baseboards were dingy and so were the light switch panels; my work-out sweats were strewn across a living room chair and some balled napkins made their way to my lackluster wood floors. I had been so infatuated that I didn't even notice I was slipping on house duties. I decided to stay up after my bath cleaning, determined to get my place back in ship-shape.

    My phone pinged as I was mopping my floors. I rushed over to the table to retrieve it, snatching it with shaky hands. It was just Amber inquiring if I had heard from Dontae.

    No, not a peep. I texted back.
    Oh no! Try not to worry. I'm sure you'll hear from him soon.
    Don't want to hear from him. EVER!
    I'm sure you don't mean that.
    You wanna bet?
    You know I'm here if you need to vent.
    I know.
    Day or night. I'm usually up early throwing up my guts.
    Lol. Okay. I'll keep that in mind.
    Love you, gumdrop!
    Love you more.

Chapter 19

I slipped into a pair of suede moccasin boots and strutted around Sonya's living room with an exaggerated sway of my hips. It was the seventh pair of shoes I had tried on that night and not a one of those seven pairs compelled me to part ways with the cash in my wallet.

"Now those are it!" my always upbeat cousin Felicia exclaimed as I twirled before her.

"They *are* cute, but my feet look wide and flat in them." I plodded in circles to demonstrate the problem.

"That's because you're probably used to heels," Sonya stated, reaching for the bowl of tortilla chips that sat on her cocktail table. She plucked up a few, dipped them into a spicy salsa before packing them into her mouth.

"I don't think that's the problem. It's not like I wear heels all that often."

Sonya owned a shoe store downtown Brooklyn. Whenever she had left over inventory from a prior season, she hosted shoe parties to try and sell off the remaining footwear. She told my cousin Felicia to invite me. I figured it was just part of a ploy to get me out of the house so I wouldn't be home incessantly wondering about Dontae. Being in the company of about fifteen other women, drinking wine, and trying on endless pairs of shoes was probably the best therapy for my devastated heart.

The next pair of shoes I tried on were fringed, opened-toe, thigh-high boots. I didn't quite get why boots would have an opened toe, but I looked cute as hell when I checked myself out in a full-length mirror.

"Now those are the bomb diggity!" A girl by the name of Myrna slurred rather loudly. She was probably on her fifth glass of wine. Earlier, I had watched her polish off an entire bottle by her lonesome.

I looked over at Felicia for confirmation. She nodded in agreement and gave me the thumbs up; in fact, everyone in the room agreed that I looked hot in them so I gave Sonya a nod to tally me up for the hundred and sixty-five dollars.

"You're so lucky. Besides a size seven, these were the only pair I had left," Sonya said while writing out the receipt.

They were a sexy pair of boots, but the thought of not having Dontae around to see me strut in them stabbed at my heart like an icepick. It was a painful reminder that I may never see or hear from him again.

"What's wrong, Symone?" I heard Felicia ask.

"Nothing," I replied cheerfully, then headed over to a sofa to pull off those boots and slip back in to my Air Maxes.

I snacked on hot wings and cheeseballs while watching girl after girl try on shoe after shoe until Sonya's entire living room looked like the ruins of a DSW explosion.

Although my phone had been mostly silent the entire day, I reached for it in my handbag hoping to see a missed call from Dontae that perhaps got lost in the loud, feminine banter. But nothing. I read the last text he'd sent to me that last Friday evening maybe for the hundredth time.

In Harlem. A few minutes away from my man's spot. Be there in a little while. See you soon, gorgeous! ☺

I discreetly slipped my phone back into my handbag and started to pack my boots into the shoebox. Sonya darted up from the sofa and rushed over to me.

"I'll do it," she said, positioning the boots neatly inside the box. "Listen, these boots are a hundred and sixty-five dollars. I paid eighty for them."

"Yes, I know. No problem. I love them," I replied digging around in my handbag for my wallet.

Sonya, who was squatted before me, placed her hand on my knee. "Just give me the eighty I paid, and I'll be glad to just break even."

I recognized what that was. Sympathy. I hated sympathy. It made me feel and look weak. I appreciated the gesture, but it wasn't like I lost a limb. I lost a man and probably for the best.

Men are replaceable. Limbs aren't. So her pity could have been better spent on someone who needed it.

I counted out a hundred-sixty-five-dollars and handed it to her. "Go break even with someone else," I stated, holding out the cash before her.

"You are one stubborn bull," she said rising to her feet.

"But you love me anyway."

"I damn sure do." She sucked her teeth and reluctantly accepted the money. "But if you buy another pair, it's half-price and it ain't jack you can do about it."

She turned away, and I sat watching her wide hips sway up and down in tandem as she sauntered away.

I stayed at Sonya's until almost midnight; until the last wing had disappeared from the platter; the last bottle of wine had been drunk; and the last of the guests had struggled through the door with boxes of shoes in tow as Sonya bade them goodnight. I hated the thought of going home to face the silence of my thoughts. I didn't want to sit on the sofa where Dontae and I had made love for the first time or punch the three eight two nine code into my front door's keypad.

I called his phone three times that day. All calls had gone directly to voicemail as if his phone had been turned off. After the third try, I decided to leave a message.

"Is this your idea of trust?"

***

That Sunday I had been lying in bed mulling over the last few years of my life and all of the events that led me to where I was—or wasn't—when my phone rang on my nightstand, triggering my heart into an erratic pounding.

I reached for it and read "Unknown Caller ID" across the screen. Initially, I thought maybe it was some solicitor, but decided to answer it anyway.

"Good Morning," I said, my voice raspy.

"Yes, Symone Alexander?" The West Indian accent sounded familiar.

"Yes, this is her."

"Good day, ma'am. This is Everett."

I took a moment to think. *Everett*? "I'm sorry, but I don't know—wait a minute!" I exclaimed, feeling as if my heart was going to beat out of my chest. "Yes! Everett! Now I know. The driver. Dontae's driver!"

He chuckled. "Now you got it."

At that point, I was elated to hear from anyone connected to Dontae, but I couldn't understand why in the world would Everett, the driver, be calling me?

"Is there something wrong with Dontae?" My throat felt as if it were constricting as I anticipated his answer.

"Actually, I'm here to pick you up. We're parked right outside your door."

I ran to the window and was jolted at the sight of the stretched Mercedes limo that appeared too big, and oddly out of place on my grungy street in daylight.

Even though it was twelve, I was just getting out of bed. I needed a shower, to comb my hair, get dressed and to put on makeup. I was in panic mode, but managed to take a moment to think about things. I was able to calm my nerves and decided to make him wait like he'd made me wait an entire week.

"I'll come down but tell your boss it's going to take me at least a half hour to pull things together."

"That's okay. You may take your time."

"Okay, see you in a bit, Mr. Everett." I disconnected the call.

I hated that I only allowed myself a fifteen-minute shower, but I was anxious to see Dontae and give him a piece of my mind. If he thought he was going to woo me with some extravagant restaurant or some off-the-wall excursion, he had another think coming.

I had no idea what to put on. If I dressed up too much, he'd most likely think that I'd overlooked his transgressions and was excited just to see him and to enjoy whatever he had planned. If I'd dressed too casually, he'd probably think that I felt he didn't owe me anything and wasn't looking forward to any grand gestures, so I aimed somewhere in the middle. I threw on a long-sleeved, thigh-high dress and a pair of platform heels. I could never compromise my sexy just because I was angry. My hair had been in pin curls, so I just undid those and raked my fingers through them. I threw on some light makeup, spritzed a subtle fragrance behind my ears, grabbed my jacket and headed for the door imagining the kind of greeting I would give him. I thought of being cold and aloof, but that would just be pouting. I thought of being loud and angry, but that would probably scare him out of any true confessions. I missed him terribly, but I was sorely disappointed in him which made me all the more confused.

Everett popped out of the driver's side and flung the rear passenger's seat open when he noticed me walking toward the limo.

My heart drummed in my ears and it took all that I had to try and keep it together.

"Good day," Everett said again as I approached the vehicle.

"Good day, Everett," I said, then tried to swallow a log in my throat.

I climbed inside the limo and gasped at what I saw. I had one knee propped up on the leather cushion staring wide-eyed at the figure sitting across from me. My brain struggled to make sense of what I was looking at. A woman. A dirty-blonde with an inch of her black roots showing, in her mid-to-late fifties, plumper than she'd probably like to be, but not fat or overweight. She sat with her shapely legs crossed, coolly puffing a slim, brown cigarette. There were small musical notes tatted on the side of her neck and her red nail polish was old and chipped. Nothing about her conveyed money except for two hefty diamond rings decorating the middle finger of one hand and the forefinger of the other; they caught a ray of light emanating through the opened sunroof and damn near blinded me. She wore a tan, suede overcoat over a suede vest, a white shirt that generously exposed her augmented bosom, and a brown leather skirt that rode up to her rather beefy thighs.

Everett had closed the door and was already back in the driver's seat. As much as I wanted to bolt out of that car, I needed to stay. I clasped the door handle, still pondering my next move.

"Why do you act so surprise? It's not like you've never been in here before," she stated, casually flicking her ashes into a tray built into the armrest.

My mouth tasted dry and pasty as my mind frantically searched for a reply.

She took one last puff, snubbed out her cigarette, and then extended her hand to me. "I'm Evelynn, by the way. It's Eve...*lynn*. Not Evelyn. Everyone makes that stupid mistake. It's a combination of my mother Eve's and Grandmother Madelynn's names."

I loosely shook her incredibly soft hand, then jerked away.

"You're Symone, right? Or is it Kara?" Her flickering eyes studied me. "No, not Kara. Kara was the otha one." I detected some kind of accent, but I couldn't discern from which region in the world this exotic woman hailed.

"You know who I am. So stop fronting."

"Fronting?" she repeated, appearing genuinely confused. She giggled. "I'm sorry, but I don't know these words."

"Stop *bullshitting* me. You understand that?"

"Now that word I can understand," she said lightheartedly.

"Good. Now, who the hell are you to show up in my hood unannounced?"

"Do you want launch?" she asked dismissively, meaning to say lunch. She wouldn't deign to answer me directly. It was the typical passive-aggressive rich person's mentality that singed me.

"I figure you probably rushed down here expecting to see your lova and made no time to eat *some*thing. There's a lovely café in City. They make these stuffed—" She broke off and brought the heel of her hand to her forehead. "It's the bread. Oh shucks! I'm sorry. I can't think of the name," she said bashfully. "What do you call these French pastries where they put the fruit and the cheese and the meat?"

"Crepes." *Bitch*.

She tittered. "That's right. Crepes. Do forgive me."

"That's okay. Dementia is a serious thing."

"What?" she asked with a smile and side tilt of her head, her face stubbornly holding on to the vestiges of a once good-looking woman. "I'm fifty-five, sweetheart. Much too young for Dementia."

"My bad. I was sure you was pushing sixty-five." That was a lie, but Evelynn had started plucking my nerves the minute I got inside the limo.

"Anyway," Evelynn continued. "They stuff them with cheese, ham, the peppers, olives. So much different stuff. Anything you can name. They're so good," she said, pressing her hand to her chest. "But I can only have half of one because they are very, very fattening. But you're okay, so you can have whole one," she said, reaching for her pack of cigarettes on the seat beside her. "You mind if I smoke?" she asked while lighting another cigarette.

The bitch was toying with me, but I had to play it cool if I wanted to find out what was really up with Dontae.

She pressed a button on the wall and spoke into a speaker. "Everett, the crepes place in the city."

"Yes, ma'am," he replied as the vehicle began to move.

I got nervous. I left my firearm in the house. I didn't know if she was trying to kidnap or kill me; but, I had already decided that if I had to go down, I would do so kicking ass and taking names.

"Apparently you and my *so-called lover* are well-connected. I just want to know what happened to him."

She took a drag of her cigarette, then blew puffs of smoke through her mouth then nose. "He's on a time out." She smirked.

"So now you're his mother? Well I guess that's not too far-fetched. You're certainly old enough to be."

"Tell me—Symone, right?"

I had a hunch that she was very familiar with who I was, so I refused to entertain her feigned forgetfulness.

"Yes, Symone. Tell me, did you like the red dress and shoes I selected for you? I hear you were very impressed," Evelynn smirked devilishly.

Her question electrified me and gripped my heart. It seemed oppressively hot and I struggled to breathe.

"Don't look so surprised. You should know a man cannot properly select clothes for woman, or even for himself in most cases. I've had to hire personal stylist for him, but he's finally learning to dress himself." She smiled and flicked her ashes in the tray.

I wanted to vomit.

"Oh, I just loved the dress and so did he since it was so easy for him to strip it off me in the Palace of Versailles."

Evelynn's eyelids fluttered at my last statement and she shifted in her seat. I could tell the image of Dontae making love to me, in what I now surmised was her home, deeply troubled her.

The Mercedes drove down Atlantic Avenue and we were coming up on the Barclays Center where I imagined we'd be turning right onto the Flatbush Extension. Even though I was in the company of vast wealth and privilege, I secretly envied passersby outside my window simply going about their ordinary lives. I inwardly ridiculed myself for buying into the whole Dontae façade. I loathed being in Evelynn's presence, breathing the same air, lusting after the same emotionally unavailable man.

"You think you can hurt me with your words, but you cannot. I am used to it. There have been many."

"Driver! Pull over!" I screamed to Everett.

He cannot hear you. You need to press speaker button behind you." Evelynn sounded amused.

My hand groped along the wall. "Everett, please stop this car! I want to get out!"

Evelynn pressed the speaker button on her side of the car. "Everett, do not take orders from this woman. Keep going."

D.D. Sherman   Rare Orchids

"So you're kidnapping me, bitch?" I could feel a burning heat rise up from within me and it took a whole lot of praying to keep from pouncing on her.

"You are free to go if you like, but you will never know about the man you've fallen in love with. And there is much, much that I have to tell you."

"Then you better start talking." I felt there was something Evelynn wanted from me, but I had yet to discern what it was.

The Mercedes never hesitated but continued up the Flatbush Extension. I felt weird, like I was caught up in some lost episode of the Twilight Zone.

"I encountered your *boyfriend* under rather unusual circumstances," she tittered wistfully and took a puff of her cigarette.

I felt my brows furrow.

"He burglarized my home," she said nonchalantly. "Stole a quarter of million in jewelry. Over one point five million in rare paintings, seventy thousand in cash, and some other things. I cannot remember everything. It was long time ago."

Every nerve in my body was rattled. I could not believe what I was hearing.

"But it all totaled up to more than one point six million dollars. I know that for sure. But who cares? My insurance covered it." She stabbed out her cigarette and blew smoke through her nostrils while I sat, lamenting the day I'd laid eyes on Dontae.

"He'd gotten away with robbing a few other houses, but I have an elaborate security system. Anyway, he got caught a month later. I saw him at his arraignment. And there he was, this thug, this criminal who had nerve to come into my home and take things! Expensive things! Irreplaceable things! The judge wanted to throw book at him. Five years. That is what Judge Bloom wanted to give him. The judge and I have mutual friends, so I asked if I can talk to Dontae. Perhaps make him pay for what he did in a more *pro*ductive way."

Evelynn lit another cigarette, inhaled and continued. "So he agreed."

197

D.D. Sherman — Rare Orchids

"Oh, how classic. White woman intervenes in the life of a black man to save him from himself or the elements. I think I've seen this movie before," I said scathingly.

"You make fun, but this is true. He did one year in prison then came to work for me, but I did not know what to do with him so I asked him, '"what is it that you like to do?"' He said, '"Plant flowers."' I laughed...at first. "But he was very serious. He said he cared for small garden in his project development for many years and would like to care for mine. I know you've been to my home in New Jersey and have seen my lush gardens."

I refused to dignify her with a response.

"They're all Dontae's designs." she said proudly. "Anyway, it doesn't matter. He had my permission to bring you there."

I could've been floored with a feather, even though nothing Evelynn said should have surprised me at that point.

"I have eight architect landscapers. They taught him almost everything he knows. But that wasn't enough for him. He wanted to learn about each and every plant. The regions in the world they come from. All the many different varieties. Everything, I tell you. Then he told me he always wanted to learn to fly plane and to go to college. It was like, my God! This young man has an insatiable quest for learning. I must help him! It is my duty as philanthropist and human being to help those less fortunate."

I shrugged. "Sounds very magnanimous of you, but you're starting to bore me. So can you please just get to the punchline?" The limo turned right off of Tillary Street and on to the crowded Brooklyn Bridge, which made me feel a bit more relaxed. If Dontae's sugar momma and—Driving Miss Daisy—tried anything at that point, I was sure there'd be plenty of witnesses with their cell phones on the ready.

"Punkline? What is punkline?"

Damn! Blondes really are dumb. Even the rich ones.

"You've got me here for a reason. What is it you want from me?"

Evelynn chuckled, probably out of nervousness. "I don't want nothing from you. You cannot give me nothing. What is it that you think you can give me?" she tittered again.

My caller tune played. Evelynn's eyes darted to my handbag. I reached in, retrieved my phone, and pressed it to my ear.

"Hey."

"Well, *thank* you for answering my call after my *fifth* attempt to reach you. I was starting to worry if you got kidnapped or something," Phil said with odd insight.

"Hmph!" I interjected. "You're not too far off."

"Huh? I was just joking...obviously."

"I'm in the Mercedes limo. Remember the one I told you about? The one Dontae came and picked me up in?"

Evelynn chuckled and put out her third cigarette in the twenty-minute car ride.

"The one with the bar and the lights and the banging sound system. Yes, I do recall."

"Just keep that in mind," I said, hoping Phil detected the urgency in my tone.

"For what?"

"Just keep that in mind, please."

"Why are you talking like that? Is everything okay?"

"Maybe."

"Okay, now you're starting to freak me out," Phil said, sounding as if he was finally catching on that I may have been in dire straits. "Is Casanova Brown with you?"

"We'll talk later."

"Symone, do not disconnect this call until you tell me you're okay."

"We'll talk later."

"Tell me you're okay," he insisted.

"I'm okay. Bye."

I disconnected the call and dropped my phone inside my handbag.

"Dontae?" Evelynn chuckled. "He has lied to you."

"Listen, ma'am." I started, looking Evelynn square in her dazzling blue eyes which were, by far, the best feature she had left. "I'm a grown-ass woman with a busy schedule and a full life. I do not have time to go joy riding with the likes of you. Nor do I want to eat crepes, converse, or even be on the same planet. So tell your driver to pull over or I'm calling 9-1-1."

The previously nonchalant and laid-back Evelynn became instantly unglued. "Don't—don't leave! Please!" She raked a shaky hand though her unkempt hair. Please!" she begged. "You must at least hear me out. Please?"

I squinted, shaking my head at the quivering mess before me.

"I must tell you that I love him. He was all that I had after my husband died. I confided in him many things and he was always there to listen. I was so lonely—even lonely many years before my husband died because he always had affairs with lots of women. He was never good to me." Her teary eyes seemed to plead for my sympathy.

"And then this young man came into my life who knew how to make me feel loved. I'm sure you can understand that. He is very good at making woman feel beautiful and loved. This is what he does better than any man I've ever known."

All I could do was press the heels of my hands to my eyes and shake my head.

"I told my otha rich friends about this man that made me feel like dream. Some of them are widows. Some divorcees. They wanted to experience same feeling. He has slept with many of them. But I don't care because he will always come back to Evelynn."

I felt drained, disgusted, and mortified.

"Everything he has I have given to him. Everything he knows I have taught him. He would be just 'notha criminal or maybe even dead if it were not for me. You—" Evelynn stopped to sniffle. "You love him because I have made him loveable."

I could not listen to another detail. My brain was on overload and I felt I had to get away from Evelynn whose name was starting to sound more like *Evil*lynn in my head. "Tell your driver to pull over...*now*."

She dug her hand into her overcoat and pulled out a folded manila envelope and shakily held it before me.

I stared at it with raised brows and mouth agape.

"Here." She nodded. "You take it. It's all for you."

"What *is* this?" I demanded.

"Twenty-five-thousand-dollars. Cash." There was now a maddening and desperate look in her eyes.

"Why would you just give me twenty-five-thousand-dollars?" Suspicions whirled in my head ad nauseam. *Was she looking to set Dontae up and wanted my help? Was she trying to bribe me or did she want me to do Dontae in myself?*

"Just take it!" she insisted shaking the envelope before me. "And promise me you'll never see him again."

I was jolted back in my seat.

"You see, I think he's fallen in love with you." She let her envelope bearing hand collapse, dropped her head, and sobbed so hard that her shoulders shook.

I laughed at the notion. "You're obviously making an inaccurate assumption. Is this how you treat someone you love?"

She whipped her head up to look at me, the whites of eyes pink, her cheeks wet with tears. "It's not assumption. He loves you. He told me that."

I tilted my head back at the insanity of it all and studied the roof of the car desperately trying to make sense of everything I'd been told.

She shoved the envelope at me. "Take it! It's probably more than you've ever seen at one time! You must need it! You must need it for *some*thing! If he should ever cross your path again, do not entertain him. Send him away. But know that if you do take him back, it will be waste of time. He will always come back to me. He will never forget the woman who's given him everything."

"Then why are you offering money?"

Evelynn's expression turned dour. "Because money makes solving problems easier."

"You are so wrong about that, *Evil*lynn." I slammed my hand against the speaker button and informed Everett that if he did not pull the car over asap, I'd be dialing 911 the next second. He promptly listened, pulling up at a curb and stopping.

Everett popped out the driver's seat and rushed to my side, swinging the door open.

"You might've bought Dontae, but I'm not for sell," I said as I scooted out of the vehicle, brushing past Everett so hard that I nearly knocked him over.

Chapter 20

After abruptly exiting that limousine ride from hell, I foggily walked the damp streets of Manhattan in heels while cool raindrops pelted my face. I didn't know where I was going much less what I was doing. The more I focused on the events of the day the less things made sense.

I had somehow ended up in midtown. I was passing a church when I noticed the open doors and groups of parishioners quietly filing through them. It was a Catholic church with arched, stain-glass windows, doors of wooden planks, and tiers of rounded steps. I lowered my head and followed a family of four—a wife and husband with their adolescent son and daughter—inside. It was even darker inside the church than it had been outside. Priests in white robes prayed in a subdued hum as I slipped onto a wooden bench and bowed my head. I didn't know what to do other than to ask God for forgiveness for heeding to my carnal desires and to have mercy on my fractured heart. Not that I did anything to warrant His mercy, but I was desperate to feel better, to be alright again. I was sure my sins paled in comparison to the sins of the wickeder of earthly beings and hoped that God would take that into account.

I must have sat in that pew an entire hour before I garnered the strength to lift myself up and go outside to hail a cab. I ended up at Phil's house. He was the only friend I could think of who would not have judged me and might have shown at least a smidgen of empathy.

"You should have kicked her windows out," Phil stated as he pushed a button on his cappuccino machine. "The nerve of her to offer you money like you're some wayward vagabond. Rich people. They make me sick. Sweetner?" he asked, reaching for a bowl in his cupboard.

"No. And you're right. I should have."

"And you haven't heard a peep from Dontae?"

"Nothing since two Fridays ago."

"That so weird," Phil said, gingerly walking over to me with a steaming cappuccino in tow. He carefully sat it on the table then rushed back over to the oven.

"Weird is an understatement."

"And to think, I was really beginning to like him for you." Phil put on an oven mitt, then slid out a pan of stuffed pastries. He closed the door with a bump of his knee and sat the pan on top of the stove burners.

I knew I looked a hot mess. My frizzy hair was sopping wet from the rain and the dried streaks of mascara staining my cheeks qualified me for initiation into the Gothic society. I had kicked my shoes off under the table to release my throbbing toes.

I leaned my head in my hand and sighed. "Please do not mention that man's name to me again. I cannot believe I fell for him. I have nobody to blame but myself."

Phil placed the pastries into a decorative dish and sat it on the table before me. "Don't go beating yourself up because what's-his-face turned out to be an a-hole. Maybe it'll all make sense one day, but you need not waddle in regret. At least you had *some* fun."

"Yeah, getting my heart broke is a lot of fun. Wee-hoo, can't wait for the next heartbreak." I popped a cheese-stuffed pastry in my mouth and chewed lazily.

Phil made himself a cappuccino then took a seat at the small bistro-like table beside me. "I think you know what I meant," he said blowing on his cappuccino then taking a sip.

"Yeah, I know what you meant. I'm just in a funky mood." I reached for a different kind of pastry and examined it between my fingers before taking a small bite. "These are pretty good."

"Don't I know it. And no matter what, you can never eat just one. *Scandalous*."

I attempted a laugh, but it only came out as a 'humph!'"

"So what are you going to do, my friend?"

My eyes wandered as I took in a deep breath. "Get on with my lonely life," I answered on an exhale. "I just have to remember how to do that."

Phil nodded.

D.D. Sherman   Rare Orchids

    I took a sip of coffee and listened to the rain and wind whip against Phil's kitchen window. It was strangely demonstrative of the turbulent emotions whishing about within me.

***

Abdullah Malik sat rigid in the armless chair across from me. He appeared staunchly neat donned in a black Kufi, pull-over sweater, slacks and dress shoes with his hairline and mustache trimmed to perfection. He was handsome, aside from the angry scar that stretched from ear tip to ear tip across his neck like someone tried to decapitate him.

    "See, my sister, not only do you work for the system, you're part of it. You think you're reforming me, but all you're doing is playing into that Willie Lynch mentality. This is all part of a grand plan to keep us pitted against each other. Now you may think that shield and gun gives you power, but it's really taking the power away from our community because it's making you think of me—and all the other brothers and sisters caught up in this crooked ass system—as the adversary. And we're *not* the adversary. You ballin' fo the wrong team, my sister. Eventually, the truth will reveal itself. And when it does, and you find out you're just a pawn in some elaborate game, I'm still gonna say," Abdullah Malik stretched his arms into a circle, "come here sis, give your brother a hug."

    He had been rambling for a good fifteen minutes and I had only been half-listening. He had been in and out of parole supervision since adolescence. Seniority in the criminal justice system had at least earned him my half ear.

    "I appreciate what you're saying, Mr. Abdullah, but what in all God's creation does that have to do with you not being at your place of residency these past three days?"

    "See, that's what I'm talkin' 'bout. Officer, I'm forty-four years old and you wanna check on me every five minutes like I'm somebody's child." He shook his head. "This is the first time you've come to my residence and found me not there."

"Yes, but I've only been to your house twice."

"Look, I'm not doing nothing illegal. I told you I spent the night at my girl's house. I do that sometimes, you know?" Abdullah stated bitterly, making me sense an undertow of built up anger.

"But your girlfriend lives within the vicinity of the complainant."

"My ex-wife is a liar. I was never violent towards her. I only struck her back in self-defense. She's just trying to destroy what I got goin' on with this new thang."

"I'm sorry, Mr. Abdullah, but you and your girlfriend will have to decide on how you're going to continue to see each other in a way that does not violate the stipulations of your parole."

Abdullah shrugged. "Whatever, man. Guess I gotta bow down to the system 'til I'm off this short leash."

"Listen, I'm going to turn a blind-eye this time, but Mr. Abdullah, you *have* to be where you say you are and you *cannot* be in the vicinity of the victim which can be construed as stalking."

"Won't happen again, sis."

"*Officer* Alexander," I corrected him.

"Yeah, right. But just remember what we spoke about," he said as he got up from his chair and ran his palms down the legs of his neatly-creased pants.

"I'll try to. Have a good day, Mr. Abdullah."

There was a bit of irony in me trying to reform and rectify the lives of strangers while my own life seemed to be spiraling in an unknown direction. I felt like a fraud.

While work wasn't affording me the benefit of peace of mind, it did distract me from constantly ruminating over the whole Dontae debacle. It had been weeks since I had heard from him and I was slowly coming to terms with the fact that I may never know what became of him let alone get all of my questions answered.

***

D.D. Sherman   Rare Orchids

I was on my way to meet Amber after work that Tuesday for her first sonogram appointment. Antoine had to cover for a sick partner which had him leaving town on a last minute business trip. I didn't mind. It was another thing to distract me from thoughts of happily never after. My life seemed dull and regimented without unpredictable Dontae in it, blowing my mind with almost everything he did.

Her clinic was in Methodist Hospital. After wasting twenty minutes searching for meter parking, I finally acquiesced and parked at the obnoxiously expensive garage across the street. I took an elevator to Gynecology and Obstetrics and found Amber in a room at the end of a hallway already lying on the exam table with a forearm propped under her head. The doctor had just started the sonogram, squeezing a gel out onto her expanding belly, then working the transducer around it.

Her eyes lit up when I walked into the room. "Honeycakes!" she exclaimed.

I rushed over to her and gave her a cheek-to-cheek kiss. "Sorry, I'm late. I couldn't find parking to save my life."

"I know. I barely made it here on time myself. Luckily, a woman was just pulling out of a spot when I drove up. Oh, Dr. Griffiths, this is my best friend, Symone."

A woman with a butterscotch complexion, bulgy but attractive eyes, and a cutesy pageboy haircut smiled at me. "Hi, nice to meet you."

"Hi, nice to meet you as well."

You wanna come around so you can get a look at your friend's little bundle of joy?" The doctor's nod indicated a space between the exam table and wall.

I slipped in between the small area and marveled at the screen. I looked at Amber to get her reaction. She gasped and slapped a palm to her mouth.

"Oh my..." she trailed off, her eyes welling with tears.

I felt like crying as well.

"Oh wow! It's so clear. Is that its big ole head?" I teased to lighten the mood.

Amber slapped my arm. "Don't be talkin' about my baby."

"Look at you. Already being smotherly and the poor child ain't even fully baked yet."

The doctor chuckled. "I can see what sex it is. Would you like to know?"

"No!" Amber responded with widened eyes. "My husband would never speak to me again if I found out before him."

The doctor tittered. "Alright, I'll just keep it to myself. My job is to help expand families, not break them apart."

Both Amber and I laughed at the doctor's good-natured humor.

As the doctor went on explaining what parts of the fetus we were looking at, a profound sadness clutched at my heart and held me in its grip. I couldn't help but wonder if I'd ever be fortunate enough to find a good man like Antoine to marry and have children with. I was turning thirty-nine my next birthday. As I closed in on forty, the picture of having a family of my own was becoming increasingly obscured.

"I want you to be the godmother." I heard Amber say in the distance, yanking me back to the here and now.

"For real?" I was genuinely surprised. She was extremely close to Ditzy Bitchy Ebony as well, and there was her younger sister, Anita.

"Don't sound so surprised."

"Well, I am. I mean I know how tight you are with Ebony and Anita."

"I'm no tighter with Ebony than I am with you."

The doctor was smiling, seeming to enjoy this quintessential girly exchange between two middle-aged women.

I couldn't help but think if this was just another act of pity being shown to the only one of Amber's friends who was still both man-less and childless.

"And it's not like this is going to be our only child. My sister can be godmother next time around, and then maybe Ebony if we have a third one. *Maybe.*" Amber's eyes wandered upward. "I mean, she is a little different."

"You think?" I put in.

The both of us laughed, including the doctor.

I craned my neck to get a better look at the monitor. "Look at my little god poo poo. I'm going to spoil you like no tomorrow."

"Yeah, that's mommy's stinky boo boo," Amber said with a wide smile that exposed her gleaming teeth.

***

I dozed off while staring at my ceiling, ruminating over the events of my life, but was soon jarred awake at the incessant ringing of my doorbell.

I glanced at the clock on my nightstand. It was eleven thirty at night. My heart quickened as I scrambled out of bed and over to my safe to retrieve Christy Black, my trusty firearm. I was a single female living alone in Brooklyn. There was no telling what trouble stood on the other side of my front door.

I flicked on the light in the foyer and cracked the door an inch. My jaw dropped at the droopy, pitiful-eyed figure staring back at me, clad in a dirty jean jacket with the hems of his blue jeans frayed from dragging the ground. The gray T-shirt he wore looked way too big, as if it belonged to someone else and his sneakers were run-down and dirty.

His right eye was swollen closed and blueish-black bruises marred his dark skin. His raggedy backpack was slung over one shoulder and though a bit taller, he appeared frail and weaker since the last time I saw him.

"Godson?" I had to blink the sleep from my eyes to make sure I wasn't dreaming.

He lowered his head. "Sorry, Miss A. I ain't got nowhere else to go."

"What do you mean, you don't have nowhere else to go? What about your foster family?"

Godson looked up at me. "But they all jumped me."

I slapped my palm to my forehead. "Why would they do a thing like that?"

"'Cause they say I'm a bum-ass nigga 'cause I ain't got no momma or no daddy."

"Well, they're wrong. You have a momma and a daddy too." *Albeit trifling and worthless.*

Godson looked up at me with a tightened face and squinting eyes. "They ain't tellin' no lie 'cause I ain't seen my momma since I was this small." He held his raised hands a ruler-size length apart.

"That may be an exaggeration. Maybe since you were this big." I held my hands a yard apart, remembering the gun in one of them and discreetly dropped it inside the pocket of my robe.

Godson studied his ragged sneakers.

"Doesn't matter either way," I said with a shrug. "Fact is, you do have a momma *and* a daddy." I shivered and tightened the belt on my robe around my waist. "Now come out of this cold air before you get sick."

A smile broke the ash on Godson's face as he stepped inside. I closed the door behind him.

"Now what's your foster parent's names?"

"Her name Miss King. She like you, Ms. A. She ain't got no husband. But she got a whole lot of kids but only three of us comes from the system." Godson said while walking over to the sofa and plopping down, still gripping the ragged strap of his backpack.

"You can put your bag down. It'll be safe here."

Godson placed his satchel on the floor by his feet and fell back against the sofa. I loved him, but worried what germs or bugs were taking up residence in his tattered clothes.

"You can't stay with me, you know?"

Godson's face drooped.

"The last time I had a friend take you in nearly cost me my job." I went for my phone in the bedroom and to secure my firearm before reappearing in the living room. "Now what's Miss King's number? I'd like to talk to her about that eye-jammy you've got going on over there. You know she's accountable for anything that happens to you."

D.D. Sherman								Rare Orchids

Godson held up praying hands. "Please, please, please don't call that lady."

"What do you mean? Why not?"

"'Cause she said I'm a troublemaker. She said she was throwing me outta her house. I told her I didn't care 'cause I was leaving anyway. And that's when I walked out and came to you. She already knows I left and I'm not coming back there no more."

With everything else out of place, Godson's neatly trimmed hair seemed an anomaly.

"Godson, you're only eleven. You're not old enough to make those kinds of decisions." I stood observing him for a moment. "Yeah, that's a nasty hit you took, but your haircut is on point."

Godson smiled one-sidedly. "Loot keep me dipped."

"Who's Loot?"

Godson sat up, arching his back inward. "He work in the barber shop 'round the corner from my house."

"And what do you mean, 'he keeps you dipped?'"

"'Cause sometimes on the weekend when I go in there and sweep the floor for him he gives me a fresh shape up. He rich. He the owner."

"How do you know he's rich?"

"Cause he be having big stacks of money," Godson said with a smile, measuring out money with the width of his hands.

"So that's why they call him Loot?"

Godson nodded proudly. "Uh-huh. That's why."

"Well, I need to call Miss King to make sure she hasn't alerted the authorities. What's her number?"

Godson searched his cracked Obama cell phone for the number then called it out to me.

"Sharhonda, Rhonda and Inez punched me in the face while their older brother Shawn held me down," Godson informed me as I listened to the phone line ringing in my ear. And they took two spinners from me."

"Hel-lo?" A lazy voice asked on the other end.

"Is this Miss King?"

211

"Yeah?" she affirmed cautiously.

"Good Evening, Miss King. I'm a friend of Godson Curry—well, I'm more like his mentor."

"Uh-huh."

"I'm just calling to let you know he's safe and with me."

"I was wondering." the groggy voice said. "I was just fixin' to call the police. He stormed outta here angry 'cause he got into a scuffle with my twins Sharhonda and Rhonda. They were all play fighting at first and then it just got outta control. When they started getting the best of 'im, Godson got mad and ran outta the house talkin' 'bout he ain't nevah coming back no mo'. And that's fine with me 'cause I don't need no mo' aggravation than I already got see 'cause I got high blood. There's seven kids here already and three of 'em is from the system. So it don't make me no never mind one way or the otha. Whateva he wanna do is fine by me."

"Okay. I see. Well, one of your children socked him pretty good. I don't think it's safe for him to return to your home with an injury like that."

"Look," Miss King continued defensively. "They all was fightin'. My twins got some pretty good lumps upside their heads too and they don't nevah be gettin' into no trouble. So I don't know where you think you're going with this!" Miss King's tone was suddenly livelier.

"Hey, listen. I'm not trying to rock any boats. I'm just making you aware."

"Well, who are you? You said you a mentor. Sounds like you oversteppin' your authority to me. You can tell me anything. How I know who you *really* are?"

My warning signals flashed. Miss King was traversing dangerous territory, so I decided to cease and desist before I blew my own cover.

"I understand your reservations and believe me when I say I don't want to cause trouble for anyone. Godson is here. Would you like to speak with him so that you'll know he's okay?"

"Put him on the phone," she agreed perfunctorily.

D.D. Sherman   Rare Orchids

The conversation between Miss King and Godson lasted all of thirty seconds. She asked him if he was okay and he responded that he was. She told him that coming back there may not be a good idea because he beat up her twins and that she would be calling his caseworker in the morning to have him placed.

"Uh-huh." Godson simply responded before handing me back the phone and shuffling dejectedly over to the sofa.

I bade Miss King a goodnight and assured her that Godson would be fine before disconnecting the call. She was a fool to trust a stranger, but it worked out in Godson's favor as he'd be getting to spend at least one night with me.

"She ain't nice like you, Miss A," Godson reflected bitterly. "I can see why she ain't got no husband, but you nice, and pretty, and sweet. You should have a hundred thousand boyfriends." He sat back on the sofa with his arms crossing his chest.

"Well, I had a boyfriend just recently." I went to sit beside him on the sofa.

Godson perked up, sitting erect and looking at me with a surprised expression. "Well, where did he go? I bet he's a cool dude who likes to wrestle and watch football."

"Well, I know he likes football." I chuckled pensively. "And he *was* pretty cool."

"Man, I wish I can meet him. And I wish you guys can be my momma and daddy. That would be really cool." He sank his chin in his palm and sighed.

I slung my arm around Godson's shoulder and pulled him close to me. "Yes, that would be nice if only we lived in a perfect world."

Godson shook his head regretfully.

"And you know what?" The tinge of excitement in my voice was evident.

Godson lifted his head to look up at me with eyes that danced in his face.

"He fly planes."

Godson darted up from the sofa and pumped a fist in the air. "You gotta be kiddin' me, Miss A. Tell me you're not lying."

I was tickled. "Of course, I'm not lying."

"He has—well, I *thought* he had—his own personal plane. He's a pilot. I flew in his plane over the New York Harbor."

"Cool!" Godson's eyes flickered. "Oh my God, that is sooooo cool," he added with a shake of his head then plopped down next to me again.

"I was scared at first. I really was. I have never flown in a plane like that. I got to see the Statue of Liberty up close. Oh my God. It was amazing! I wish you were there."

"I wouldn't have been scared 'cause I'm gonna fly planes myself one day."

I ran my palm over his neatly-shaved head. "Yes, you will...one day," I said, despite not being sure of anything in my own life let alone someone else's.

Godson twisted his torso to face me. "Can I meet—" he broke off and squinted an eye. "What's his name again?"

"His name is Dontae."

"Oh right! Dontae," Godson said as if he'd forgotten. "I think he'll like me 'cause I like football and planes and I like to do fun things."

"I'm sorry, Godson, but that's never going to happen."

"Why?" his eyes seem to plead for a logical answer.

I sighed. "Because we don't speak anymore. And I found out that he's not the nice person I thought he was."

Godson's excited expression took on a heavy sadness. "But I thought you said he showed you how to fly?"

Chapter 21

But I thought you said he showed you how to fly? Godson's words played in my head like a song on repeat. I thought about those words all night and even as I showered and dressed myself for work.

    The next morning, I met Miss King at the Little Flowers Foster Care Center. I had called again to remind her that she was technically still responsible for Godson and that it'd be in her best interest to explain to the social workers how Godson ended up with a shiner than to have Godson wander in there by himself.

    Upon seeing her, Godson sucked his teeth, grunted and dropped his head. "Don't know why I can't just stay with you, Miss A?" he mumbled ruefully.

    "Because that would be a conflict of interest."

    "What's a conflict inches?"

    "Never mind. I'll explain it to you another time."

    When the portly Miss King approached us, I extended my hand. Instead of obliging me, her chubby fingers gripped Godson's shoulder to lead him inside the building.

    I relaxed my suspended arm at my side. "Nice to meet you. I'm Symone Alexander."

    "Uh-huh," she replied, ushering Godson through a revolving door.

    "Godson, you have my number!" I yelled after them. "You can always call me if you need—!"

    Before I could finish my sentence, they were already inside the building with Miss King rushing him over to a bank of elevators.

    My heart sank to my stomach as I watched a pitiful Godson glance longingly over his shoulder at me. I bid him goodbye with a wriggle of my fingers and reluctantly proceeded to work.

***

D.D. Sherman   Rare Orchids

It was nearing lunchtime and I still had three more clients to see. The fact that one of my coworkers had broken his leg created an even bigger backlog for all of us.

    I pressed a button on the intercom system near my desk. "Xavier Reynolds! Room five, please."

    I quickly scanned the contents of Reynolds's folder to re-familiarize myself with the details of what had been my injured coworker's case. It was a simple probation violation, which was a shame since he had been in his final year. He was charged with burglary in the third degree and was sentenced to a one-to-three because the judge took two prior misdemeanors into consideration; but it looked like he'd only spent a year in jail. Mother died when he was nine. Raised by a grandmother. Father unknown. Seven other siblings raised by various family members. High school dropout. GED…

    "Bachelors of Science?" I had to re-read that aloud just to convince myself it wasn't a typo. "Hmmm, very impressive," I said under my breath.

    When I looked at Mr. Reynold's photograph, I was stunned beyond words. My head vacillated between the picture and the man entering my office.

    I swallowed to keep the contents of my stomach down as I felt I would vomit. I became faint as a sudden wave of heat made me break out in a profusion of sweat.

    My mind whirled with a million questions, scenarios, statements and swear words but I couldn't unclamp my lips to speak.

    "Well, I'll be damned! My horoscope said I was to have a run of good fortune." Dontae dropped in the chair across from me.

    My eyes latched onto the specter sitting before me, all decked out in a leather blazer, distressed jeans and a pair of Gucci lace ups.

    "Hel...loooo?" Dontae sang, waving a hand before my eyes.

    A subtle scent of coconut and fresh almonds wafted past my nostrils instantly weakening me.

    "You bastard!" I retorted, snapping out of my stupor.

"There you are!" His eyes gleamed. "You had me worried for a second," he said, sitting back in his chair and crossing his legs.

"Xavier Reynolds?"

He squinted at the folder on my desk. "Guess so, if that's what it says there."

"You're a fuckin' liar!" I was seething to say the least.

"Hey, let's try and keep things professional. Shall we?"

"Don't be facetious with me."

He fumbled for his phone in his pocket, took it in his hands, and began to poke around at the screen. "Facetious. Hold on, lemme look that up."

"For fuckin' real? You're going to sit here and play dumb with me, Mr. Bachelors of Science!" I shouted.

Dontae pressed the air with his palms, as if to quiet me down. "Please, no need to set off false alarms."

Just as he'd completed his sentence, McIntyre rushed in with her gun holstered at her hip. "I heard someone shouting. You alright, Alexander?" She asked, shooting Dontae an accusatory look.

"Oh yeah, I'm fine McIntyre. Was just here reading Mr. *Reynolds* the riot act about violating probation. You know how animated I can be." I chuckled, hoping my white lie was sufficient to ease the tension.

McIntyre relaxed, letting her shoulders drop. "Okay. I'm over in the next office if you need me." She turned to leave but not before giving Dontae a warning glance.

He waited until she was out of sight then continued in a whisper. "What's up with that? Tryna get me killed? You hate me that much?"

"Nobody's killing nobody."

"Well, that's good. Didn't plan on dying today. If I had, I'da wore a suit."

"You just don't get it, do you?"

"Oh, I get it, Officer Alexander. If anybody's *not getting it*, it's you."

"So is this what you do? Go around breaking women's hearts? Do you derive some sort of sick pleasure out of it? Just so you can go to bed feeling in control?"

"Please, one question at a time."

Dontae's cavalier attitude irked me to the white meat. I collapsed against my chair with a shake of my head.

"Look, I'm here as Xavier Reynolds. So ask me questions pertaining to Xavier Reynolds. If you want to ask me questions about Dontae Cummings, you can do so over a dish of Confit de Canard."

I scrunched my brows.

"It's French for duck." Dontae looked around before whispering. "I know this great restaurant in the city. I'm on a first-name basis with the owner. It's a small, discreet little spot that only caters to—" he broke off to make quotations signs with his fingers. "…A certain kind of people."

"I decline." I said, throwing my arms across my chest. "I've had about enough of eating off Evil lynn's dime."

Dontae sat back in his chair and pulled one leg over the other. "It's not *her* dime."

I chuckled at his feckless attempt to persuade me otherwise.

"I know she came to see you, and believe you me, I'm furious. I don't need anyone speaking for me. Look, I'll tell you the whole truth about everything if you give me the opportunity to."

"The opportunity to hurt me again? Don't think so." I objected, slamming my desk drawer closed.

"See, that's it. That's all you're concerned about."

"What do you mean *'that's all I'm concerned about'*?"

Dontae took in a breath, let his eyes wander to the ceiling then rolled them back down to look at me. "You're so on guard against being hurt that you can't help but to be hurting all the time."

I studied the desk, ingesting the poignancy of his statement then shook my head to clear my thoughts. "Go 'head. Blame the victim."

"See, that's exactly what I'm saying. You can't tolerate even the *thought* of being played."

"Who tolerates the thought of being played?"

"People who can't be in the moment because they're so guarded against the past and so afraid of the future 'til the only place left to be in is a state of constant fear. Baby, the moment is all we ever have."

"How soon we forget. Weren't you the one who finagled your way into my life with all the poetry, flowers, fake promises, and lies? I was perfectly fine as a single woman."

Dontae smirked. "Okay." He shrugged. "If you're selling it, I'll buy it. And by the way, I'm here as a client. Xavier Reynolds, remember?

I squinted at him, flaring my nostrils as I searched my mind for an appropriate comeback.

"Fine, Mr. Reynolds." I pushed a sheet of paper across the wooden desk. "These are the stipulations of your new probation agreement. Violation of any one of these items can be cause for your immediate apprehension and the revocation of said agreement. You are to maintain a permanent place of residence and phone number where you can be reached at all times. Failure to report any changes in the aforementioned circumstances can result in the revocation of this agreement. You must obtain *legitimate* employment and refrain—"

Dontae snatched the sheet of paper I was reading from, folded it in to a medium-sized square, and placed it the inner pocket of his leather jacket.

"I've heard this song before. If you want the truth, the whole truth, and nothing but the truth, let me take you to dinner tonight?"

I sucked in a deep breath while mulling over his proposal then, after a few moments of deliberation, shook my head.

"Okay, then I'll give you some of the truth now. Truth is, I fucked you on the couch in your living room, but I made love to you in the Serengeti. Truth is, I've fucked Evelynn in every room in that house, but I've never made love to her. Not a one time."

I shook my head, but I couldn't discern if it was out of disgust, disbelief, or both.

Dontae paused. His eyes seemed to search mine for understanding. "I'm a male escort," he volunteered with a shrug. "I fulfill fantasies. It may be wrong. It could be right, but either way, it's what I do."

"I seem to recall you saying that you'd be willing to change all that."

"*Change*...is a process. If you want to get the ball rolling then have dinner with me tonight?"

I shook my head again. "Fool me once, shame on you. You know the rest of it, I'm sure."

"Not trying to fool you. Just trying to get you to *be* in the moment before it passes us by."

I sat pensively. *But I thought you said he showed you how to fly?*

Chapter 22

Maybe it was the succulent five-course meal or the fruity notes of the Château Lafite that played upon my palette; perhaps it was the rickshaw ride through a vibrant Times Square or the seven bushels of flowers that Dontae purchased, one from every street vendor we'd passed. It could've been his masculine scent intermingling with the crisp, night air or the way the reflection of the city lights dazzled in his laughing eyes. It could have been the whispers of I love you that permeated my heart and burrowed within my soul, or how secure I felt resting my head against his firm chest as his gentle hand stroked my cheek.

Whatever magic Dontae worked on me led us to a rapturous night of lovemaking incomparable to anything I'd ever experienced.

Dontae's tongue explored the spot between my thighs as my fingers dug into his chiseled shoulders. He flipped me onto my stomach and I could feel the sensation of his warm tongue starting at the small of my back, finding its way to the nape of my neck, snaking into the canal of my ear, and then entering my mouth hungrily. We kissed deeply, wildly and I could feel his pulsating organ entering my oozing love canal. Our bodies moved in perfect synchronization as we drifted on clouds of simmering ecstasy.

He nibbled the lobes of my ears, ran his fingers through my thick tresses and planted soft, moist kisses on every area of my décolletage. His large hands clutched my sumptuous cheeks as he thrashed his pelvis into mine, contorting my body into positions that ignited a flame of passion only his sexual prowess could extinguish.

He lay on his back allowing my generous thighs to straddle his waist. I thrusted my hips as his large hands cupped my breasts and his thumbs stroked my nipples. I bit my lower lip, struggling to savor the moment as Dontae roared out in convulsions. I soon followed, clawing at his chest as I screamed his name. I collapsed on top of him, feeling his heart pulsing against mine.

"Thank you," he said, kissing the top of my head.

***

After a shower together I lay with my head against Dontae's chest, listening to the strong rhythm of his heart. Now that all our itches had been scratched, I had the clarity of mind to ask the question that had been haunting me since he sauntered into my office that morning.

"How did you allow yourself to go back to jail? You were almost there."

Dontae sucked his teeth. "It was Evelynn who snitched that I'd been driving with an expired license."

I sat up on my elbows. "Is it Dontae or should I be calling you Xavier? And why are you going around using aliases anyway?"

"Xavier is actually the alias. It's the fake name I gave to the cops when I got locked up the first time. It all started with a fake driver's license I was able to obtain from the state of

Pennsylvania. I had been up there looking for work, but I was too young for the job I wanted. A friend showed me how to fudge some documents. I ended up getting a fake license that essentially made me three years older—I was eighteen at the time. And from that, I was just able to build this whole other person."

"But why would Evil lynn have you locked up?"

Dontae tittered, then propped his arm behind his head. "Because of you."

"Me! What do I have to do with anything?"

"Evelynn knows that you are not just a fly-by-night chick, or some older woman I'm just trying to trick out. She knows what I feel for you goes much deeper than that because I told her I love you. No sense in being dishonest since her and I had, more or less, a business arrangement. She threatened that if I saw you again she'd call my parole officer. 'Trust me, I've got friends all throughout the legal system. You don't want to fuck with me,'"

Dontae said, mocking Evelynn. "I'm serious, those were her *exact* words," he declared as if I doubted him. "She found out I was meeting you at my friend's restaurant that evening and—not coincidentally—that same day some random cop pulled me over for failing to signal, searched my car and ran my name via my expired Xavier Reynolds license. Next thing I know, dude's throwing cuffs on me."

I sighed. "Baby, why didn't you just get a license under your *real* name?"

"I was getting around to it."

"An ounce of prevention is—"

"Worth a pound of cure. Damn! You sound like my grandmother and that ain't sexy."

"Shut up!" I said, playfully plucking his nose. I laid back, snuggling my head against the pillow. "She tried to pay me off, you know? Twenty-five-thousand-dollars."

Dontae sucked his teeth and rolled his eyes. "Damn! Is that all she thinks I'm worth?" he teased. "But seriously, that's just like her to think she can just pay her way out of everything! So sorry that happened to you, babe."

"Oh, don't be. I was tempted to take it."

Dontae's expression turned serious.

I tried to contain myself but burst out laughing. "Come on babe, you know I can't be bought."

Dontae's expression remained serious. "I never meant to hurt you, Symone," he confessed, reaching over to brush my hair behind my ear as his eyes studied mine. "You really are a genuine person and I'm a better man because of you."

I sighed as my eyes wandered away from his. "This will have to be our last night together."

Dontae darted up in bed. "Why do you say that?"

"Oh, for a lot of reasons. Most important, this interferes with the integrity of my job."

"How so?"

"I'm not supposed to be having personal interactions with my clients. Trust me, I nearly lost my job just recently for fraternizing with a client."

"Why are you trying to make me jealous? Who is it? I'll find him and run his ass out of town."

"No, nothing like that. He's just a kid. A very special kid by the name of Godson." "Well, *technically*, I'm not your client. Mr. Jennings is my P.O."

"Yeah, but he's out on injury and no one can say for how long."

"Baby, nobody has to know. I won't tell if you won't tell."

I sat up in bed beside him. "That's not the point. It's an integrity thing."

Dontae shrugged. "So. I'm the only other person who knows, and I'm not judging you."

I shook my head at his lack of understanding. "I also don't feel like being caught up in all this Evil lynn drama. Seems like she's willing to go all out for her man and the last thing I need is for her to be meddling around at my place of employment."

"Correction, I'm not her man."

"Well, she thinks you are."

"Well, I'm not," he insisted. "Look, I'm going to fix things between us. I promise you that."

"How you gon' do that, Dontae? Are you willing to give up a life of luxury just to appease me?"

"I'm willing to give it a try."

"That doesn't sound too promising."

"Change is a process, baby. Remember? Look, I have legitimate money saved up that I've earned honestly. Do you know how many gardens I've designed for rich people and big corporations?"

I pulled a deep breath into my nostrils, held onto it a moment or two and exhaled deeply.

Dontae slid down in bed and flung an arm over my thighs pulling me to him. "Ready for round two?" he asked on a yawn.

"Ding! Ding! Ding!" I responded, slipping under the sheet then pulling it over our heads.

Chapter 23

"Okay, so who's the smart ass?" Amber asked holding up a box of No-Doz. She looked as if she was adrift on her own island sitting on a chair made to look like a throne and surrounded by a sea of gift boxes of all shapes, colors, and sizes.

Her younger sister, Anita, who had recently given birth to twin girls, held up her hand and wriggled her fingers. "It's not like you're going to be getting any sleep once the baby's here, so I figured I'd help you out with that."

We all laughed. Anita's actual gift was a multifunctional stroller that had been revealed to us earlier.

Amber's small apartment was crammed with at least fifteen women, not to mention the seven men, including Dontae, watching the game with Antoine in their bedroom.

"I'm next!" Arlene's petite frame sprung from the sofa with gift box in hand. "Sorry to jump the line ladies but I have to be at work in an hour."

"It's all good, sweetums!" Amber said, tearing off the beautifully crafted wrapping paper. "Oh, isn't this sweet."

She raised a box containing a high-tech baby monitoring system; one with a small monitor so that you can see as well as hear.

"Thank you, Arleeeene," Amber crooned.

"You know I got you, momma," Arlene replied, leaning over to hug Amber. She reached for her handbag on the sofa, bid us all a goodnight, and then hurried for the door in her typical urgent fashion.

My mind wandered in the midst of all the chatter and the *oohs* and *aahs* as Amber continued to unwrap gifts and hold them up for all to see. Amber was not just a happily married woman on the verge of becoming a mother. She represented the tape that one breaks through at the end of the finish line of love; a bullseye on the target of marital bliss; an esteemed scholar of the Kama Sutra; the possessor of love's Holy Grail.

"And this is from my bestie and my baby's future godmother," Amber said, looking in my direction while holding up a placard-sized check for five-thousand-dollars. "The first deposit in our baby's tuition fund."

The room thundered in applause, apparently impressed with the generous gift. Admittedly, thirty-five-hundred of it came from Dontae despite my protests that fifteen hundred was sufficient. I cringed to think how Evelynn's money was probably tainting my good intentions, even though Dontae swore up and down not a dime of it came from her.

We'd recently started dating again. After our last night together, I refused to see him personally so long as he was my client. During that time, Dontae had strictly adhered to all stipulations of his probation agreement. He even went so far as to find legitimate employment working with Antoine on a few projects. Jennings had returned to work after three months of being out sick; by that time, Dontae had successfully completed his probation.

Though things were looking up for us, I still refused to let my guard down. I hadn't gotten over him just disappearing without a trace and that limousine ride from hell with Evelynn. Since then, my relationship with Dontae always felt precarious and I often found myself bracing for some catastrophe that would end things between us for good.

"Oh, how cute!" I heard Amber sing. She was showing us a collection of onesies and matching bibs. "Thanks, ginger snaps." Amber was referring to Ebony, who smiled broadly then got up and sashayed over to her with opened arms.

I got a little teary-eyed at the sight of them embracing. Although I wasn't a member of Ebony's fan club, I respected her loyalty to Amber. She really was a good friend to her. Besides, my aversion could've been tempered by the fact that her and Devin had finally broken up, so I no longer viewed her as a man thief. According to Amber, Ebony had met some rich, white guy through none other than her baby brother and dropped Devin like a hot potato. The guy had already bought her a Maybach, furnished her new condo, and took her on trips to Paris and Tahiti while a devastated Devin begged and pleaded for reconciliation. When I told Dontae about what had happened, he reminded me of the Lycaste Orchid and I laughed heartily at his keen insight.

"Open mine!" Lacey urged with her grey eyes twinkling. She was kicking a huge box nearly half her size over to Amber.

"Oh my, honey cakes! Looks like you went all out!"

Amber pulled the lid off the box, reached in and slid out a beautiful rocker trimmed in lace with all the bells and whistles to go with it.

As if on cue, everyone *oohed* and *aahed* at the extravagant gift.

"Now, I've never seen a rocker like this! It's amazing, Lacey, thank you."

"Oh, I just couldn't resist," Lacey said, slapping a palm to her chest. "That vintage design had me at hello."

We all laughed, I suppose more out of courtesy than anything else. Marisol got up to help Lacey move the box out of the way as Amber reached for the last few gifts.

Bibs and diapers, strollers and car seats, gift cards and bath sets littered the floor around Amber. I wondered where she'd plan to store all that stuff in her small apartment especially since she'd gotten two and even three of the same kinds of gifts.

Music blared from a Bluetooth speaker, courtesy of Rasheeda's streaming service, and somehow all fifteen of us managed a line dance right there in Amber's living room, traversing gifts and trying our hardest not to collide into one another. Amber led the dance, bumping almost everyone she encountered with her pregnant belly. To a bystander, we probably resembled a cluster of dancing clowns, uncoordinated and half-inebriated.

The giggling raucous caught the attention of the men who happily joined in, making for an awkwardly tight situation. Dontae moved in perfect synchronization to the music, right on beat and never missing a step. I, however, went right when the record said left and when it was time to turn around, I found myself facing opposite everyone else. That was my cue to get out of the way and go refresh my drink.

I stood on the sidelines sipping champagne and watching Dontae take turns dancing with at least four women. The ratio of women to men was two to one and four of the men were busy entertaining their own women. Those were the little things that hopelessly drew me to him. He had a genuine concern for people, particularly women. I think if it were up to him, everyone woman in the world would have a permanent smile on her face.

Terence Trent D'arby's "Sign Your Name" floated through the speakers. Dontae brought me into the dancing circle and whirled me around to the sultry voice filling the room.

'Fortunately you have got someone who relies on you. We started out as friends, but the thought of you just caves me in. The symptoms are so deep. It is much too late to turn away. We started out as friends. Sign your name across my heart. I want you to be my baby.'

Soon, we became the center of attraction. Dontae pressed my body against his while our hips swayed to the silky smooth rhythm. Dancing with him felt very natural and I found myself deeply in tune with every movement of his body. I could feel all eyes on us and I took full advantage of the moment, swirling my waist and swaying my booty against his manhood. I reached up, encapsulating his neck from behind, and I could feel his soft, moist lips against my ear and the firmness of his nature imprinting my backside.

Dontae sang along. *'Sign your name across my heart. I want you to be my baby. Sign your name across my heart. I want you to be my lady.'*

Antoine and Amber joined us with him grasping her waist from behind. The four remaining couples, Manuel and Marisol, Roderick and Lacey, Anita and Craig, Amir and Rasheeda—who'd recently started dating—made their way to the floor, catching the bridge of the song. Dontae and I were so engrossed in one another that I hardly noticed. Then came that old, familiar high of falling in love; that blissful emotion that rockets you from center gravity and sends you soaring though the stratosphere; that feeling that makes the roses rosier, the sun brighter, and the sound of rain splattering the earth a symphony. In those moments I was experiencing love in love's most potent form. That much, I was certain of.

***

Amber's little sister Anita, my cousin Felicia, Dontae, and me stayed to help clean up. Felicia and Anita were putting away leftover food and tidying up the kitchen. I was assigned to replacing the gifts back in their boxes and helping Amber find a proper place to store them which gave us the opportunity to catch up on things.

"So I see Mocha Choca Hotté Latté has got you back in his good graces," Amber said, folding onesies in her lap while sitting on her pretend throne.

"I didn't get the chance to tell you, but he was locked up all that time."

Amber looked up at me and gasped. "Locked up? What do you mean you didn't have the chance to tell me?"

"Well, you've been busy with all this baby stuff and I've been busy with work and things."

"Come on, sugah dumplings. This is your best friend you're talking to. Just admit that you were too embarrassed to tell me that your man got the collar."

"That too. And the fact that you can be so damn judgmental at times," I replied, pushing Lacey's large box into a corner of the room.

"Well, what did he go to jail for?"

"Remember that crazy stalker chick Evelynn I was telling you about?"

"The chain smoker who tried to kidnap you. Yes, I remember."

"Well, *she's* the one who had him arrested."

"How?" Amber stopped folding to look up at me, her attention piqued and her eyelids stretched.

"She threatened him to stop seeing me or else. Turns out she's got friends in high places within the legal system. She was having him followed. Cop pulled him over that day we were waiting for him at the restaurant for failing to signal—of all things—and *boom*, next thing you know, he's being carted off to jail."

"People don't go to jail for just failing to signal. Has to be more to the story," Amber said, her voice heavy with disbelief.

"There is." I confirmed, glancing over my shoulder then lowering my voice to a whisper. "He was driving with an expired license."

"Okay, but that still doesn't sound severe enough to go to jail," Amber said, waving that explanation away.

I hesitated, considering if I should tell Amber the rest of the story and sighed before continuing. "Yeah, but he was on probation."

"On probation?" Amber blurted.

I shushed her with a finger pressed to my lips.

"I'm sorry, honey cakes," she whispered. "But all this stuff you're telling me just sounds so overwhelming. What was he on probation for?"

"Robbery. Third degree. Listen, that's all behind him now and he's trying like hell to give back in every way he knows how."

Amber dropped her head. After a few moments she looked up at me with what I interpreted as pity in her eyes. "I'm so sorry, Symone."

Dammit, I was right. I loathe pity. Any form of it. "So sorry for what?" I casually answered, stacking a few boxes in another corner of the room.

"I feel like this is all my fault. I mean, I'm the one who brought him into your world and now to see you going through all of this is heart wrenching."

"See me going through all of what? I'm having the time of my life with Dontae." I asserted, even though I couldn't swear to confidence in what we had.

"I just don't want to see you get hurt like I have so many other times. And trust me, it ain't pretty watching you mourn," Amber said as she resumed folding small outfits.

"See." I reached for another box lying on the sofa.

Amber whipped her head up. "See what?"

"That's what I mean about you. Judgmental," I said, sliding the over-sized placard gift behind the sofa.

"You've fallen in deep, girlie pearly. I mean *real* deep. He was just supposed to be a hookup. A way for you to work out them stiff legs." Amber chuckled. "How it came to all of this I'll never know." Her eyes wandered upward. "Damn, maybe I should've tested the merchandise before I made the purchase."

"You really should have," I said, then playfully stuck my tongue out.

We both laughed.

"Nah, I'm just having fun. Antoine is all I'll ever want and need."

I took a seat on the sofa. "And that is why you are so blessed. Amongst all the other things in your life that makes you special, of course."

"Thanks, snookums!" Amber replied, sending me air kisses. "Look, Symone, if you really care for this man, then I'm going to pray real hard that it all works out for you. I mean, I can see how he's captivated you. Hell, he captivated almost every chick in the room tonight. I mean, I get it. I just want you to be as happy as I am."

I leaned back into the sofa marinating on Amber's words. She made it sound simple as if all one had to do was adhere to a certain recipe like add a dash of salt, a sprinkling of pepper, then bring to a boil to be happy. I was happier than I'd been in years during the time I'd spent with Dontae, which was to be expected, for happiness is simply a byproduct of love. Love is what complicated my life, muddied the waters of rationale and rendered me vulnerable.

"I don't quite understand how to measure happiness, but if it's on a scale of one to ten, I'm probably at a hundred."

"Well, if it's like that, then I think it's time to start—" Amber broke off and wriggled the fingers on her left hand causing her rock of a diamond to shimmer. "Securing your investment." She smiled widely, exposing her gleaming white teeth.

"Hmmmm," I sighed, thinking of Dontae in ways that never occurred to me.

Chapter 24

Phil and I stood in the midst of a floor covered in sawdust while our eyes wandered over a ceiling of dangling electrical wires, walls of exposed brick, slats of wood framing the future walls of a room, paint speckled ladders, drills, saws, and other construction materials.

"It's pretty big on the inside. Maybe a little too big for a flower shop," Phil said, his head swiveling as he took in the enormity of the room.

"I think it's the perfect size. I'm planning on displaying as many different kinds of orchids as I can get my hands on. You do know there's over twenty-five thousand species of orchids?"

"Yes, you've often reminded me," he replied, exhaustingly.

I spun around. "I can't believe I'm going to be a business owner!"

"I still think this is risky business. I mean vesting out on your career to become a florist just doesn't add up for me."

I placed my hand on my hip and looked at Phil. "That's because you're not an idealist. You're afraid to take chances."

"Call it what you want. Doesn't change my mind one iota," Phil said, rocking back on his heels as his eyes roamed over the surrounding walls.

I placed a hand on Phil's shoulder and looked deeply into his eyes. "Look, I need you to be supportive. You don't have to agree with me, but just be supportive."

"I think I can manage that," he said, throwing his arms across my shoulders.

"Thank you." I rubbed his back. "Besides, I'm thinking of adopting Godson and I can't do that and work for the Department."

"Really? Are you sure about that?"

"I'm not *sure* about anything. I'm just following my heart. And since Dontae and I have gotten back together, I just don't feel right about covertly dating my co-worker's ex-client behind his back."

D.D. Sherman — Rare Orchids

Phil sighed. "William Shakespeare. I just can't believe how quickly he's squirmed his way back into your life."

"It's not just that. The biggest reason of all is that the job just isn't right for me—or better yet, I'm not right for the job."

"I can't agree with you there. You are one of the finest probation officers I know. And I'm not just saying that because you're my amazingly beautiful friend."

"I'm a bleeding heart, Phil. I can honestly say my emotions and empathetic tendencies have over-ruled my authority on myriad occasions. A lot of my clients are from the hood. I'm from the hood. They speak a language I'm all too familiar with. I get their struggle. How can I ever be truly impartial?"

"So...what are you calling the place?" Phil was obviously trying to change the subject.

"Rare Orchids, of course."

"Clever. I like. So I suppose this was lover boy's idea?" Phil said with a sniffle.

"Nope. In fact, I haven't even told him yet. This is something I wanted to do on my own although I'm kind of hoping he'll consider coming on as a partner or maybe even as a consultant."

Phil lowered his head and sneezed into the bend of his arm. "Well, he does seem to know a whole heck of a lot about flowers," he said, sniffling.

"He doesn't know a lot about flowers. He knows *everything* about flowers," I stated dreamily, imagining my finished store bursting with customers hovering over endless rows of exotic plants.

"I'm sure. But can we go do lunch now? I'd rather see the completed space without all this sawdust around. It's triggering my allergies."

Phil's words instantly transported me back to an unfinished room cluttered with construction supplies. "What do you feel like?"

"I don't know. Sushi?"

"What about a good, old-fashioned burger? Haven't had one of those in a while."

"Okay. I can do burgers. Since you're picking the restaurant are you picking up the tab?" Phil asked jokingly.

"Of course. As long as you promise to help me plan the grand opening."

"I'm all over it. Just tell me what you need me to do."

As we exited the store front, I looked back at the space. I saw an apron-clad Dontae in a made-believe room working on an arrangement of orchids as I waited on customers at the register. I flicked off the lights, then closed the door.

***

I leaned over the railing, marveling at the gently swaying sailboats and flamboyant yachts docked at the North Cove Marina. In the background, a cityscape of disparate skyscrapers jutted from the harbor and lit up the night in a theatrical display of lights. The sea took on a hue of violet and an occasional gale troubled the waters. The nearby restaurant was aglow with chattering patrons and bustling wait staff while new age and jazz tunes poured from speakers.

I had the grilled salmon while Dontae feasted on fresh oysters. We had walked a few feet over to the dock's railing to get a closer look at the boats with our watermelon cocktails in tow. It was the end of April and coming up on spring. With the exception of that one hiccup with Dontae getting arrested, we had been consistently seeing each other for going on eight months. Most of his things were at my place; by all accounts we were cohabitating except for the few times he left town to visit a brother or some other family member.

"I've got something to tell you, sweetheart," I said, turning around to face him.

"You're pregnant." He said matter-of-factly.

"Um...no."

"Oh."

"Don't sound so relieved," I said jokingly.

Dontae tittered. "Sorry, didn't mean to sound that way. Just don't think I'm ready to be a father. I've got too much work to do on myself before I can call myself raising someone else."

"I agree. Besides, that won't be happening no time soon."

"Everything in its time." He said, pecking me on the lips.

"But I *am* considering adoption."

Dontae's eyes widened. "Adoption? Why would you want to adopt? Can't you have your own babies?"

"I suspect I can. But it has nothing to do with that."

"I'm sorry. You lost me."

"Do you recall that kid I was telling you about? The one I almost lost my job over?"

Dontae's brows furrowed as he tried to remember. "Oh, you mean lil dude with the funny name."

"Godson."

"Yeah, Godson. What about him?"

I went to sit on a nearby bench. Dontae followed, taking a seat beside me.

"He's really a good kid, baby. I mean he's smart, and ambitious, and polite. It's just that he's been in the system for years and it seems the older he gets the harder it is for him to find a family that's willing to adopt him."

Dontae looked empathetic. "That's messed up. Well, you know my childhood wasn't all gravy."

I nodded.

He reached for my hand and placed it in his lap. "I mean, baby, if that's what you want to do, I support you a hundred percent. You know I'm all for giving back. Someone gave me a shot—hell, plenty of people gave me a shot."

"You mean that?" I squeezed Dontae's hand, grateful for his support.

"Of course I do."

I grabbed him into the tightest hug I could muster.

"That is why I love you so much, Symone. That heart of yours is like gold. I mean you put on this tough exterior, but I know what that is."

"Tell me what it is, Dr. Cummings?"

"A wall of protection."

I was jolted. I strongly related to what Dontae was saying but chose not to reveal that to him.

His face inched up to mine. "But I think I'm tearing it down. Brick—" he broke off to kiss me. "By brick," then kissed me again.

"You have been putting in the work. I'll give you that much. But baby I saved the best surprise for last." I'm sure my widened eyes were twinkling.

Dontae rubbed his palms together. "Oh, I can't wait to hear this. Does it involve hot oil, sexy lingerie, blindfolds, and handcuffs?"

I playfully socked him in the shoulder and pointed a finger at him. "Get yo' mind out the gutter."

"No, seriously. I can't wait to hear this."

I sat up. "I quit my job and bought a business."

"Quit your job? Why in the world would you do that?"

"Because it no longer felt like something I wanted to spend the next ten, fifteen years doing."

Dontae tittered, his impeccably straight teeth gleaming in the oncoming darkness. "What kind of a business?"

"A flower shop."

He chuckled again. "A flower shop? Baby, why would you do that? That's a very tough and not very lucrative business. Besides all that, you don't know much about flowers."

"Yes, but you do." I bit the corner of my lower lip.

"Wait, hold on a second. I never said I had any interest in going into the flower shop business," Dontae said, taking a sip of his watermelon cocktail.

"Come on, baby. Think about it. It'll be legitimate work doing something you love to do and something I've come to love to do."

"Babe, I like gardens in big, open spaces and watching flowers grow in their natural state. I love stumbling over different species of plants as I'm running a trail or frolicking through the tulips."

I couldn't help but laugh.

"I mean I'm the guy who plucks wildflowers growing in random places and challenges myself to name all the different species of plants in Central Park. My love of flowers is at a whole 'nother level, babe. It's intricate and...*spiritual*."

"Well, I'm not there yet and I don't know if I'll ever be. I just want to be free to do the things I enjoy. If I can make money at the same time, all well and good."

"Look, Symone. I'm there however you need me to be. I'll support you in any way that I can."

"I don't want you to think I'm imposing on you. This is my dream. Really, it is. You just gave me the idea."

"So what's your concept for this flower shop?" he asked, crossing his legs, finishing off his cocktail, then leaning back against the bench.

"Orchids."

"Just orchids?"

"Just orchids."

"Well, can you answer me this, flower lady? How can one orchid stand out in the midst of thousands of other ones?"

I smiled as I recalled the day Dontae kissed me for the first time. "It would have to grow tall."

"Tall is a good way to get noticed."

"It'll have to smell delightful."

Dontae nodded, turning the corners of his mouth down.

"It would have to be a very good looking orchid, strong with large petals."

"I'm with you on that."

"And it would have to be able to withstand strong winds, rainy days and fluctuating temperatures. But more than anything else, it would have to convince me that there is none other like it on earth."

Dontae smirked sexily. "Have I convinced you of that?"

"Keep doin' what you do. You're almost there." I replied, pressing my lips against his sumptuous mouth. His tongue met mine fervently.

I was adrift again, wafting somewhere amongst the stars with the smell of fresh coconuts and almonds filling my nostrils and Amy Winehouse's, "Some Unholy War," serenading me through restaurant speakers.

Chapter 25

The grand opening of Rare Orchids was only two days away. The shop had been clinically cleaned with exposed brick walls, glass door refrigerators containing shelves of colorful corsages, a back room with a large wooden table for flower arranging, and my jaw-dropper counter-top fashioned of gneiss rock with alternating layers of greys. The extravagant showpiece was Dontae's gift of good luck which he had custom made. As if that had not been enough he'd stocked the store with Phalaenopsis recognizable by their dappled petals of white and yellow, and the anatomy of what resembles an opened mouth; paradise jewels, a crowning flower flanked by two folded petals that appear to be taking a bow; diamond crowns with their cottony white petals, ruffled edges, and golden centers, and their sister, the Hawaiian wedding song virgin. He'd had shipped loads of freckled-faced Fred Tompkins with their deep red flowers and pink centers; bushels of soft-pink Barbara belles, Beaumesnil parmes, sweet chocolate drops, Empress Fredericks in gentle shades of white and pink, and cloud-white little angles.

 Despite reiterating that I was becoming a business owner for my own edification, Dontae poured his heart and strength into the realization of my dream as if it were his alone. He was uber focused, intentional and kept the contractors on schedule. The most I had to do was figure out the aesthetics of the place.

 I walked into the back room where Dontae was teaching Godson how to play chess. They were seated at the wooden picnic-like table which was topped with loose lady slippers. I had planned on making an arrangement for my counter-top.

 "See, lil man," Dontae began picking up the queen. "Even though the object of the game is to put the king in check, it's the queen that has all the real power."

 "How can a girl be stronger than a boy?" Godson asked, wrinkling his brows and wriggling in his seat.

"Oh, but she is. You see," Dontae put the piece on the board to demonstrate. "The queen can move in almost any direction she likes—diagonally, straight ahead, back and forth, and side to side across any number of ranks."

"Wow! That makes her really powerful!" Godson exclaimed while sitting erect.

"Indeed, it does. But the king here can only move one square at a time."

"That's it?" Godson asked, slumping his shoulders.

"Yep. That's it. The queen can easily be ranks ahead of the king, but if she can just understand that it may take some time for him to catch up to where she is, then the both of them may have a shot at winning the game." Dontae looked in my direction.

"Hi, Mom!"

"Hey, Godson."

Although I was still going through the process of adopting Godson, he'd been cleared to live with me three weeks prior.

"I see you're learning the fascinating game of chess?" I said, taking a seat on the bench beside him.

"Tryin' to." Godson pouted.

"Don't get frustrated. It's not going to happen overnight. I've been trying to learn for years and still don't have it down pat."

"Okay, Mom. I won't."

It was odd to hear Godson refer to me as Mom, but I was slowly getting used to it.

"Yeah, lil man. Don't let the game intimidate you. You'll have it mastered in no time at all." Dontae plucked Godson's cheek.

Godson twisted his body in my direction. "Mr. Dontae's a cool teacher and he knows everything about everything!"

I tittered. "It certainly appears that way doesn't it?"

"Uh huh," Godson agreed, rigorously nodding his head.

"You're ready for a snack, son?"

"Pizza?"

"Just a single slice, you hear me?"

"Okay, Mom."

D.D. Sherman　　　　　　　　　　Rare Orchids

Dontae reached in his pocket, extracted a ten-dollar bill from his wallet, and handed it to Godson before I had the chance to grab for my purse.

"Ten dollars!" he exclaimed, looking at the bill with eyes wide. "Thanks, Mr. Dontae!" Godson got up from the table and made a dash for the doorway when I caught his shirt.

"Yes, Mom?"

"One slice." I reiterated.

Godson nodded his head and darted off.

Dontae chortled. "You know, babe. I see a lot of myself in that little guy. Curious and adaptable. Tough as nails, but sweet as honey. He's been bumped around quite a bit in life, but he still hasn't given up. He still has that fiery determination to make lemonade out of lemons."

Dontae had a very old soul and it was hard to believe I was dating a man eleven years younger than me. "Absolutely, honey. Those are some of the same things that I see which is why I stepped out of my comfort zone to do what I did."

Dontae reached for my hands across the table. "And I commend you for that. Not a lot of people would have."

"Thanks, babe. I can't thank you enough for everything you've done to make my vision a reality. I mean all the gorgeous flowers, the killer counter, and keeping the workers in check. There's no way I could've got this all done without your help. I'm so grateful."

"Look, you're one of the only people I can still be myself around. One of the only ones that's not smitten with money and material things and I deeply appreciate that. You're just real and real is so hard to find these days."

"I don't know how else to be."

"I don't want you to be anything else."

I smiled, squeezing his hands in mine. "So...two days to the grand opening. I'm nervous."

"Don't be nervous," Dontae said patting the top of my hand. "You got this."

"I'm just worried if we'll sell enough flowers. It's not like orchids last a long time and we've got so much inventory."

"Stuff like this usually works itself out. You'll see."

"Hope you're right, 'cause I've been doing a lot of praying. Oh, and I don't know if I should wear a simple A-line dress for the grand opening. Or maybe some overalls and a head scarf to look real hippie and organic? Or just jeans and sneakers to keep it hood?"

"I'm sure you'll look amazing in anything you decide to put on."

"You're too sweet." I raised up on my elbows, leaned over the table, and gave Dontae a peck on the lips.

"Can I have another one?"

"Sure." I kissed him again and sat back down.

"Everybody's going to be here. Amber and Antoine. Rasheeda and Amir. Amber's little sister and her man, my cousin Felicia and her friend Sonya. And of course, Phil and some of my other former co-workers. And they've all committed to buying something."

"See. So what's with all the fretting?"

"Babe, I just want everything to go right."

"It will. I promise."

***

Amber had delivered her baby boy two months before and was already prancing around the store in heels and a mini dress. Except for a hardly noticeable pouch at her mid-section, one would never have guessed she'd recently given birth.

"This place is gorgeous!" she exclaimed as her and Antoine conducted a quick tour of the store. "And look at all of these orchids! I never knew there were so many different ones!"

"Yeah, y'all hooked this spot up," Antoine agreed.

"I take it back," Phil started. He was standing at the counter helping me arrange flowers in a vase. "I think this store is the perfect size for a flower shop when you consider all the different varieties of plants you have here. A lot of them are absolutely stunning to look at."

My cousin Felicia had started the music, a throwback to the early seventies Rhythm and Blues era, while Anita and her husband put a spit shine to the storefront window. Stephanie from court and my cousin Felicia's friend, Sonya, stood outside handing out flyers while Ebony and Lacey assembled hors d'oeuvres on artisan paper plates.

It really was all-hands-on-deck. With all the love and support being shown, I could feel the tension dissipating from my stiff neck and joints.

"I have to try one of these deviled eggs," Amber said, popping an egg half into her mouth. "Oh, they're so good!" she exclaimed, reaching for a second half.

Antoine went for a crab bite. "Delicious," he said, sucking his fingers.

"Those are Phil's recipes. He's an amazing cook, but he'll never admit to it."

"Oh stop it!" Phil arched his wrist. "I can do a *little* something."

"See, I told you."

"You the man, Phil," Antoine said, making Phil's cheeks turn red. I half-expected Phil to correct him, but of course, he didn't.

"Ooh, let me try." Felicia walked over to where the food was set out and picked up a puffed pastry, tossing it into her mouth. "Mmmm, these are tasty, Phil."

"Oh, I didn't make those. I got them from Costco."

I elbowed him. "Don't be giving away your secrets!"

We all laughed.

"I finished Mom," said Godson dragging from the back room with a plastic spray bottle in hand.

"Hey Godson!"

"Hi, Mr. Phil."

"You've watered them all?" I asked Godson.

"Yep."

I placed my hands on my hips. "The way that I showed you?"

"Yes, ma'am."

"Good job. Now, go see where else you can help out. Looks like Stephanie and Sonya can use a hand giving out the rest of these flyers."

Godson reached for the stack of flyers in a box on the counter then rushed off.

"He's so good," Phil said, wiping the glass vase with a cloth.

"Yep. He can be a handful though. That's why I'm always trying to wear him out. Kid's got an infinite supply of energy."

"I'm first in line if he's got some of it to spare," Phil said on an exhale.

We both laughed.

"Auntie Coretta!" I looked up from the floral arrangement to notice my cousin Felicia running for the door.

My eyes instantly flooded with tears and I became too choked up for words. I was absolutely stunned to see my mother Coretta and sister Charmagne coming through the door.

"Wow!" Phil gasped. "Your mom and sis are here. How lovely."

I ran from behind the counter and threw my arms around both of them. "Mom, you told me you wasn't feeling well?" I cried.

"Yes, but I wouldn't have missed this for the world."

"Hey girl!" Charmagne exclaimed hugging me tightly.

"Y'all drove all the way here from South Carolina?" My cousin Felicia asked.

"Nope. Momma wouldn't have been able to stand the long trip so we flew," Charmagne replied.

"This day is so perfect and it's such a blessing to have my family here supporting me. I'm just overwhelmed with joy." I sniffled as tears trickled down my cheeks.

I grabbed my mother and sister by the hand to show them around.

"Oh honey, this is lovely." My mother's eyes seemed to twinkle.

"Yes indeed, baby sis. You did a remarkable job. And look at all these exotic plants!" Charmagne's jaw dropped.

"I'm really proud of you, Symone." My mother beamed.

"Thanks, momma. It means so much to hear you say that."

"And where's my new grandson?" she asked, looking around.

I waved Godson back inside the store. He raced over to us. "This here is your nana, Godson, and your auntie Charmagne."

Godson threw his arms around my mother's waist. "Hi, Nana."

She slid a hand over his head. "Hey, Godson. I'm so glad I'm getting to put a face to that sweet voice over the phone."

"Me too, Nana," Godson said, continuing to hug my mother tightly.

He darted over to my sister and grabbed her around the waist.

"Oh, he's so precious, Symone."

"Thank you, Auntie." Godson's voice was muffled against Charmagne's mid-section. I was choked up at seeing how ecstatic Godson was to finally be able to have a family of his own.

Charmagne leaned over to whisper in my ear. "So, where's Dontae? I'm excited to meet him."

I'd been so wrapped up in making sure everything was perfect for the grand opening I hadn't noticed Dontae's absence. It was half past eleven and we were planning to open the doors to the public at twelve.

"He's probably still home getting ready. We were here late last night."

"Home getting ready?" Charmagne jerked back. "Y'all living together?"

I shushed her, hoping that my religious mother hadn't heard, but she was a few feet away chatting it up with Felicia and Amber plus the music was pretty loud so I didn't think she had.

"Something like that," I replied quietly.
"So this thing has gotten serious?"
"Yep! We're getting there."
"Well, call and tell him to get himself over here. I want to see what dude looks like. I want to see if he lives up to *everythimg* I've been hearing about him."
I chuckled. "I'm sure he'll be here soon."
I asked Felicia to lower the music, then called everyone into a prayer circle. I'd asked God for a successful grand opening, longevity and prosperity in my new venture. I'd thanked Him for the opportunity to open a business and for the unwavering support of all my friends and family. I'd thanked Him for blessing me with Godson and for granting traveling mercy to my mom and sis.
After a resounding Amen, we all went outside to unveil the store awning. Passersby stopped to watch the ceremony and a few customers filed inside. It pained me that Dontae was not there for the sign reveal, but I kept reminding myself that this was my dream and something I was doing for myself.
"Hey, Symone." Antoine tapped my shoulder.
I turned to face him. "Hey, wassup? Having a good time?"
"Yeah, everything's perfect. But where's my man?"
I glanced down at my watch. It was going on three o'clock. Something clenched at my heart and I swallowed to moist my dry throat.
"Guess, he overslept," I answered, chuckling it off.
Antoine looked serious. "Look, it's not my style to be sticking my nose in other folks' business, but you're like family to me and Amber. I'ma let you know that I'ma have a real problem with dude if he's pulling another one of his disappearing stunts. I mean, I think he's a real cool brother, but if he's in, he needs to stay in and if he's out, he needs to stay out and stop playing games."
I tried hard to remain stoic, but I knew Antoine noticed the tears welling in my eyes.
Amber came up from behind him and placed a hand on his shoulder. "What's with the somber looks?"

I cleared my throat. "Nothing. Antoine was just asking about Dontae."

"Yeah, where is he?"

"On his way, I'm sure."

I could see that Amber wasn't convinced and excused myself to go wait on a customer.

After ringing up a few customers, I slipped into the back room to call Dontae. His phone didn't even ring; it went directly to voicemail. It was going on four o'clock and I was terrified at the thought of Dontae not showing up at all. None of this was making sense. Why would he invest so much time and money into the shop just to bail when I needed him the most? My apprehension was quickly melding into anger and anger was quickly becoming rage no matter how hard I tried to convince myself that this was my venture alone.

Phil peeped his head in. "Heeey, girl!"

"Wassup, sweetie?" I tried to seem upbeat, but I could tell by Phil's face that he wasn't buying it.

"Just wanted to let you know that I'm checking out." He said walking into the room.

"Awww...all ready?"

"Yeah, it's my sister's birthday and we're all going out to dinner."

"Oh, that's right. I remember you telling me that." I walked over to him and threw my arms around his neck. "You've been a tremendous blessing to me today." I rubbed my cheek against his. "Thanks for everything!"

"You're very welcome," he said, hugging me back. "You do know I'm pissed."

I stood back from him and slapped my palms to my face. "I'm at a loss for words, Phil." I lowered my hands from my eyes. "I mean almost everything you see here is the result of Dontae's hard work and financial investment. I think the most I've spent on this place is a few thousand dollars. It just doesn't make sense."

"Maybe he got picked up on another violation." Phil shrugged.

"No. He completed the remainder of his probation period without incident."

"Well, you've got a lot of soul searching to do. Is this really the precarious relationship you want for you and your son?"

I sighed deeply. "Of course not."

"Well then, you've got to make some serious decisions about how you want to spend the rest of your life."

I nodded, feeling my eyes well up again. My lips quivered uncontrollably. I hated appearing so weak before Phil.

"I'll call you tomorrow." He kissed me on the cheek and sauntered away.

I plopped onto the bench marinating on Phil's words. After a few moments of introspection, I gained the gumption to rejoin the festivities.

I scurried over to about three customers standing at the counter waiting to be rung up. When I completed the transactions, my eyes searched for Dontae amongst my few remaining guests. In doing so, I accidentally caught Charmagne's eyes. Her brows darted up as if remembering something and then she rushed over to where I was at the register starting to count the day's take.

"And where is Mr. Dontae? It's after four."

"Your guess is as good as mine," I replied, thumbing through a small stack of twenty-dollar-bills.

Charmagne gasped. "That really sucks."

"Oh, that's just putting it way too mildly."

"You think something happened to him?"

I slammed the drawer closed. "Listen up!" I shouted. Only a few people noticed, so I stepped out from behind the register, stood in the middle of the floor, and clapped my hands. "Listen up, everybody!" Amber and Antoine, my mother and Charmagne, my cousin Felicia and her friend Sonya, Rasheeda and Amir and a few stragglers from my former job all turned their heads in my direction.

"For those of you who are wondering where Dontae is, I have absolutely no idea. Okay? I've been stood up—yet again, bamboozled, hoodwinked, played, made the fool or whatever you want to call it. I am an idiot. Plain and simple."

Rasheeda gasped, putting a hand over her mouth and Amber sadly turned the corners of her mouth down. A worried looking Godson ran over to me and grabbed my hand.

My mother darted up from her chair. "Don't you say that about yourself!"

I sent Godson to the backroom to tidy up.

"It's true Mom. And I take full responsibility for my stupidity."

Charmagne went to hug me, but I stopped her. "I love you, big sis. But you know how I can't stand pity."

"That's right," she said, sighing then dropping her arms to her sides.

"Now that that's over with I'd like to thank each and every one of you from the bottom of my heart. You guys did a tremendous job and I would not have gotten through the day without you." I paused to take in the smiles inching across the faces of my family and friends. "I mean if I stood here all night I couldn't put my gratitude into words. I just want to let you know that I love every last one of you with all that I have and all that I am."

Everyone responded with their own *I love yous*, well wishes, and continued blessings. I waited on a few customers that had come through the door at the last minute then promptly closed shop at six.

Chapter 26

I heard Godson struggle through the door with his five-speed bike in tow and rushed out of the kitchen with dishrag in hand. I had been cleaning the house from sunup to nearly sundown.

"Okay, young man, you've got some explaining to do," I said, placing my hands on my hips. "It's half-past seven."

Godson closed the door and dropped his head. "Yes, Mom. I know," he mumbled, rolling his bike over to a corner in the living room.

"It's near eight o'clock and you've got day camp tomorrow."

"I'm sorry, Mom. Won't happen again."

Godson trudged in the direction of the bathroom to clean up and prepare for dinner. It was a routine he'd already grown well accustomed to—shower the minute you hit the door!

"You've been out there looking again, haven't you?" I asked his back as he drug his feet up the hallway.

He turned to face me and let out a protracted sigh. "I went to five barber shops," he said, throwing up his hands in resignation. "And rode my bike to the park where they're always playing chess. And when I didn't see Mr. Dontae there, I rode *all* the way to the Brooklyn Botanic Gardens 'cause I know how much he loves flowers."

"That's too far. You should never have gone there looking for anybody."

"And when I couldn't find him in any of those places, I stopped in front of a church to pray for him to come back to you." Godson shrugged. "I hope God answers my prayers 'cause I can see you're sad without Mr. Dontae around. And I am kinda sad too."

I walked over to Godson and hugged him tightly. "Listen, I don't need you risking your safety out there looking for folks. Yes, I miss Dontae, but it's been over a month and I'm steadily getting used to the idea of him not being around and I'm okay with that.

The flower shop is doing great, you're doing great. I can't ask for much more. So go get showered and ready for dinner. Maybe we'll have enough time to get in a movie."

Godson's face lit up as he dashed up the hall and into the bathroom.

I lied to Godson. I was nowhere near getting used to Dontae's extended absence. I wasn't even past his sudden disappearance, that again, left me with no explanation or even a clue as to what happened to him. He still had clothes at my house and even left behind some expensive watches which baffled me even more, but not as much as his phone being disconnected. I had searched every crevice of my mind trying to recall if there were any clues to his abrupt exodus, but there were none that I could remember.

And then I had an epiphany that somehow never occurred to me prior. I felt nauseated at the thought—weakened by the probability, enraged by the vision—of him going back to Evelynn. There was no other explanation. A few days after his disappearance, I had Phil run his name through the police department's computer to see if he'd been locked up again and that search turned up nothing. I called all the area hospitals and went to places he frequented to no avail. I was beginning to think Dontae had reverted back to his old ways because he could not envision himself living an ordinary, middle-class life with one woman.

Whatever the reason, I no longer planned to stand by in regrettable silence while that man philandered with the likes of lonely, rich women and played paramour to the desperate housewife. He was welcomed to go about his prodigal life of rolling between satin sheets with his middle-aged admirers or skinny dipping in Evelynn's hot tub while her self-indulgent cronies lustfully looked on, but he wasn't going to do it without hearing a few choice words from me.

***

The following weekend, I decided to close the flower shop early and make good on my intentions to confront Dontae and his deranged Madame head-on. Although I had been on a love-induced high that evening I spent with Dontae, I remembered a sign that read Saddle River/Woodcliff Lake as we got off the exit. I recalled that the house wasn't too far from the expressway and the limo making a lot of short left and right turns. Evelynn's sprawling property was situated on a bit of an incline and could easily be spied from the main road. After having circled every block within a three-mile radius, I finally hit pay dirt. There it was, the structure that longed to be a French chateau, loomed in the distance. My heart thumped so violently in my chest I thought I would faint. I had not anticipated being so nervous, but anger obviously clouded my judgment. The wrought-iron gates were open, and I boldly drove up the sinuous path leading to the circular driveway and stopped in front of the house. I anticipated being accosted by a legion of bodyguards and felt vulnerable that I no longer carried a firearm; but to my surprise, the only greeting I got was from a few colorful birds twittering in the surrounding trees.

    After a few moments of deliberation, I garnered the courage to get out of the car and rang the doorbell which chimed out musically. Old lady Alda answered in her requisite grey uniform and gaping orthopedic shoes. She gasped upon seeing me and her eyes darted maddeningly as if she'd been at a loss for what to do or say.

    "Hi, Alda."

    She opened her mouth, but could only mutter indecipherable words. She swallowed hard to compose herself then said, "Mr. Reynolds, he no here."

    "That's fine. I'd like to speak to the lady of the house, please. Is she home, Alda?"

    "Si. Si. You wait here one minute," Alda said, closing the door in my face.

    I stood taking in my opulent surroundings and breathing in the aroma of lush trees while trying to organize my thoughts and the words I wanted to say to Miss Evil Lynn. I wiped my clammy hands on my jeans and tried to slow my breathing using a counting system taught to me many years ago.

The door swung open, and a disheveled looking Evelynn appeared all aghast to see me at her doorstep.

"What are you doing here?" she demanded.

"Selling girl scout cookies. Why do you think I'm here, Evil Lynn?"

"If you've come for the money, you are too late."

"You know, Evil Lynn—"

"Stop sayin' my name like that! It is Evelynn! I've told you that before!"

"Okay, Evelynn. No sense in me being as tacky as you are. As I started to say, there is much more to life than the millions of dollars you seem to swim in. But the irony of it all is that you are the most miserable person I've ever encountered. You and Dontae were made for each other. You bait him with money crumbs and he can't help but follow the trail right back here."

Evelynn laughed. Hysterically. Psychotically. A frisson swept through me and I had the urge to back away and run to my car.

"You do not know. You are so smart, but you do not know."

"Know what?" I asked, frighteningly anticipating her reply.

"Xavier is dead. Motorcycle accident."

Something had come along and knocked the wind out of me so hard that it dropped me to my knees. I was panting, trying hard to catch my breath; trying desperately to regain my bearings, but it felt as if everything around me was off-kilter.

"So you see? Now we are the same. Neither of us have the man we love." With that, Evelynn slammed her door in my face.

After what seemed like forever, I found the strength to stand and noted Alda looking out one of the huge, arched-shape windows at me. Her expression appeared worried almost as if she wanted to tell me something, but instead, abruptly turned away, releasing the curtain she had held aside.

D.D. Sherman   Rare Orchids

    I drug myself to my car with my heart swelling in my chest and suppressing the urge to vomit. I slid into the driver's seat and slumped down in the chair studying my sad, teary-eyed face in the rearview mirror.

    "She did it!" I said to myself. "I just know it." I covered my face with my hands and bawled like I never had before. I felt defeated in life like Dontae had been my last chance at happiness. I was lost and felt disconnected from anything meaningful. The world appeared to be an illusion and it was as if I were in the midst of a nightmare and couldn't wake up. I didn't know what to think or what to do or even how I would go on with the thought of never having said goodbye. I stuck the key in the ignition. Somehow, I managed to find my way home.

Chapter 27

Losing Dontae had taken a serious toll on me. I had lost weight and had even closed the flower shop for a week after learning of his demise. I just couldn't bear to be around all the things that reminded me of him, especially the orchids. But it had been months and somehow I was finding ways to get on with my life. I had babysat a couple of times for Amber and Antoine and Godson was back in school doing exceptionally well. He and I were in the back room filling a few orders for floral arrangements. The business had been thriving but slowed after I closed shop for a week, so we were playing catch up to try and get things back on track.

"Think we need another bag of Spanish moss," I said wearily.

Godson darted up to get it, running over to a storage shelf.

"You're a really big help to me, Godson. You know that?"

Godson rushed back over to the table. "Yes, ma'am," he replied, tearing into the bag.

"I don't know what I'd do without you."

"Don't worry, Mom. I'm not going anywhere like Mr. Dontae did. It was a mean thing to leave you all alone like this."

"I told you before, Godson. Mr. Dontae did not leave me. He just got into trouble and can't come back."

"But what kind of trouble?" Godson asked, pinching up Spanish moss and adding it to an arrangement I'd just finished.

"Just some kind of trouble that I'd rather not tell you about."

"Okay, Mom." Godson replied sadly.

"Well," I said, getting up from the table. "I hear customers outside. Keep working on those arrangements." I instructed him, making my way over to the front of the store.

"You see, the thing about the lady slipper, is that she has to be rooted ever-so precisely or this very delicate and deciduous flower will shed her petals prematurely. Oh, and these are the

D.D. Sherman   Rare Orchids

Vanilla orchids. There's an entire history lesson behind them that most people aren't even aware of. It's about pollination and a slave named Edmond Albius."

I felt so weak in the knees that I had to grab hold of the counter to keep from falling. I wanted to say something, but my mind was dizzy with a million thoughts swirling through my head. All I could do was stand there leaned over as if someone had siphoned the air from the room. I was desperately trying to discern if the person I saw before me was truly Dontae Cummings, a ghost, or an identical twin brother I never knew about.

The two women touched the petals then leaned in to smell the rare orchids as Dontae kept them engrossed in detailed explanations and fascinating stories. Though I was in utter shock, I somehow managed to keep my composure for the sake of not scaring my customers away.

Both women had bought bushels of different kinds of orchids and complimented me numerous times for having a well-versed employee saying that they'd never had such an enlightening experience simply buying flowers.

I thanked them for their patronage and gave them each a lady slipper. As soon as they exited the store, I picked up a glass vase and hurled it in Dontae's direction. He ducked just as it careened over his head and crashed against the floor.

"Wait a minute!" he exclaimed, still squatted with his hands raised.

"No, *you* wait a minute!" I said, launching another vase at him. He'd sprung out of the way and it shattered against a wall.

Godson ran out of the back room. "Mr. Dontae!" he exclaimed, starting in his direction, but I ordered him back inside with what I knew was a crazed look in my eyes.

"You bastard!" I said, picking up yet another vase. Dontae rushed over to me and wrestled it out of my hand, so I beat his chest with my fists instead. "*This* is what you call trust?" I said through clenched teeth still pounding on his chest. He grasped my elbows to halt the assault, but I managed to wriggle away.

"Give me a chance to explain, dammit."

258

D.D. Sherman   Rare Orchids

"A chance? Haven't I given you enough chances?" I shouted.

"Well, just listen. If you decide to never speak a word to me again, I'll understand, but just listen!"

I wiped the tears from my eyes. "Is this some kind of sick mind game you and your madame Evil Lynn are playing with me? The both of you are sick psychopaths that get off on hurting people!"

"Are you going to listen to me or not?"

"For months, I've mourned for you. Thinking you were dead!"

"I did die."

I shook my head. "Now I know you're a sicko."

"Hear me out, Symone." Dontae said sternly. "Xavier Reynolds *is dead*. Don't you get it?"

I shook my head. "No, I don't get it," I replied, pumping my fists at my sides to keep from using them on him again.

"Look, I couldn't keep living a double-life. In order for me to be a hundred percent Dontae, I had to kill Xavier. Baby, Xavier was the man who slept with rich women for money; the thug who went to jail; the dude who couldn't conceive of spending his life with one woman. Trust me, it's Dontae you want, not Xavier."

"I don't know what I want anymore! Especially when it comes to you!" I fired back.

"That's a lie and you know it. You want to be happy. Baby, everyone does. And you want to be happy with me. Dontae."

"And this is the unhappiest I've been my entire life!" I shouted.

"Symone, happiest is not a rite of passage. Someone once said that happiness is to be pursued. Look, it's not handed to us on a silver platter."

"That cold-hearted bitch, Evelynn, really believes you're dead."

Dontae dropped his head, then after a few moments looked up at me. "And I want it to stay that way."

I sighed deeply. "Isn't that kind of cruel? I mean, even for Evelynn?" I asked, swiping a streaming tear.

Dontae grasped my arms and looked deep into my eyes. "If I had not faked my own death, I truly believe she would've had me knocked off anyway. She threatened me with violence the last time I refused to see her. Things were becoming unsafe for me. I was desperate to get out of the mess I got myself in. Desperate for a start-over." Dontae's eyes scanned me from head to toe and then back up again. "Desperate for you."

I shook my head in disbelief. "I mean she seems crazy, but it's hard to believe she would've done something to you as much as she professes to love you."

Dontae looked deeper into my eyes. "Trust me, she *is* that crazy and don't think she'd stop short of hurting you. I couldn't continue to put you at risk, babe."

I cringed to think of it. I had never considered that before, but as desperate and unhinged as Evelynn seemed during that limousine ride, it could've easily been true.

I wiped stinging tears from my eyes and cleared my throat. "How did you do it? Fake your own death that is?"

"You sure you want to know?"

I thought about it a few seconds, then nodded.

"There are a lot of John Doe's out there—"

"Okay, stop!"

"Anything can be bought, even a dead man's identity...but at least some unclaimed, homeless drug addict got a proper service."

"I said stop! I don't even want to think about it. I just want the answer to one last question."

"Shoot!"

"How did you manage to fool Evelynn?"

"With the help of Alda."

"Old innocent lady Alda?"

"Old innocent lady Alda."

"But how?"

"A distraught Evelynn just couldn't bear to go down to the city morgue to identify her beloved Xavier, but motherly Alda was all too willing to attest that a stranger she'd never laid eyes on was, in fact, Xavier Reynolds. For twenty-thousand-dollars that is."

I couldn't help but chuckle at the thought of old lady Alda having a gangster side. *That's probably why she gave me that strange look as I was leaving Evelynn's house that day.* I thought. My mind was whirling to the point that I felt dizzy. I collapsed against the counter. Dontae stood in front of me, but somehow, it was still hard to believe that he was actually there.

"Look, Symone. I'm not making any grandiose promises, but I'm willing to work hard helping you out here in the shop and helping you to raise Godson as well as doing the things I need to do to better myself. I can't keep pretending. I don't want to go on living a lie, no matter how much money I stand to gain."

I sighed deeply and wiped the streaming tears from my eyes. "But I don't know how to trust you again."

"Trust is a process, Symone. All I ask is for the time to catch up to where my queen is."

***

Dontae and I sat in the rear of the plane while Godson sat in the pilot seat next to the instructor as the teacher went over flight deck controls and repeated some last minute instructions. He was fourteen years old and had been accepted into Aviation High School after scoring a ninety-nine on the admissions test. Dontae had taken him flying on myriad occasions, but that was the first time he had flown the plane himself.

After a few static-ridden exchanges with Tower Control and jotting down the wind directions, fuel levels, and other information onto a notepad, we taxied up the runway and were soon airborne.

"Perfect lift-off, son," Dontae said through his headset.

"Thanks, Dad!" Godson replied with a proud grin on his face.

I suspected Dontae felt a little strange being called Dad, but I knew he'd soon get used to hearing it like I had gotten used to Godson calling me mom, just in time for the birth of our second child, a girl, due in three months.

"Thanks, Dad." Godson repeated through his headset.

"Thanks?" Dontae asked, puzzled. "For what, son?"

"For showing us how to fly."

Dontae gazed at me. "And thanks to you for giving me a safe place to land."

THE END

D.D. Sherman

Rare Orchids

D.D. Sherman graduated Cum Laude, obtaining her degree in Creative Writing from Brooklyn College. She was a regular contributor to the Black Romance and True Confessions magazines under the umbrella of Sterling and MacFadden and have been a finalist in the American Black Filmmakers Foundation (ABFF) and Cynosure screenwriting competitions.

She has been featured on the show, "How To Make It In The City," with Ama Karakari-Yawson, WBAI 99.5FM, where she discussed how she used writing as a catharsis to escape the violence of a dysfunctional home life and urban upbringing. She spearheads her own burgeoning writer's group entitled, "Novel Ideas," based in Brooklyn. In her group, she shares her valuable knowledge and her vast experience with novel writing with other hopeful authors to help them bring their stories into fruition.

Printed in Great Britain
by Amazon